SO-AVE-646

PRAISE FOR

COFFIN'S GOT THE DEAD GUY ON THE INSIDE

"I LOVE THIS BOOK. . . . A highly original and
entertaining novel that treads with insouciance the narrow line
between comedy and life-threatening danger."
—Meg Chittenden, author of the
Charlie Plato mystery series

"Snyder delivers dialogue that is often strikingly original and
adroitly paced. His edgy, appealing characters and deft
evocations of seedy Southern California urban life make return
visits with Keltner and his cohorts a welcome prospect."
—*Publishers Weekly*

"THINK OF SEINFELD ON SPEED: RAZOR-SHARP,
RESOURCEFUL, REFRESHINGLY ORIGINAL. Did I
mention plugged-in? Great sport, with all the twists and turns
you can handle. Don't be left behind."
—Richard Barre, award-winning
author of *The Innocents* and *Bearing Secrets*

"With its computer guys, snappy dialogue, car chases, and
California backdrop, it suggests what might have happened if
Hammett's Sam Spade had been a computer geek." —*Booklist*

"HIGH-VELOCITY PROSE . . . The novel's brilliance
springs from the intelligent banter of Jason and his friends. . . .
A highly artful mystery." —*ForeWord*

"SUCCESSFUL HUMOR—AT TIMES DRY, INANE,
WITTY, AND SLAPSTICK. Jason's spontaneous, often insane
antics will appeal to most readers, especially those who enjoy
Donald Westlake's comic mysteries." —*Library Journal*

"Set in Pasadena, this book is a quirky, hip, down-and-outers'
Rose Bowl of computer skullduggery and deadpan quippery."
—Lev Raphael, author of *The Edith Wharton Murders*

Books by Keith Snyder

Show Control

Coffin's Got the Dead Guy on the Inside

COFFIN'S
GOT THE
DEAD GUY
ON THE
INSIDE

A JASON KELTNER MYSTERY

KEITH
SNYDER

A DELL BOOK

Published by
Dell Publishing
a division of
Random House, Inc.
1540 Broadway
New York, New York 10036

ISBN: 0-440-23541-3

Reprinted by arrangement with Walker Publishing Company, Inc.

Printed in the United States of America

Published simultaneously in Canada

August 1999

10 9 8 7 6 5 4 3 2 1
OPM

For La Diva on our paper anniversary

ACKNOWLEDGMENTS

Thanks to Richard Bugg, Bill Pomidor, Michael Nunley, John Schramm, Joel Weise, and Sita Lazenby for facts, Michael Seidman for demanding risk, and Lillian Roberts, who could have kept it for herself.

1

The heat and smog would hit in early morning and cling to the floor of the San Gabriel Valley like a gritty blanket. Evenings, the blanket lifted a little, and a dirty, stifling warmth filtered in to supplant the shattering heat. Pasadena was almost unbearable in the summer. Pretty bungalows and tree-lined avenues didn't matter.

Jason Keltner was sitting at a table in a bright, untrafficked alley on a Thursday afternoon, reading *Cosmopolitan*, sipping weird hibiscus iced tea, and half-listening to the Neil Young cassette the Espresso Bar counterperson was playing, when Norton Platt came around the far corner and walked toward him. Platt was wearing faded jeans with an old brown belt and new sneakers, and his long brown hair was down, loose. His expression was as Jason remembered it: vaguely amused, as though God tried out

His new comedy material by beaming it directly into Platt's brain.

Jason was wearing his only good shirt, white linen with metal rims on the buttons, with the sleeves rolled halfway up his forearms. His hair wasn't quite as long as Platt's, and it was darker. He had it back in a soft black ponytail band. He lowered his *Cosmo* a little, raised one eyebrow, and said, "Aha. A tricky case of international intrigue has you stymied. You have come to beg for my insight."

Jason hadn't seen Platt in a long time and hadn't expected to see him at the E-Bar. Platt pulled out the other chair, sat down, and said, "What's the difference between a musician and a savings bond?"

Jason said, "A savings bond eventually matures and earns money. What do you call a musician without a girlfriend?"

" 'Homeless.' What did the drummer get on his IQ test?"

"Drool. Uh . . . did you hear about the drummer who locked his keys in the car?"

"They had to break the glass to get the guitarist out." Platt thought for a moment. "You know the difference between a cello and a coffin?"

"Yeah, I know that one."

"I have a job for you if you're interested."

"What kind of job?"

"Hold on, let me get some coffee." Platt got up and went inside. Jason picked up his magazine and read an article about how to make men better in bed. Apparently, some of the dim oafs could be taught to sign simple words and not drool on the mattress.

Platt came back with a glass of iced coffee, sat down, and said, "You never struck me as a *Cosmo* girl."

"Man should have an open mind," Jason said. "I don't

read this magazine, and it occurred to me that I had no good reason not to."

Platt pursed his lips as though that made sense. "So?"

"Now I have a good reason." The perfumed air that puffed out as he closed the magazine smelled like a dump site for hazardous orchids. "What's the job?"

"Baby-sitting Paul Reno. Interested?"

"No."

"Before you answer, let me tell you more about it."

"No."

"His girlfriend is kicking him out of her apartment."

"Paul would be a better person if more people kicked him out of their apartments."

"I noticed there's an empty room at Marengo Manor."

"I don't want to live with Paul."

"It's a paying gig."

"I don't want to live with Paul."

Platt named a weekly figure. It was a little higher than what Jason had earned when he was patrolling pipelines for Municipal Water.

"Um," he said. His post-employment benefits had expired, and the few thousand from his retirement account was gone. Rent was two months overdue. Iced tea at the E-Bar in a white linen shirt was the day's conscious luxury.

"Plus expenses," Platt said. "And mileage. I'll pay standard mileage. Is the odometer in your Plymouth accurate?"

"Sure, for about six seconds every hundred thousand miles."

"Well," Platt said. "You could conservatively estimate the mileage."

"So the job would be just for you, not subcontracted for some secret agency or something."

Platt shrugged unforthcomingly.

"I see," Jason said.

"Reno's been hanging with a new crowd lately."

"Yeah, Paul switches crowds with increasing frequency as they keep inconsiderately figuring out that he's full of it."

"I want to know what he's up to. The new crowd is a little seedier and a little more serious than his usual."

"I don't know."

"I need an answer now, before he finds a new place."

"Who's supposed to convince him to move into the Manor?"

"You are."

"How?"

"That's your problem. Tell him you want to repair your relationship with him. Tell him you forgive him for sleeping with your ex-wife. Offer him free Factory-to-Paul incentives. You know him better than I do. Whatever you do, it has to be quick; I've encouraged three apartment managers to turn him down, but I can't keep doing that." Platt tried his coffee and looked not-disapproving. "I'll give you a two-thousand-dollar discretionary budget for friendly dinners, accomplices, decoder rings, stuff like that if you need it."

"Um."

"Try not to need it."

"I see."

"I need to know now. Sorry to push, but that's the deal. Do you want the gig?"

"For how long?"

"Indefinitely. Maybe shorter, maybe longer."

"I was actually thinking of leaving town and getting some composing done."

Platt waited. Jason sipped his coffee and looked at the table. He had none of what they used to call "prospects."

"Okay."

"You're hired." Platt took a folded notepaper out of his shirt pocket and put it on the table. Then he took a last sip of his coffee and stood up. "I'm hard to reach right now. Drop me some e-mail on MUSE if you need me."

"Okay."

"Save all your receipts, and I'll need your social security number for your 1099." He stood. "Gotta go. Talk to you soon."

Jason said, "Factory-to-Paul incentives?"

Platt smiled and said, "I'm trying to nail your sense of humor. I made that up on the drive over."

"Oh. Do I get royalties?"

"Nope. Parody is fair use."

"So is plagiarism, apparently."

Platt smiled. "See you."

He went down the alley. Jason picked up the folded paper and opened it. A blue check fell out. Paul Reno's phone number was written on the notepaper, and the check was made out to Jason, in the amount of three thousand dollars. The notation at the bottom of the check said, "$2000—expenses, $1000—advance." He put them both in his pocket, finished his iced tea, went to the pay phone inside the E-Bar, and called Paul at the apartment out of which he was being kicked.

2

The day after next, Paul moved into the Manor, the huge, wrecked remains of a turn-of-the-century boarding house where Jason and his friends Martin and Robert lived. In its long history, people had certainly made love and died in it, but the romance had sloughed off long before Jason moved in, and it mostly just seemed urinated in. Jason had been one of the first to move in and nail drywall onto the rotting, blackened timbers. Rent was cheap.

Martin, an occasional graphic artist, had recently moved off Jason's couch and into Robert's room upstairs. Jason didn't understand the rationale, which had something to do with Robert going on acting auditions and Martin working days, and fractions of rent, but he was glad to get his front room back and so didn't request clarification. Robert and Martin had disappeared for the day, and weren't helping Paul move in.

Paul's old beige Toyota hatchback was parked next to the dilapidated wooden staircase by Jason's back door. He and Jason carried boxes up the loose stairs, past the old white tilted refrigerator where Chuck, a tenant who worked as a key grip, kept beer, and into the doorway at the end of the landing.

At two-thirty in the afternoon, Jason stood on the landing in Paul's doorway and said, "How much more is there?" He was wearing a colorful Bob Marley T-shirt with the sleeves ripped tastefully off. The unwelcome promise of the warm morning had been fulfilled with a stifling noon, probably 95 degrees Fahrenheit, with little motion in the air.

"That's it," Paul said, sitting on a stack of two boxes. He was tall and skinny in black sneakers and pants and a dark brown sleeveless shirt.

Jason leaned against the warm doorframe, his sweat-damp arm sliding a little against it. "Hungry?"

"Sure, what've you got?"

"Nothing. I meant we should go out and get something. How's Mexican food sound?"

"Is it close?"

"Walking distance. Everything's walking distance."

PASADENA WAS ENDURING a blight of improvement; turn-of-the-century houses with fascinating crackly paint vanished mysteriously every few weeks, replaced by flimsy-looking condos with semi-cylindrical orange roofing tiles. The condos were supposed to hearken stylistically to the California bungalows that had once stood in mighty herds in the San Gabriel Valley. A living tribute to Pasadena's historic past. Jason thought they looked like the old triangular orange Tast-E-Freez stores that sold chocolate-dip cones made with paraffin. Most of the few remaining older houses had cheap plywood nailed up over their windows and doors.

As they walked the three blocks into Old Town, Paul said, "Well, I guess the neighborhood's okay." He soaked sweat off his temples with the shoulder of his shirt. The light reflecting off the white sidewalk was dazzling.

"Yeah," Jason said. "You'll like it. You can walk out your door and be at the mall or the movies or the museum in ten or fifteen minutes." They crossed Marengo and walked west on Colorado, toward Old Town. "And as much as I hate all those trendy little boutiques on Colorado Boulevard, the restaurants are great."

"Then why are we getting Mexican food? What else is there?"

"Chinese, weird Chinese, French, Malaysian, Thai, two kinds of Italian, expensive American, Cuban, Mexican, sort of French, uh, couple of cafés, pizza, whatever you want."

"How's the Italian?"

"Good."

"It's not subs and spaghetti, is it? I don't want to have subs and spaghetti."

"No subs. There's probably spaghetti."

"It's good, though," Paul said, giving Jason a making-sure look with the eyebrows up.

"No, Paul, it sucks. Big gobs of sputum in the pesto." Jason turned toward Paul as they walked and held his hands about two feet apart to illustrate.

Paul's expression became one of annoyance. "A simple 'yes' would have sufficed."

A little jolt of adrenaline up near the sternum. Jason didn't say, *You already got a simple yes.*

He said, "So what would you prefer?"

"I don't care," Paul said. "Hey, I'm easy."

They ate pasta at the Italian place, drank iced tea, and had tiramisu for dessert. It cost forty-three dollars, plus tip. Jason forgot to get the receipt. Then they walked to a record store on Colorado Boulevard and browsed through the used CDs without buying anything because they'd spent all their money on food, and then walked back to the Manor.

The front door took some persuasion. Upstairs, Bill Cosby was telling the story of the Monster Chicken Heart in a scratchy voice in Robert's room. With Paul behind him, Jason went up the old, painted brown stairs, around the corner at the landing, and into Robert's entryway, threading his way through stacked dusty boxes of dusty books.

Robert's door was open, and he and Martin were sitting on the wooden floor against their respective beds, laughing at the Bill Cosby record, which was playing on a turntable atop a wobbly tan card table with a torn vinyl surface. Kinked brown wire ran to two faux-walnut speakers with stained wicker faces.

Robert was six foot five and light-skinned, with dark hair and eyebrows, and he was wearing tan corduroy shorts and a geeky blue shirt with white trim around the pockets that Antonio Banderas would look like a doofus in. He sat cross-legged next to a pocket-sized two-dollar chess set with undersized plastic pieces that stuck to it magnetically. It had been two weeks since Jason had seen Robert without a solo chess game going.

Martin sat against the wall with his legs crossed casually in front of him. He held a shiny, jointed butterfly knife in one hand, practicing a little twirling maneuver that made the parts of the knife click together. He was short and coffee-colored, in a white V-neck T-shirt and jeans.

Jason knocked on the open doorframe, and Martin motioned them into the room with his free hand. The wooden floor was strewn with dropped clothes and boxes of paperback books. Robert got up and lifted the tonearm.

Jason said, "Where'd you get the turntable?"

Martin said, "One of the ladies from the condos was having a garage sale. She got tired of sitting out in the heat, so we got it for four dollars, and a whole stack of old Bill Cosby records and some old Motown for two dollars more. Robert, put that Temptations album on again. You gotta hear this."

Robert slid the Bill Cosby record carefully into its torn, yellowed paper sleeve and gently put another record on. The needle went *skritch* through the speakers, and the Temptations started singing "Just Another Lonely Night."

Jason smiled. "That is great."

Paul snorted. "Yeah, right. It's not even in stereo."

Martin looked at him. Jason said, "It's not *supposed* to be, Paul."

"But you can get it in stereo now," Paul said. "Just go buy the CD."

Jason said, "It's not supposed to be in stereo, Paul. That's not how it was arranged."

"Yeah, well, just listen to this. The signal-to-noise ratio sucks, it's all scratchy, and it's in mono. Why would you want to listen to that?"

Martin said, "Tell you what, buddy. I'll listen to my Temptations in yucky mono, and you go listen to your Yanni in wonderful digital blah blah stereo, and we'll see who goes to Music Hell when he dies."

Robert snickered and looked at Paul.

Paul shrugged. "Hey, you know me. Audiophile to the bone. Well, see you around, roomies. Some of us have things to accomplish."

"Later," Jason said.

"Later," Martin echoed. He twirled the butterfly knife.

"See ya, roomie," Robert said cheerily. Jason glanced sharply at him. Robert had his I'm-a-friendly-guy face on. Paul waved and went out between the books and down the old stairs.

Still with the cheery face, Robert said, "Some of us have things to accomplish!"

"Asshole," Martin muttered, flicking the butterfly knife.

Jason didn't say anything. The Temptations sang "My Baby," which helped, but it was still too hot.

3

I gotta ask you," Paul said. He narrowed his eyes and looked at Jason. They were sitting in rickety red plastic folding chairs on the porch of the Manor. A warm early-evening breeze ruffled the dead leaves on the dead lawn somberly without actually dislodging them. "How come you asked me to live here?"

"You needed a place."

Paul shrugged. "Okay."

They sat and watched the traffic. A sparkly blue mini-truck drove by with Snoop Doggy Dogg thumping in its camper shell.

"Stupid song," Jason said.

"You're not black."

Jason said, "No, it's a stupid song." The truck turned at the corner of Del Mar. "Nice feel on those triplets, though."

"So what are you up to tonight?"

Jason said, reluctantly, "I've got a weekly jam session, down around Crenshaw. West Africans, mostly. I have a real gig Saturday night with some of the regulars."

Paul looked interested. "What time?"

"I figured I'd leave around nine-thirty."

Jason looked out at Marengo. Two women were walking on the other side of the street with a baby carriage. The front wheel of the carriage had a faint white mark on it, and the mark played a visual rhythm every time the wheel spun. The wheel's movement over the regular intervals of the concrete sidewalk grooves made a second visual rhythm. Jason tried to hold both rhythms in his head.

"That's cool," Paul said. "I mean, it's not as good as doing your own stuff, but sometimes I can get into that off-the-wall shit. Should I bring anything tonight?"

The women's feet made two more rhythms. Jason tried to layer them with the carriage rhythms, but it was too much to hold at once and he lost all of it.

He shook his head distractedly, still partly in the rhythms. "Nope."

FIFTH STREET DICK'S didn't have a lot of square footage, but there were stairs up to a loft, where the musicians were. As they went in past men playing nighttime chess at outdoor tables, Paul said, "Wow, I never expected you to come to a place like this."

"Why?"

"Well, just look around."

Jason looked around. Two women were drinking coffee and chatting at the long counter that ran the length of the room, a man with a knit hat was talking on the pay telephone, the guy behind the counter looked bored, and an offhanded scatter of casual hand drum sounds floated easily down from the loft. A metal bookshelf held flyers and community newspapers. One of the newspapers was turned so Jason could read the headline: Louis Farrakhan and Lyndon LaRouche agreed about the Anti-Defamation League. It was a clean, neat place, and the dark, empty street showed through the front windows.

"What," Jason said.

"You're the only white person here."

Jason looked again, irritated. Now he'd notice everyone's color for the rest of the night. The counterperson watched them indifferently as they went up the stairs.

The loft was ten feet wide by twenty feet long, and half of it was a performance area that barely contained two conga players, an electric bassist, an electric guitarist, and a talking drum player. The talking drum was an hourglass-shaped drum slung over the player's shoulder on a strap. A cylindrical web of tight cords stretched from the drumhead to the drum bottom, and by squeezing this web under his arm, the player could raise the pitch of the drum while it was being played. It was called a talking drum because languages existed that could be articulated in its playing. Sometimes during a jam session, some of the Africans would all crack up simultaneously, and Jason would find out later that the talking drum had been insulting the dancers.

An electronic keyboard sat on top of an old, battered, brown upright piano. The other half of the loft was filled with a dozen folding chairs in rows. Somebody's grandfather's uncle's old brown floor fan that he was just going to throw away anyway sat to one side of the performance area, impersonating a functional cooling device and making a racket.

All the musicians were black, Jason noticed, annoyed again with Paul for making it matter. Some were African and some weren't.

The bass player said, "Aay, Jason!" and put out his right hand. Jason said, "Hey, Pete," gripped the hand, and slid through a three-part handshake. Paul's presence made him self-conscious about the handshake.

He took a black box the size of a small encyclopedia volume out of his backpack and used a cable to hook it into the back of the synthesizer atop the piano. The box contained piano sounds that could be played from the keyboard. Jason used it instead of the real piano because the real piano was never in tune. He always found a measure of ironic pleasure in seeing his electronic emulation of a piano perched atop a real one.

Paul gestured at the keyboard and said, "I see you have a DX-7. I used to have a couple of them, but all my stuff got seized. I miss my DX-7s, though. Great boards."

The DX-7 was responsible for the sappy electric piano sound on every schmaltzy pop song from the 1980s. Jason thought it was a good thing the government had finally come to its senses and started seizing them.

Paul did a rueful head shake. "I rented my warehouse in Chicago to these people who were using it as a crank lab, but I didn't know it. So to make a long story short, when the cops busted them, they got all my stuff along with the meth stuff. They got everything—my Linn drum machine, sixteen-track, all my microphones, the warehouse itself, and everything. It'll be years before it all gets sorted out."

The needle on Jason's internal bullshit detector pegged itself to the right. He carefully did not react.

"That's really a shame," Pete said.

"Yeah," Paul said, "it really set me back. But I got some money coming now."

"You should sit in," Pete said.

"Hey, I'd love to."

Jason said, "I'll just finish connecting my stuff."

On the way home afterward, on the freeway, Paul said, "What's eating you?"

"Nothing," Jason said. "Just tired."

"Whatever," Paul said, as though Jason's emotional instability wasn't his problem. He looked out the passenger window at the tall downtown buildings that barely moved in the distance as the freeway rushed by.

JASON GOT IN a little after midnight, turned on the television in his front room, and sat on his wooden piano bench to watch the news. The lead story was about a "high-speed chase" that had caused "terror on Southland freeways." There were pictures from several angles of a car going fast. The next story was about a "controversial decision," which hadn't been made yet, but which was going to affect the "Southland bail-bonds community."

"Controversial," Jason said to the screen after the newscaster said it. *"Terror on Southland freeways. Bail-bonds community."* He tried to get Important Reporter Cadence in his voice, but it probably took years of practice in front of a mirror and a lot of determination and lack of anything worthwhile to do.

The weather idiot pointed at things on a bluescreened map and said the heat wave would break the next day. When the newscast ended, Jason closed his eyes and concentrated to see whether he was any smarter than he'd been before it started. He wasn't.

4

At two in the morning, somebody stomped up the stairs to Paul's room, knocked on the door, and waited. The person's shifting weight was clearly audible as creaks in Jason's front room. Paul's footsteps crossed Jason's ceiling, and then Paul's door rattled open. Muffled male voices exchanged soft words. Then somebody went down the stairs, the door closed, and Paul's footsteps recrossed the ceiling.

Was Paul dealing? There was that comment about his coming into money soon.

Bothered, Jason sat again on his piano bench in front of the music equipment that occupied a black L-shaped rack system that loomed like a jungle gym in the corner of his front room. His laptop Macintosh computer was powered up, the little indicator lights on his keyboards glowed, his software beckoned, and he had no musical ideas at all. A black wire spiraled from his headphones to a little mixing board that perched on the rack next to the keyboards. The piece he was trying to work on was called "Untitled #23," and it said so at the top of his screen. It was one of thirty-odd incomplete fragments of music that he'd created in several months. It was his favorite of the bunch, but it wasn't working. What it really needed was for him to get out of town for a while, to get away from familiar surroundings. But he'd taken the job from Platt, so now that was out of the question.

In light of the unique challenges posed by the unfinished composition, he reassessed his options:

He could order pizza, but he knew of no pizza delivery at two-thirty in the morning.

He could walk to the Salt Shaker and eat a chili omelette, but he lacked the motivation necessary for such an involved plan.

He could undergo a creative epiphany that would grip him in an artistic frenzy of incandescent intensity.

He could check his e-mail.

He quit the music program, shut off his keyboards, and dialed in to MUSE.

```
HELLO NOTE ON
You have 1 new mail message.

From: METAMUSIC
To: NOTE ON
Subj: party

Call me at Light Wizards in Glendale
when you can.
_*_
MUSE DISCONNECTED
```

When the computer broke the connection, Jason picked up the phone headset, got the number from 411, and called.

Platt's voice said, "Light Wizards."

Jason said, "Hello, is this White Lizards?"

"That's funny. Are you available tomorrow night?"

"Tomorrow's Friday. It's date night all over the country."

"Good, then you're free."

"Sure."

"There's a party at L.A. Arts College on the second floor of the Cage building. There'll be a guy there named Huey Benton. Take Paul with you and see if anything happens between them."

"Why would it?"

"It just might."

"Ah."

"Benton is either a brilliant genius or a total flake, depending on who's talking. He's heavily into the whole virtual reality wave-of-the-future multimedia interactive BS research thing, and he's gotten some grants, but now he's in with a not so nice crowd, maybe for research money. Some of them are those seedy, serious friends of Paul's I told you about."

"So is he a genius or a flake?"

"Beats me."

"Know any geniuses?"

"No."

"So I'm supposed to see if they exchange meaningful glances, fisticuffs, sloppy tongue kisses, subtle tip-offs like that."

"Right."

"Okay. If Paul can't go, should I still go?"

"Only if you're interested in virtual reality."

"Is there free food?"

Platt chuckled. "I forgot what motivates you. Probably so, though it may just be controlled substances and smart drinks."

"What the hell's a smart drink?"

"B-vitamins and wheat grass and all that stuff in high concentrations, liquefied in a blender."

"Oh barf," Jason said. "So how do we get in?"

"There should be no problem. These things are generally loose. Drop my name if you feel you need to. Oh, and you can't miss Huey Benton. Look for a six-foot dread-locked Viking with a red beard. Prefers tattooed brunettes and drinks tequila and Midori."

"Can't these guys ever come up with anything original?"

"Right."

"What's Midori?"

"Sweet melon liqueur, most often combined with vodka and orange juice to make Melonballs."

"Tequila and melon liqueur? That is totally disgusting. So, what does White Lizards do?"

"Let me know what happens."

"Okay."

Platt hung up. Jason powered all his stuff down and went to bed. Chuck who lived upstairs walked around for an hour and made Jason's ceiling rattle and creak. After Jason fell asleep, Chuck dropped something hard on his floor and Jason woke suddenly, tangled in a damp sheet with jittery adrenaline amplifying the pulse that pounded through bone induction in his ears. The dropped thing rolled across the floor and went *tunk!* against a wall. Chuck creaked around some more and then stopped, and Jason swore, threw the damp sheet off the bed, and went raggedly back to sleep in the still warm air.

5

The heat didn't break the next day, but at ten o'clock in the morning, it was only eighty degrees. Jason ground some hazelnut coffee beans and started coffee brewing in the coffeemaker he'd given his ex-wife for her birthday before it turned out she wasn't very nice. The coffeemaker sat on top of a large, wheeled dish cabinet made of particleboard that was insufficiently rigid to support its own weight, so the top surface bowed in the middle, exposing an unpainted strip along the vertical back piece. Next to the cabinet, a battered green Coleman stove perched atop its propane tank. Jason called the arrangement a "pseudo-kitchen," and used it instead of the Manor's real kitchen because it was closer.

He went outside to look at the sky. It was sky blue, a noteworthy event in the San Gabriel Valley, and even had little wispy white clouds. Hidden in the trees at the edge of the parking lot, a small flock of parrots cackled and talked, and a slight wind ruffled the leaves. People who moved to Pasadena were always surprised by the parrots.

He tried to think of something whimsically literary and gently ironic to muse aloud to the pretty sky, but all he could think of was, "A man, a plan, a canal: Panama!" He said it. It failed to evoke the desired mood. He resolved to do more reading.

Waldo, the gray-and-white cat who lived somewhere in the condos past the parking lot, lay sprawled on his back in some dead grass at the bottom of the staircase, his legs splayed in four different directions. He regarded Jason upside-down and blinked slothfully. Jason squatted next to him and said, "You're fired." Waldo yawned cross-eyed and rolled in the dead leaves, flagrantly indifferent to his faltering career. "Okay," Jason said, "but this reprimand is going in your file." Waldo sneezed decisively at him. Jason looked around for a thin stick that Waldo would want to chase in the grass, but there wasn't one. He scratched Waldo on the ribs and then decided it was time to compose. He went back into the Manor and sat down on the piano bench.

He played a few notes and then realized his coffee was gone, so he got up and went into the pseudo-kitchen and poured more. He noticed that the strip of veneer on the front edge of the dish cabinet was coming loose, and looked through the apartment for some glue. There wasn't any, so he went outside and rummaged around in the storage space under the sagging exterior staircase. There wasn't any there, either. He went back in the house and found a hammer and some little nails, and drove one of the nails through the veneer and into the particleboard behind it. The particleboard split when the nails went in, and looked as though it would have to be glued.

His coffee was gone again, so he poured some more,

went back into the front room, and sat down on the piano bench. The little work surface that the computer sat on was very dusty. He got up to look for a dust rag and some glue for the dish cabinet.

Feet thudded down the interior staircase, a door opened and closed, and there was a knock on Jason's front door. He got up and opened it. Robert said, "Are you busy? What are you doing?"

"Composing," Jason said.

"Cool," Robert said. "Can I hear it?"

"It's not done yet."

Robert squinched his left eye shut and peered at Jason. "Mine either."

Jason waited. Robert peered.

"What," Jason said, "do you want?"

"I wanted to either see you working industriously at your work so that I would be inspired to work industriously at mine, or see if you wanted to go get some used records."

Jason hesitated.

"Clearly," Robert said, opening his left eye and squinching his right, "you are working industriously indeed. I would not want to be the cause of the interruption of such industrious—"

Robert made a big show of groping for the word.

Jason waited for the punchline, which he predicted to be "industry."

"—industry," Robert said. He looked one-eyed at Jason and waited.

Jason looked behind him at the computer and synthesizers and the dusty work surface.

"I can take a break," he said. "We walking?"

Robert opened both eyes and smiled happily. "No, you're driving."

ROBERT STOOD OUTSIDE the Plymouth's passenger door while Jason got in the driver's side.

"It doesn't lock," Jason yelled when Robert continued to stand outside.

Robert opened the door and got in. "And I should know this how?"

It took a few tries to start the Plymouth. Once it was going, Jason had to tickle the accelerator to keep the irregular engine rhythm from becoming too rough, coughing, and dying. Desiccated remains of the original green cloth headliner drooped from the underside of the metal roof, exposing rotten gold acoustic insulation. Jason had tried to sew up the headliner, but the fabric was too old, and the thread sliced through crosswise when pulled, leaving dangling strips. Robert angled his head so that the strips lay across his face and politely asked, "May I?"

"Go ahead," Jason said. Robert tore down the strips. The motion dislodged some of the acoustic insulation, which came apart into fine dust, made him sneeze, and stuck to his forehead.

"Have you thought about a new car?" Robert inquired. "I'm just asking."

"Nope."

Jason shifted into reverse and the Plymouth went about four inches before the engine shuddered and died. He shifted into neutral and started it again.

"These old engines have to warm up first," he said.

"Yes they do," Robert said. He sneezed again. Jason tromped on the accelerator. The crumbling floorboard under his heel gave a little, but the engine rhythm became a little less rough.

"There we go," Jason said. "The automatic choke was

just stuck." He shifted into reverse and backed out of the parking space. Something in the back of the car clunked loudly when he braked, but the clunk sounded the same as it always did.

The Plymouth wouldn't stop at the end of the driveway, so he quickly let up on the brake pedal and then stomped on it, throwing Robert forward.

"Sorry," he said.

"We could walk," Robert said. "It's not all that far."

"Nah," Jason said. "I'm probably just low on brake fluid. I'll check it later."

They drove to the used record store. Jason had to pump the brakes every time he wanted to stop, and the engine throbbed and sputtered. Robert bought some Benny Goodman and Mike Curb Congregation records in the original cardboard jackets for seventy-five cents each. Jason offered him two dollars for each Mike Curb Congregation record he'd promise to destroy, but Robert called him a Philistine, an enemy of art, and a cheesehead, and haughtily refused.

They parked at the Manor without incident. Robert went in, and Jason went up the back stairs and knocked on Paul's door.

The door had a flimsy plastic window and a small set of white plastic miniblinds where there had originally been the topmost of three wood panels. The blinds moved a little, and Paul opened the door.

"What's up," he said.

Jason said, "Want to go to a party tonight at L.A. Arts?"

Paul looked at him blankly for a few seconds and then said, "Sure. What time?"

"Leave at seven-thirty, get there around eight-fifteen?"

"You'll drive?"

"Sure."

"Okay." Paul shrugged with his eyebrows. "I got nothing else to do."

Benny Goodman started playing his clarinet in Robert and Martin's apartment. Paul looked pained and said, "I hope those guys get off this old music kick and get back to the nineties soon."

"Right," Jason said. "Play some good music. Some Marilyn Manson, maybe some Jewel. Enough of this moldy crap. Some Spice Girls, maybe."

Paul said, "You know, you really got some attitude lately."

Jason said, "I like Benny Goodman."

"If you don't mind my saying so, what you really need is to get laid."

Jason said, "See you at seven-thirty."

"Later." Paul went back into his room. Jason went down the creaking stairs and scratched Waldo on top of the head for a while until Waldo got sick of it and clawed Jason's hand. Jason retaliated by flicking Waldo's snout with his forefinger, and Waldo growled and ran under the Manor.

Jason put hydrogen peroxide on the scratches, leaned against the sink, and watched it fizz. When the fizzing became less fascinating, he went into his front room and sat on the piano bench most of the day, listening to Paul move around upstairs and writing halfhearted music.

At seven o'clock, he gave up. Until he could leave town, he wasn't going to get anywhere with it. He deleted the day's music and switched everything off. In the bathroom, he took an old pair of pliers from the soap dish in the shower stall, turned the stripped knobs on either side of the bath spigot, and took a shower in a trickle of lukewarm water. At seven-thirty, carefully shaven and dressed in jeans and his good shirt, he went upstairs and knocked on Paul's door. Paul was ready to go in black jeans with extra-wide belt loops and a purple polo shirt.

"Wow," Paul said. "You shaved."

The Mike Curb Congregation started singing "The Candy Man" in Robert's room. Then Robert and Martin started singing along. Paul bugged his eyes out in horror and said, "Shit! Let's get the hell out of here!"

"HEY, NICE CAR," Paul said as he got in.

The Plymouth died when Jason put it into gear. He started it again and nursed it into the street. The engine vibration had a rough, rhythmic surge to it, as though one cylinder might not be functional.

"Feels like it's missing," Jason said.

"You sure we'll make it?" Paul said.

"Nothing is certain, Grasshopper. We could always take your car."

"Hey, I'm not complaining," Paul said. "Just wondering."

On the onramp to the 134, the Plymouth shuddered and pulled as its nearly bald front driver's side tire rolled into a pavement seam and stayed there until the seam ended at the top of the ramp.

At the Interstate, they almost ran into the back of a brown Buick Skylark when the brakes failed to work properly. Jason pumped the brake pedal and wrenched the wheel to the left, coming to a stop partly out of his lane.

"Ought to fix that," he said to Paul in a casual voice.

"No shit."

When he pulled back into traffic, something didn't feel right. He stopped in the emergency lane and got out to look. The front driver's side tire, its tread worn completely through to frayed steel belts, had blown its sidewall to shreds.

Paul exuded sincere helpfulness but did not help. While he was unearthing his spare tire, Jason's gas can and a bunch of oil and coolant bottles and general clutter from the trunk ended up strewn on the ground. Then when the new wheel was on and the blown tire back in the trunk, the other junk wouldn't fit back where it came from, so the trunk wouldn't close. Jason leaned against the side of the car and tried not to be angry.

"I thought you were going to do that," Paul admitted.

Jason said nothing, tossed the bottles and clutter onto the back sat, and said, "Let's go."

IN A BAD mood, Jason found a parking space on the small L.A. Arts campus, got a tube of mechanics' hand soap from the junk on the back seat, and walked with Paul toward the sound of throbbing electronic music. A metal plaque affixed to a two-story brick building said "Cage." The music pulsed from within the building, mixed with the sound of party chatter.

A strange mix of people milled around on the wide interior stairway, spillover from the party. Middle-aged professorial men held forth for younger men in ill-fitting shirts and young women in either no makeup or severe makeup. There were a lot of soft fringed boots, floppy hats, dreadlocks, bits and pieces of touristy-schlocky ethno-trinkets, nose rings, and pierced eyebrows and tongues; self-conscious attempts to create personal trademarks, something someone would mention. At the top of the staircase, more of the same people stood near an open classroom door, through which came the loud music and more party hubbub.

Paul said, "I thought we were going to a real party."

"We've been here maybe thirty seconds," Jason said. "How do you know what kind of party it is?"

"Get real."

"You want to leave?"

"We're here," Paul sighed. "We might as well make the best of it."

Jason said, "Think positive. Maybe they'll play Naked Pictionary."

Paul looked at him as though he were dripping mucus. Jason spotted a men's room.

"I need to clean up."

"Sure."

PAUL WENT INTO the loudest classroom and watched. Then he went out to Jason's Plymouth with a square glass bottle. He looked through the rear window at the trunk clutter and the container of coolant and opened the un-lockable door.

AFTER FIVE MINUTES of scrubbing with the last of the mechanics' hand soap and the powdered stuff in the men's room dispenser, Jason figured his hands weren't going to get any cleaner. Paul wasn't there when he came back out.

The electronic music ended, and another piece that sounded just like it began. Some of the young women in the hallway recognized the new piece and moved their shoulders a little over their drinks, as though unable to muster sufficient natural rhythm for distribution over an entire body. Some of the young men looked approving of the new piece of music and bobbed their heads coolly to it without moving anything below the neck. Nobody actually danced.

Paul appeared next to him.

"White people," Jason said, looking at the non-dancers and shaking his head.

"That was a racist remark," Paul said. He didn't sound as though he actually cared. Jason didn't respond, but he decided to think about it later.

The music went *thump thump thump thump*, and some of the upstairs windowpanes buzzed in their slider tracks. Everybody not danced.

Huey Benton came out of the classroom with a small, tattooed, dark-haired girl under one arm and a squarish glass bottle of greenish liquid in the same hand. Platt's description was accurate; Benton was big, with a red beard and reddish-blond dreadlocks. He looked about twenty-six years old, and wore a buttoned shirt with red-and-white candy-cane stripes over gray no-iron pants that sagged in the crotch and needed ironing or possibly immolation. His face was flushed, and he brandished the sloshing bottle aggressively.

"Steamafuggn drngwooja!" he slurred. He stood unsteadily in the doorway for a few seconds with his bottle, swaying, and then pitched over onto the floor in the hallway, scattering a small group of younger people.

"There," Jason said to Paul. "See? It's a real party."

Paul rolled his eyes.

Jason said, "You'd rather be back at the Manor, singing along with Robert and Martin?"

Paul made a sour face. "Listening to fucking Pat Boone?"

"Fucking Mike Curb," Jason corrected. "Not fucking Pat Boone. If you can't be bothered to learn the subtle differentiations, I'm not loaning you any more of my Up With Fucking People records."

"Whatever," Paul said. "What a couple of racial stereotypes, anyway."

"Who?"

Paul looked at him as though he'd admitted he didn't know who Wilma Flintstone was. "Who else? Your little roomies there. The black dude with the knife and the Jew with the books and the chess set. Talk about your racial stereotypes."

"Yeah, Paul, they're a regular Amos and Abraham."

The dark-haired girl with the tattoos was kneeling next to Benton. She jerked away from him. "Oh my god!" She looked around in a panic. "Does anyone know CPR?"

A young man with short thick hair said, "Here, let me get in here." She moved aside and stood, and he felt to the side of Benton's Adam's apple for a pulse. Then he felt the other side.

"He's got no pulse," he said.

Jason gave Paul his keys and said, "Get the first-aid kit from the trunk." As Paul left, he got on his knees next to the young man.

The young man said, almost panicked, "You know CPR?"

"Yeah." Benton had hit his head on the upright metal doorstop when he fell, and there was a lot of wet, slick blood in his hair and on the floor. Jason looked up at the gathering crowd. "You," he said to a young woman with a yellow crystal necklace, "Find a telephone and call the paramedics. Tell them there's a man here with a head injury and no pulse who's probably had way too much to drink. When you've done it, come back and tell me."

The young woman said, "Okay," and left.

The young man was kneeling next to Benton's chest,

beginning CPR. Jason checked for a throat pulse, found none, moved to the side, tilted Benton's head back, and started mouth-to-mouth resuscitation through the strong, strange odor of sweet tequila, counting to coordinate with the young man and moving periodically to listen for breathing. There was none. Benton's abdomen distended as they worked and he started turning purple. At some point, the yellow crystal necklace came back and said the paramedics were on their way. At another point, Paul and the first-aid kit showed up, but there was no use for it. Paul kept trying to help, but he just got in the way and Jason had to tell him to move back. The paramedics came and took over from Jason and the young man, who got to their feet shakily and leaned against the wall next to the classroom. Jason's legs were wobbly. The paramedics gave up shortly thereafter, put the body on a gurney, covered it, and rolled it away. Somebody started in about alcohol poisoning, and someone else said no, it was obviously the blow to the head that did him in.

Jason shook hands with the young man. Then he and Paul went outside and leaned against the building.

"Where'd you learn that?" Paul said.

"When I used to be on the pipeline crew." Jason's knees still shook, and he felt distracted.

"You stay here," Paul said. "Give me your keys and I'll get the car."

As Paul walked away with the keys and the first-aid kit, Jason put his hands on his knees and leaned against the building that way. A few minutes later, Paul came back and said, "I can't drive that thing. It keeps dying."

"That's okay." Jason straightened and took his keys back. "I doubt anybody could drive it but me." They walked back to the car, which jutted a little out of its parking space.

Jason started the engine and put it in reverse, tickling the accelerator to keep the engine from dying. The rear brakes went *clunk* and the engine died.

"Engine seems to have gotten worse," he said. His hands were still shaking. He started the engine again, revved it for a while, and stomped on the accelerator to try to close the automatic choke. His foot sank into the floorboard a little, and when he moved it, he could see the pavement through a rough hole the size of a dime where his heel had been. He put it in gear and drove back to Marengo Manor.

6

Back at the Manor at eleven o'clock, Paul went upstairs, and Jason went into his front room and called Light Wizards. His hands were steadier and his knees were no longer wobbly, but he was in a weird mood, removed, as though someone had shrink-wrapped his brain.

Platt answered.

Jason said, "When can we meet?"

"Midnight," Platt said. "Denny's."

"Which Denny's?"

Platt gave him directions. Jason said, "See you there," and hung up. It would take twenty minutes to get to Denny's. That left forty minutes to kill. He opened up the laptop computer and turned all his synthesizers on. Then he turned them all off, closed the laptop, got his jacket, and went out the back.

As he locked the rickety back door in the dark, Paul came out of his upstairs room in a black leather jacket. He headed down the staircase with a casual step that faltered almost imperceptibly when, halfway down, he saw Jason looking up at him through the gaps between the stair treads.

"Going out?" Jason said.

"You know me. The night is young." Paul stood on the staircase and breathed in the young night, as though casting for the spoor of a good party. He shrugged and looked down at Jason, "Why should I let one piece of bad news ruin the rest of it?"

"Where you off to?"

"Oh, here and there. I got some parties to hit, maybe score some weed, maybe get a little lucky. Hey, I meant to ask you. How do you guys feel about weed?"

"An insidious suckhole for creativity if used habitually. But—" Jason shrugged. "Your business."

Paul nodded and said, "That's cool." He descended the staircase and went to his beige hatchback as Jason got into the Plymouth.

Paul turned right onto Del Mar, and Jason turned left and nursed the shuddering Plymouth toward the freeway. The engine rattled and shook like an amateur death scene. In twenty-five minutes, Jason was sitting in the yellow light of a Denny's restaurant, sipping coffee and waiting for a slice of apple pie with cinnamon ice cream on it or Norton Platt, whichever showed up first. The booths were an ugly pastel purple that had been popular for about nine minutes in 1983, and they were hideous in the yellow light.

The slice of pie showed up first. Jason ate most of it before Platt slid into the vinyl booth and said, "Don't tell me yet. I'm starving." He got the waiter's attention and ordered coffee, soft-boiled eggs, and a short stack of pancakes. The waitress went away and then came back with his coffee.

Jason said, "So what does White Lizards do?"

"Contracted visuals and audio for a company called Synervision that does CD-ROM games." Platt put sugar in his coffee and stirred it.

"And you're doing—?"

"Sound for one of their CD-ROM games."

"Oh."

Platt looked up from his coffee. "A note of surprise?"

"I guess I never thought you could just . . . get up and leave the cloak-and-dagger biz."

Platt raised one eyebrow. "You've been reading way too much John le Carré."

"I guess. So what's this CD-ROM game?"

"*Devils of Alpha-Six.* They're shooting little latex space monsters this week. Next week it's miniature spaceships with little missile launchers on them. I'm making whooshes and screaming monster noises and explosions."

Jason looked at him.

Platt looked back.

Jason said, "Uh-huh."

Platt said, "Yes, it's dumb." His eggs and pancakes came. He peppered the eggs. When he'd eaten half of them, he said, "Okay, the fog is clearing. Tell me what's up."

"I took Paul to the party. Huey Benton fell over dead."

Platt's fork paused on its way to his mouth. "Tell me."

Jason told him everything he could remember, concluding with, "Somebody said it seemed like fatal alcohol poisoning."

"Did it seem like fatal alcohol poisoning to you?" Platt said.

"Got me. What does fatal alcohol poisoning look like?"

"Initially, like being extremely drunk."

"Maybe. He was up, then he was down. Then he was dead."

"Obstruction to the air passage?"

"No, it was clear."

"The head wound?"

"I didn't really see it. It was serious enough to bleed a lot."

"That doesn't necessarily mean anything with a head injury."

Jason spread his hands apologetically. "I didn't have the presence of mind to inspect the wound."

"So it's most likely that he got really drunk, lost his balance, fell over, and received a fatal blow to the head."

"Okay."

Platt ate his pancakes. Jason said, "You think that's what happened?"

"We won't know until I see the coroner's report." Platt sipped some coffee. "It's most likely. Occam's razor generally holds true; the simplest explanation is usually the correct one. But . . . sometimes not. It could be that someone injected him with something, tampered with his drink, or any number of other things. What about Paul? Did he seem to know Benton?"

"There wasn't time to find out. I didn't see anything meaningful, though. What do you want me to do next?"

"Back to Plan A. Just baby-sit Paul. Where is he?"

"Out trying to score some weed," Jason said. Then he felt like a fool and said, "Duh. I should have gone with him. You ask me to take him to meet Benton, Benton falls over dead, Paul takes off by himself, and I go out for pie."

Platt nodded. "Pick it up tomorrow and keep better tabs on him."

"Okay." Jason picked up his pie fork. "So if you're out of the cloak-and-dagger business, how come you've got me following Paul around?"

Platt smiled. "Well," he said. "I'm not *totally* out of the cloak-and-dagger business."

"Good to have something to fall back on," Jason said, "in case the screaming monster market dries up." He ate the remains of his pie, and Platt finished his eggs and coffee.

On the way to the cashier, Jason asked how you could hear monsters screaming if they were in a vacuum, and Platt nodded and explained that it was partly because the clever monsters were ingeniously able to disseminate coherent vacuum waves and mostly because the producer's girlfriend wrote the script.

The cashier overheard him and said with some heat that all producers' girlfriends should be banned from the set.

"Actors except for Robert are annoying," Jason said when they were outside, "but without them, the West Coast food service industry would founder."

7

At the sound of a car in the lot, Jason went to the back door, moved aside the orange towel that hung over the window, and looked out. The beige hatchback was in its space, and he could hear Paul going up the rickety back stairs. Jason went out. Paul was on the landing above, going through his keys. He looked down at Jason.

"Hey," he said.

"Score some good stuff?"

Paul came down the stairs. "Nah. Not tonight. Why, you want some?"

"Nope."

"It's been a weird night. I could see you wanting to relax."

"Not for me."

"Oh, right. I forgot. You never relax."

Martin's little CVCC pulled into the lot and Robert and Martin got out and walked toward them.

"How was the party?" Martin said.

"Short," Jason said. "A guy died."

"Died like died?"

"Yeah."

"You saw it?"

"Yeah."

Paul said, "He tried to save the guy. Totally heroic. I was impressed."

"That's why I was doing it, Paul," Jason said. "To impress you."

"Hey," Paul said. "Don't take it out on me that it didn't work. Look at the bright side. At least we didn't die on the way home in that car of yours. That would have really sucked."

Robert said, "But, since it wasn't you who died, it didn't suck."

Paul looked at him without saying anything.

Robert said, "I'm just trying to understand."

Paul glared at him. "All I said, Robert, is that it would suck. You have some kind of fucking problem with that?"

After the briefest pause, something in Robert's face seemed to click to a different setting.

He leaned closer to Paul.

Martin shuffled back to give him a little space and looked as though he expected to enjoy whatever happened next.

Robert paused.

Then, "That word!" Robert emoted intensely, his gaze burning into Paul's. "What was it? What *was* it?" He shut his eyes and concentrated. Paul gave him a look that could decapitate capybaras.

Robert pressed his fingertips to his forehead and concentrated fiercely.

"That jewel of meaning," he keened. "That tiny, shimmering perfection of poetry . . ." He half-opened his eyes in pleasure and touched the tips of his forefingers to his thumbs. " *'Suck!'* " He drew in a great breath, as though filling his lungs with sheer beauty. " *'Suck!'* Angels weep. Bards forsake their souls! The simple magnificence of that mere utterance conjures images of such scintillating splendor, such coruscating opalescence—"

"Shut up," Paul said. "You knew what I—"

Robert silenced him with one upheld hand. "Suck," he entreated, savoring the word deliciously.

Martin said, "You're a weird guy, Robert."

Robert sang, "Suuuuuuuuck!" in a loud, trembling falsetto.

Paul went *humph* and said, "Weird is an understatement."

"Suck," Robert insisted. "Suck. Suck. Suck. Suck. Suck."

Jason froze his face in a casual expression, clamped his jaw so he wouldn't crack up, and didn't look at Martin.

"Robert—" Paul began.

"Suck," Robert hissed murderously.

"Suck!" Robert ululated warblingly.

"Suck?" Robert implored querulously.

"Ro—" Paul began.

"Suck!" Robert interrupted. He nodded his head wisely and looked like a dog waiting for the next throw of a stick.

Paul said, "Ro—"

"Suck," Robert interrupted joyously.

Paul gave him a tough look. Robert twisted his lips around and snuffled like a warthog.

Paul shook his head in superiority and disgust. "Later." He turned and went upstairs.

Robert's face clicked back into a normal expression. No one said anything until they went into Jason's back room and he closed the door. Then Martin lost it, spinning on one heel, slapping his thighs, and cackling.

"And they say vaudeville is dead," Jason said.

"Paul is my favorite person," Robert said nicely. "Also, I win."

JASON DIDN'T FEEL like being by himself, so he got Robert onto the subject of books. Then they spent forty minutes making Martin defend his offhanded assertion that there were comic books equal in literary value to books by Ernest Hemingway and Maya Angelou. Despite the fact that Martin probably didn't believe his own assertion or even really care about the issue, he argued doggedly. It ended when Robert got him to admit that he'd never actually read anything by Hemingway or Angelou.

"Hey," Jason said, "you're getting pretty good with that butterfly knife."

Martin snorted through his decaf. "I figure if I just get that one move down, I can intimidate people enough so they never find out I don't know anything else."

"Sounds a little risky to me," Jason said. "What if it doesn't intimidate them?"

Robert said, "Then I sing the timeless classic 'I'm Only Thinking of Him' from *Man of La Mancha*."

He demonstrated. Martin said over the singing, "Or I could show some mercy and just slash their throats."

At three-thirty in the morning, Robert and Martin left and went upstairs, and Jason sat on his piano bench, put on just one side of his headphones so he could hear if Paul left again, switched all his music equipment on, and opened "Untitled #23."

He moved the mouse so that the onscreen cursor was positioned over a picture of a button labeled Play, and clicked. The music began to play in his headphones. It was all wrong, and he couldn't leave town to work on it like he really needed to. He stopped playback in mid-note and began tinkering with it, disliking the fact that he was doing so at home in Pasadena, and wondering whether the death earlier that evening would affect the creative process.

DAYLIGHT CAME IN from outside, and Jason's ears hurt from the headphones pressed against them. He pulled the headphones down so they sat around his neck, pushed his ears forward to their approved, upright positions, brought up the laptop's onscreen clock, and was shocked to find that it was 8:26 in the morning. Clunks in the plumbing and creaks in the ceiling evidenced housemates walking around and taking their scheduled showers, and a clock radio alarm was beeping somewhere in the house.

Someone knocked on the front door. Jason got halfway across the room before the headphone wire pulled taut and nearly strangled him. He extricated himself from the headphones and tossed them on the sofa.

Upstairs, Patrice's voice yelled, "Turn off the damn alarm clock!"

The alarm clock stopped. Jason opened the door.

There was a short, unshaven man there with blue eyes and copper-colored hair, wearing a brown wool jacket.

"Good morning," the man said.

"Good morning," Jason agreed.

The man didn't say anything else.

Jason said, "Would you like a *Watchtower*?"

The man said, "I beg your pardon?"

"I thought maybe you'd forgotten your line."

"No."

"Well, that's good."

The man said, "Is it safe to talk?"

Jason said, "Is it ever?"

"Ah," the man beamed. "Very true."

"Yes," Jason said. "Who are you?"

"Ian Hibbit," the man said, in a surprised tone. "Shall I come in, Mr. Reno, or would you prefer that I stand on the porch where anyone can see me?"

"Aha," Jason said. "The source of confusion swims into view. I am not Mr. Reno."

Ian Hibbit blanched. "I see," he said. "I'm terribly sorry. Is this not 'Marengo Manor'?"

"Yes it is," Jason said, "but Paul lives up around back."

"Ah," Ian Hibbit said. "Terribly, terribly sorry. Thank you very much."

He went off the porch to Jason's right. Jason sat down at his piano bench and considered the possibility of a bassoon part. He clicked on the record button, and a metronome countoff clicked from the computer's little speaker. His hands were poised over one of his synthesizers, ready to begin playing a bassoon sound, when there was a knock at the back door.

The countoff ended, and the music started on beat without Jason playing the bassoon part. He stopped the music, went through his apartment to the back door, and opened it.

"Upstairs," he said to Ian Hibbit, pointing at the exterior staircase.

"So sorry," Hibbit said, and went up the stairs. Jason went into the front room again, sat down, put his headphones on, and couldn't remember the bassoon part he had intended to record.

A few minutes later, he'd found another part for the bassoon. As the countoff reached its end, and he began playing, there was another knock at the back door. Jason ignored it and kept playing, but now he was tense from the knocking, so he flubbed the part. He sighed in exasperation, gave up on getting anything else done, went to the back, and opened the door. Ian Hibbit was standing on the back step.

"Terribly, terribly sorry," he said, aiming a small, shiny semi-automatic pistol at Jason's face. "I'm afraid I'm going to have to come in after all."

8

Paul's much more fun to shoot than I am," Jason said.

"Of that, I have no doubt," Ian Hibbit said. "Please back slowly into the house."

Jason stepped back into his pseudo-kitchen and Hibbit followed him, kicking the door deftly when they were both in. It would have neatly closed the door had the doorframe been square and the door correctly hung, but the lower edge scraped against the thin carpeting on the floor, leaving it two inches ajar. Hibbit banged it closed with his rump.

"You sure you don't want a *Watchtower*?" Jason said.

His pistol aimed at Jason's chest, Hibbit said, "Where is a chair?" The pistol was very shiny. Jason said, "Did you polish your gun before you came over? It looks great."

The pistol moved a little and Hibbit fired it. It was loud and sudden, and Jason, startled, convulsed away from the noise. The pistol was aimed at his chest again when he straightened up. Still bent half-over at the waist, Jason looked behind him. There was a new hole in his closet door and his right ear rang, which scared him nearly as much as the gunshot itself. Very loud noises could permanently damage hearing.

Patrice's distant voice from upstairs yelled, "Shut up down there!"

Hibbit said, "Where is a chair?"

"In the front room."

The pistol jerked toward the front room. Jason straightened up and backed into his front room through the short passage with bookshelves.

"Where is the chair?" Hibbit said.

Jason pointed at the piano bench with his thumb.

"That's not a chair," Hibbit said in an exasperated tone.

"Oh, you meant a chair chair. What do you want it for?"

"To tie you up in."

"I don't have a good tying-people-up chair."

Hibbit sighed. "Certainly you have a bed. Where is the bedroom?"

Jason inclined his chin toward the back of the apartment. Hibbit jerked the pistol. They went back through the short passage and the pseudo-kitchen, through the bathroom, and into Jason's bedroom.

"That's not a bed," Hibbit said, looking at Jason's futon.

Jason said, "Are you new at this?"

Hibbit gave him a dirty look. "I will now search your apartment," he said. "More to the point, you will search your apartment whilst I supervise."

Jason said, "What are we searching for?"

"Just do as I say."

"How am I supposed to search for something when you won't tell me what it is? Maybe I already know where it is and we can save a lot of time."

Hibbit's eyes narrowed and he looked intently at Jason. "And where might that be?"

"Where might what be?"

"The . . . the item. Where is it?"

"The 'item,'" Jason said. "Why would I want to give you the 'item'?"

Hibbit raised the gun so that it pointed at Jason's forehead. "It's outside," Jason said. "Out there." He pointed toward the parking lot. "In my car."

"Right," Hibbit said, waving the pistol again. They went through the bathroom and into the pseudo-kitchen to the back door.

With his hand on the doorknob, Jason said, "Training of the deadly side arm on my person whilst out-of-doors seems antithetical to the *raison d'être* of the whole secrecy mien, yes?"

Hibbit seemed undecided. Then he flourished the pistol and said, "Be assured I can reach it quickly. I don't want to kill you, but I certainly will, if necessary." He put it in the pocket of his wool jacket. They went out. Hibbit closed the door behind them.

In the parking lot, Jason said, "So did you have a nice conversation with Paul?"

"Yes, thank you, very pleasant," Hibbit said. "The item, please."

They stopped at the Plymouth. Hibbit said, "This is your car?"

"It's going to be a classic next year," Jason said. Around the front of the Manor, someone opened and closed the porch door loudly. A few seconds later, Robert and Martin strolled around the side of the house, laughing, with their hands folded casually behind them.

"Oh damn," Jason said, patting his pants pockets. "I left my keys inside. We'll have to go back in and get them."

"No funny stuff," Hibbit said, suspiciously.

Robert and Martin got closer, and Robert said, "Hi, Jason. Something wrong?"

"Yeah," Jason said. "I left my keys in the house."

Martin said, "Bummer."

"Bummer," Robert agreed.

Hibbit said nothing.

"Who's this?" Martin asked, smiling at Hibbit.

"This is Ian Hibbit," Jason said. "Ian, Robert and Martin. Robert, Martin; Ian. Ian's a friend of Paul's."

"Heya," Martin said. "Put 'er there." He extended his right hand. Hibbit looked unhappy, but he took his empty gun hand out of his pocket and put it out. Martin gripped him firmly around the wrist, and as Hibbit realized he'd been tricked and tried to yank his hand back, Robert hauled back and clouted him on the side of the head with a nice geode bookend. Hibbit reeled and tried to pull away, and Martin's left hand came out from behind his back, whipped his butterfly knife through a blur of clicks and whirs, and stopped at Hibbit's throat.

"I really, really, really, really wouldn't," Martin said. He moved closer and planted himself more solidly on his feet. "Get his gun, Robert."

Robert said, "I don't want his gun."

Martin looked exasperated and said, "Robert."

Robert said, "Okay."

"Right-hand jacket pocket," Jason said. Robert got the pistol from Hibbit's pocket and held it gingerly. Jason stepped behind Hibbit, reached around Hibbit's head, and got a good grip on the hair just above his forehead. Blood was trickling down the left side of Hibbit's head, where his skull had encountered the geode bookend. Martin was in front of him, and Jason was in back. Hibbit was going no-where without them.

"Unload it," Martin said to Robert.

Robert examined the pistol. "How?"

Jason said, "Just hold on to it and keep your finger out-side the trigger guard thing."

Robert moved to stick it in front of his jeans, looked suddenly concerned, and just held it in his hand.

Jason said close to Ian Hibbit's ear, "Privacy's a little dif-ficult in this house. Everybody can hear everything. Mu-sic, things dropping, conversations, sneezes, death threats, gunshots, everything."

Hibbit said nothing.

"The gunshot idea was somewhat dim," Jason said.

With his butterfly knife still against Hibbit's throat, and his right hand still clamped around Hibbit's wrist, Martin said, "How long are we going to stand out here like this? I feel like that Iwo Jima statue."

"Let's get inside," Jason said. "Easy now. Nothing sur-prising. No 'funny stuff.' Gentlemen, ready with the left foot; and . . . *one*-two-three." They began to move slowly as a group toward the back door of the Manor.

The door to Paul's second-floor apartment flew open and a big man with bushy dark eyebrows came out onto the rickety second-floor landing, holding Paul in front of him as a shield. Paul's head was sideways in the crook of the big man's elbow, and he looked unhappy. The big man had a massive handgun the size of an Atlas rocket, which he pointed in the general direction of the group down on the pavement. The handgun had been customized with a silver grip, gold trigger, and a long, black, evil-looking thing perched atop a blue barrel, and looked as though its stopping power might be appropriate for defense against a PCP-enraged cement truck.

The big man yelled, "Everybody freeze," in a *basso profundo* voice. Everybody did.

"Now drop the knife and let him go." He moved the gun so it was against the top of Paul's head. "You got three seconds. Two. One . . ."

Nobody moved. With his head sideways, Paul said, "Fuck, Jason!" in a wavering voice.

Jason said, "Zero."

Nobody moved.

"Gee," Jason observed. "That was fun."

Hibbit suggested, "Perhaps some kind of agreement?"

"I'll fucking waste him," the big man said. "I will."

Paul choked, "Jason . . ."

Jason said, "No you won't. You'll lose your human shield, unless you want to drag around what, a hundred and sixty pounds of deadweight, one-armed, and you can't shoot at us because you might hit your boss here, and even if you did shoot Paul, you'd probably bleed to death up there when the bullet went through his head and into your own other arm. Shooting Paul, as overwhelmingly attractive as that may often seem, serves only to weaken your position."

Waldo the gray-and-white cat trotted out from under the Manor and lay down in the dead grass under the dead tree.

"Tactically speaking, that is," Jason said.

The parrots cackled, invisible, at the edge of the parking lot. Paul blinked and swallowed. Martin held his butterfly knife firmly against Hibbit's throat and glared at him. The knife had fake mother-of-pearl grips. Robert stood with Hibbit's pistol. The day was sunny, a perfect kite day with a nice breeze and fluffy white clouds, full of the promise of liberty and the pursuit of happiness.

"Back off," the big man said, "and let him go."

Waldo rolled over onto his side and yawned. Jason heard a car pull into the parking lot entrance, but he couldn't turn to see it. It stopped behind him and honked with the engine going, and he jumped a little. All the parking spaces assigned to the Manor were full, so Jason figured it was someone from the condos who could see only their backs. The engine sounded well-tuned.

The car honked again. Waldo looked up for maybe a second and then closed his eyes and rolled in the dead grass. The big man looked uncomfortable. Behind Jason, a car door opened and an impatient male voice said, "You guys mind moving so I can get into my space?" Footsteps got closer.

Jason said without looking around, "Can't move. Busy thwarting Sasquatch up there with the anti-aircraft pistol. Appreciate it if you'd call the police."

The footsteps stopped and an arm snaked in from behind Jason, holding a stubby revolver with a walnut-brown grip, which it positioned against Martin's temple. The arm was pale and hairy. The voice yelled, "Put the knife down or I'll blow your brains all over the asphalt, motherfucker!"

Jason sensed slight motion behind him, and Robert's voice said, "Put the gun down or I'll blow your brains all over his brains, you squirting pus festering ulcer with maggots ripe garbage-sucking bursting boil leprotic Republican stool eater."

Martin's eyes closed to slits, and he looked at Jason, but he kept the knife where it was.

Hibbit said, "If you do that, Jeffrey will shoot you and Mr. Reno."

"If he does," Martin said through his teeth, "I'll slit your throat and Robert will shoot Jeffrey."

Everyone thought about that. The pale, hairy arm had a mole on the back of its wrist.

"Let's see," Jason said. "Who does that leave?"

"You," Robert said. "And Waldo the cat."

Jason said, "Does anyone have a problem with that?"

No one said anything. The parrots cackled.

Robert said, "No, wait a minute. Martin and I die twice in that scenario."

Jason said, "How about we all just stand here and bristle with armament until someone in a condo glances over, sees her worst fears confirmed about those losers who live in the Manor, and calls nine-one-one. Cops race up in two, three hours, and that's that."

In a few moments, Hibbit said, "Please lower your gun, Jeffrey."

Jeffrey didn't move. Then he slowly lowered the gun, keeping Paul in front of him. Sunlight glinted gold off the trigger and silver off the grip.

Hibbit said to Jason, "Now the knife, please."

Jason said, "Oh, Ian, what a card! All your weapons go down before we even start thinking about ours."

Hibbit said, "That's hardly fair."

Jason hummed "Holiday for Strings." Before he got to the part he could never remember, Hibbit said, "Lowell, put your gun down," and Jason stopped humming.

The hairy arm with the mole and the stubby revolver pulled back to where Jason couldn't see it. Robert's voice said, "Now put the pointy end in your mouth, hold it with your teeth, and take your hand away so it dangles."

Lowell's voice said, "You gotta be fucking kidding."

Robert said, "Jason?"

Jason said, "Ian. Baby. Sweetie."

Hibbit said, "Please do as he requests, Lowell."

Lowell said, "Shit."

"Okay," Robert said a few seconds later. "I have his gun. Ew, it's kind of gross."

"Okay," Jason said. "Keep yours pointed at him."

"Mine, you mean," Hibbit said.

Lowell said, "You gave them your gun?"

Robert said, "At least he didn't get his all slobbery, Dribble Boy."

Hibbit said, "Now the knife."

"Jeffrey still has his ugly gun," Jason said. "Jeffrey, give it to Paul."

Jeffrey continued to scowl down, and then seemed to click on the fact that the conversation had expanded to include him. "No way," he bellowed.

"No way," Robert bellowed too. "Jeffrey not give gun!"

Martin let his glance flick momentarily toward Jason, a tiny gesture devolved from eye-rolling during the years they'd known Robert.

"Please, Jeffrey," Hibbit said. "Let's get this over with."

"No way," Jeffrey reiterated. "I don't give my gun to nobody," he elaborated.

"Well, that's a problem," Jason said, "because we're not moving until that gun is out of the picture, neutralized, rendered *in absentia*."

Jeffrey glowered and bellowed, "No way," again.

"Not give gun!" Robert bellowed. "Not give gun!"

Jason said, "I wonder how long it will take for the cops to get here."

Jeffrey's lips and forehead compressed, and he said, "Shit."

"Give it to Paul," Jason said.

Waldo rolled upright with dead grass pieces stuck to his fur, trotted across to Jason, and meowed at him.

Hibbit said, "I'll double your fee, Jeffrey, just give him the gun."

"Triple it," Jeffrey said.

"Yes, very well," Hibbit said.

Jeffrey's eyes narrowed. The effect was not pleasing. "You welch on me and you know what happens."

Waldo stopped meowing, plopped down on his hind-quarters, and began to lick his anus.

"Yes, Jeffrey, fine. Just please give him the gun."

Jeffrey did something to the gun and a magazine slid out of it. He handed the gun, butt-first, to Paul and then shoved Paul toward his open door. Paul tripped, went down onto his backside on the landing, and scuttled backward into his apartment.

Jason said, "Now Jeffrey comes down the stairs, and he and Lowell get in Lowell's car and drive away."

"Please, Jeffrey," Hibbit said. Jeffrey looked mad and descended the loudly creaking stairs with the cartridge in his hand. Jason and Martin pivoted with Hibbit so they could watch Jeffrey as he passed them, and Jason saw the rest of Lowell, which was just as pale and hairy as his arm. Lowell was wearing gray corduroy shorts and a Kensington shirt and aviator sunglasses, and his car was a blue metallic Ford Escort rental. Robert was standing next to him with Hibbit's pistol pointed at Lowell and Lowell's revolver at Jeffrey, a look of intense concentration on his face as he kept the two guns trained independently on two targets.

Glaring, Jeffrey and Lowell got into the Escort. Lowell put it into reverse and backed out of the parking lot.

"Now what?" Martin said.

"Anybody feel like pizza?" Jason said.

"No olives," Martin said.

Jason said to Hibbit, "If I send Robert up to see after Paul, who's he going to meet?"

"No one," Hibbit said. "I brought only those two."

Jason kept looking at him.

"I'm in no position to lie," Hibbit said.

"Robert," Jason said. "Go up and see how Paul is and get him down here. Be careful."

Robert nodded.

"If you would, please," Jason added, suddenly aware he'd been giving orders. Robert nodded again in acknowledgment of the courtesy, went up the back stairs in a half-crouch with a gun in each hand, and crossed the landing. Outside Paul's open door, he said, "Paul?"

There was no answer from within the apartment. Robert looked down at Jason. Jason gave him a beats-me look.

Robert stepped to the inside edge of the open doorframe and peered around. Then he went in a little farther. Then he stepped through the doorway. Then he went into the room.

Waldo stopped licking his anus and began licking his chest. His tongue got stuck in his chest fur.

"Cats are so mysterious," Jason said, watching Waldo try to get his tongue out of his chest fur.

A minute later, Robert walked out from around the front of the Manor.

"Paul's not in the house," he said.

"Oh, wonderful," Jason said. "I blow it again. Okay, search Ian for additional weaponry, and then everybody in the car."

9

Martin and Ian Hibbit sat together on one side of the dark walnut-veneer table, and Jason sat on the other. The clamor of noisy children at the pizza place was augmented by the loud beeps and zooms of arcade games. Jason's right ear still rang from the gunshot, but not as much. Robert was in the arcade area, trying to hit plastic gophers on the head with a plastic mallet as they popped out of their holes and emoting periodically as he missed. He seemed to be the only baritone in the game area.

One slice of pizza remained on the metal pan. Its pepperoni was curled up at the edges into little red cups of congealing grease, and the cheese had hazed over and begun to harden. Four glasses of half-melted ice cubes stood on the table.

Jason wadded up his paper napkin, dropped it on the

table, and said, "There. We have plied you with exotic delicacies. Entertain us now. Tell us a story."

Hibbit said, "A story?" His hair was wet and unkempt where they'd rinsed the blood off in the men's room.

"A nice story," Jason said. "With bunnies. Or bluebirds. Bunnies or bluebirds, which one, Martin?"

Martin said, "Bunnies."

"Sorry, I don't follow," Hibbit said, frowning slightly.

"Or if not bunnies, then how about 'items'?" Jason said.

"I'm sorry, I still don't follow—"

Martin's left hand was out of sight, under the table. His shoulder moved a little. Hibbit stiffened and didn't finish his sentence.

"Martin," Jason said. "You're not being impolite down there with that very sharp knife, are you? Miss Manners would belt you one right in the chops for that."

Hibbit said, "Mm."

Martin said, "What would she say about Almost Dickless here threatening to shoot you in your own apartment?"

"Interesting perspective," Jason reflected.

"Right on," Martin agreed.

Jason put his chin on his hand and looked at Hibbit. "So," he said. "Seen any good 'items' lately?"

Hibbit said, "I don't believe you've any idea what the 'item' might be."

Jason said, "What's your interest in the 'item'?"

Hibbit looked reticent. Martin's shoulder moved again. Hibbit jerked and said, "Financial," with a brief look at Martin. With his right hand, Martin rattled the melting ice cubes in his glass and drank the weak cola at the bottom.

"Aha," Jason said. "Which tells me nothing. You want it so you can sell it, or you want it because you can make money using it?"

Hibbit didn't say anything.

Robert slid in next to Jason and said, "Guess what, I got high score on the gophers." He bent over to look under the table in Hibbit's direction and then straightened up and said brightly to Martin, "Think he'll manage to hang on to the ol' dongle?"

Hibbit looked at Robert sharply and narrowed his eyes, searching Robert's face. His reaction didn't fit, somehow. Jason glanced at Martin. Martin had caught it too.

Jason said, "The dongle issue remains unresolved."

Hibbit gave Jason the same searching look. Jason smiled pleasantly and waited for Hibbit to say something.

Hibbit came to some kind of decision and said, "Why this charade? Are you simply toying with me?"

"Martin might be," Jason said. "But I'm too far across the table."

Hibbit looked at Martin. Martin, expressionless, looked back at Hibbit. Jason motioned a little with one hand, and Martin moved slightly away from Hibbit.

Hibbit relaxed and let his breath out dramatically, like a flabby man who is finally out of sight of people on the beach. "Thank you. What do you want?"

"Can't really say," Jason said. He had no idea what they were talking about.

Hibbit looked irritated and said, "What can we possibly discuss, then?" Then his face showed dawning comprehension. "I see. There is still the question of Mr. Reno."

"Ah," Jason said. "You see that, do you."

"Of course."

"Then you understand."

"Entirely. Now, I shall ask you this. What might you consider, were I to deal directly with you?"

"Well," Jason said. He had no clue what to say. He

pretended to weigh the question. He looked up at the ceiling and pursed his lips. He tapped on the tabletop. He put his hands up at angles to each other, in a question-pondering V. He nodded to himself. "I think—" he said, and pretended to think some more. He nodded again, as though confirming whatever it was he had thought of. "—that if the situation were to change, there might be more variables introduced than would make it wise for me to commit to specifics at this point in time."

Hibbit said, "Throwing it to me now, are you? All right, I'll get things started. Shall we say . . . ten?"

"Ten?" Jason said. "Please!"

"Ha!" Robert burst out. "Ten!"

Hibbit laughed with them. "Of course not. Fifteen, then?"

Robert shook his head sadly. Martin picked up his glass of melting ice and drank the quarter-teaspoonful of new water.

Jason said, "Get real."

"I have been more than forthcoming," Hibbit said. "I'm afraid we cannot progress until you've done same."

"How can I possibly do same?" Jason said. "You don't even seem to be serious. Ten?"

"All right," Hibbit said. "What say you to seventeen?"

Jason and Robert looked at each other. Robert shook his head in sorrow.

"Seventeen?" Hibbit said.

"Seventeen," Jason said, and sighed.

"Seventeen," Robert said sadly.

"I can go no higher than seventeen," Hibbit said sincerely.

Jason smiled. "You know where to reach me." Robert

scooted off the seat and stood up. Martin did the same. When Hibbit was standing, Jason said, "By the way: Anybody breaks into my place, roughs up my friends, taunts my cat, or buys Manhattan from the Indians for a handful of trinkets, I'll go elsewhere. Even if you're offering high bid, I don't need to go with high bid to be happy."

Hibbit said, "Why, of course," and inclined his head. "Ah, the small matter of my little pistol?"

Robert started to move toward the pistol under his shirt, but caught himself. Jason said, "Surely, Mr. Hibbit, you must be joking."

Hibbit looked as though he were going to speak, but then looked as though a thought had dawned. He regarded Jason appraisingly and then turned and threaded his way between the tables and out the door.

Jason said, "He figured it out. He knows we don't know anything."

Martin said, "Do we have to follow him?"

"No," Jason said. "We have to find Paul. Ian Hibbit will find us again all by himself."

Robert said, "Seventeen what?"

"Beats me," Jason said. "Seventeen thousand? Seventeen quintillion? Seventeen Billy Dee Williams *Revenge of the Jedi* trading cards? Who knows?"

Martin said, "You are planning on explaining all this, right? At some point? So I know why I'm threatening to neuter people at Chuck E. Cheese's?"

"Yes," Jason said. "As soon as we have a few minutes."

"I'm also real curious about what this 'item' is."

"I don't know what it is."

Robert said, "Probably some kind of . . . thingy."

Martin looked at him patiently.

Robert said, "Probably . . . some sort of . . ." He gestured gropingly. Jason and Martin waited because Robert's feelings would be hurt if they didn't.

". . . valuable black bird statuette," Robert concluded.

Martin sighed.

Robert said, "If we're not going to follow him, I'm going to get stuff with my gopher tickets."

10

They went back to the Manor in case Paul had come back. He hadn't. There were no phone or e-mail messages. Robert sat on the floor in Jason's front room and played with his new rubber tarantula while Jason called Light Wizards. Platt wasn't expected until later that night. Jason didn't leave a message.

He sat on his piano bench and told Robert and Martin everything that had happened.

Martin looked displeased. "Last time we had a little meeting like this, things went totally off the deep end."

"I know," Jason said. "I'm just telling you all this so you'll know what's going on, not so you'll get involved again. All I was hired to do was watch Paul. Now things are getting strange."

Martin slid off the sofa and sat on the floor.

Robert said, "Maybe you ought to consider quitting this job."

"Believe me, I might," Jason said. "But I'm really curious about what Paul's up to."

"Gotta go with Robert on this one," Martin said. "I don't trust Paul."

"Me neither," Jason said. "But I still want to know what he's up to."

"But why?" Robert said. "Say you find out. Then what will you do, ground him? Take away his TV privileges? No Backstabbing Weasel Channel for a week?"

Jason didn't have a good answer. He said, "I don't have a good answer."

Robert said, "You guys were once close. Maybe you need to accept that both of you have changed."

Martin said, "I got to admit. I never really understood what you saw in him."

"I still kind of think he started out with the potential to be, I don't know, a good guy."

Robert guffawed. When Jason looked at him, he said, "Everyone starts out with that potential. The question of what screwed up Paul is something we could dwell on for a long time. It's usually family, but whatever it was—" Robert held the rubber tarantula as though it were talking and ventriloquized in an Alec Guiness voice, "Hasn't he already chosen the dark side of the Force, young Luke?"

"Maybe that's why I can't write him off, Obi-Robert Kenobistein," Jason said. "Maybe the only difference between Paul and me is our families."

Robert put the tarantula on the floor and said, "The good brother and the evil brother? I think maybe you're getting a little too serious with myth structures here."

Martin said, "If this is a myth structure, then what does that make us?"

"I believe the myth structure breaks down on that question," Robert said.

"No it doesn't," Jason said. "You're the hero's stout companions."

Martin said, "Who's the hero? You?"

Robert looked down at his long six-foot-five body. "Stout?"

"Forthright," Jason said. "Trusty. Faithful. Stalwart."

"Puke," Martin said. "Vomit. The rainbow yawn. To toss one's cookies. It is to ralph."

"Anyway," Jason said, "we all agree that Paul's a toad at best and a poisonous toad at worst. I'm a little afraid of him. I think he's going somewhere I don't want to go. Maybe someone should try to prevent it. Maybe that job falls to me." Jason half-turned toward his laptop and tapped a few keys. It started an e-mail run.

Martin said, "Who died and made you catcher in the rye?"

Robert looked interested. "Stop him from doing what?"

"I don't know. I'm just running my mouth. Hey, I have e-mail."

Robert and Martin moved closer and watched as the e-mail message scrolled up the screen.

```
From: METAMUSIC
To: NOTE ON
Subj: Benton


The coroners report is unambiguous—a bone frag-
ment severed a meningeal artery and caused
```

brain compression leading to death. No apparent skullduggery. Self-bludgeoning. Stupid way to go. FYI.

He was talking big before he died about some big breakthrough hed made. He was supposed to unveil it in the next few days or weeks. Most likely, it had something to do with interactive media and/or virtual reality.

He was apparently something of a security freak. All the data on his computer was always encrypted. He had some kind of little pocket-sized homemade encryption/decryption device that he carried with him at all times. Its possible that the breakthrough was spurious. It was in Bentons best interests to keep people thinking he was on the cutting edge of something big, so as not to dissuade potential financiers.

I dont expect things to get dangerous, but it can always go that way, so stay on your toes. If you want out, let me know. Also, I'm not sure how secure the email here is, so don't send me anything important.

Dont forget to save your receipts. I cant reimburse you without them.

—*—

MUSE DISCONNECTED

"So it wasn't foul play," Martin said.

Robert nodded.

"That's good to know," Jason said. "As for Paul, I guess I'll stay with it for the time being." He stood. "I have to start packing my gear. You guys going to make it to my gig with the Africans tonight?"

"Aah!" Robert said, pretending to see the rubber tarantula for the first time. He snatched it up and dashed it against the wall. It fell behind the couch with whatever else was back there.

Martin said, "My hero."

"You're going?" Robert said to Jason. "After all this, you're going to go out and do your gig?"

"Yes."

"Jason—"

"I'm going."

"But Jason—"

"I'm going."

"But—"

"Look, I don't like being held hostage by circumstances. I can either sit scared or I can adhere to my existing plans. What else would you have me do? I don't know where to look for Paul, I don't have whatever Hibbit wants, and I'm fed up with not accomplishing anything. I can sit here and not accomplish anything, or I can go out tonight and accomplish some music. You want to go?"

Robert said, "Jason—"

"You want to go or not?"

Martin said, "Forget it, Robert. He's not budging. Sorry, Jase. I can't make it."

Robert looked worried, but turned to Martin and said, "Why, you got an art job?"

"Depends on what you mean by art," Martin said. "I'm doing carpet-cleaning coupons. You'll get my work in your mailbox in about a week and throw it away."

Jason said, "Robert? You want to go?"

"I have an audition," Robert said. "Sorry. I'd come by afterward if the bus didn't take three hours."

Martin said, "An audition? For what?"

"Some sort of big tall person."

"There's a stretch," Martin said.

Robert shrugged sadly. "When you're six-five, you can be a thug or you can be a very tall alien. If I'd been shorter and handsomer, I could have been Mel Gibson, but I'm not and I'm not, so I'm not. Are you really going to go out and play music?"

"You're going to an audition. Martin's going to his job."

"*We,*" Robert emphasized, "weren't hired to keep track of Paul Reno. And *we* weren't held at gunpoint in our own house today."

"Well, *I,*" Jason said, "was. And *I* am going to take *my* keyboards and play *my* music as though everything's normal."

"It's not."

"Paul knows about the gig tonight. Maybe he'll show up. There, see? I'm on task."

Martin said, "Sorry I'm gonna miss it. You play good when you're obstinate."

11

In a bachelor apartment in the Hollywood Hills, Paul Reno said, "So that's it. I got out of there and came straight here."

"Without it," said the other man. Jeffrey's gargantuan patchwork handgun was in his right hand, and he was sighting through the scope with one eye. He put it down on the table. The tabletop was wooden, and it stood on straight wooden legs with flat metal feet in a small, neat room with a single bed and a small oak bookcase. The bookcase held mostly hardcovers, with a few oversized paperbacks: *The Anarchist's Cookbook, Mein Kampf, Fischer on Chess*. The books were clean, with sharp, straight edges to their spines and covers. Atop the bookshelf were a Spanish sailing ship in a polished bottle, a small rack that held three smoking pipes, and a small black stereo set with no dust on it. A single window was covered by a well-fitted black-out curtain, and the floor was wood. A small kitchenette adjoined the room, and the opposite wall sported a doorway to a small bathroom. The small stereo played "Summer" from Vivaldi's *The Four Seasons*. The empty orange cassette box lay open atop the stereo, and the room kept the odor of pipe tobacco.

The man was of average height, stocky, with a neatly clipped beard, and older than Paul. His hair was medium brown and thick, of a length that someone over sixty might call long, and someone under forty might call short. He occasionally moved it back from his steel-rimmed glasses.

Paul said, "It'll be no problem. It's safe."

"Are you sure you weren't followed?"

"Look, I told you already I wasn't followed."

"Summer" ended and the stereo set went *clunk* when the cassette tape wound to its end. The man pushed his chair back and went to the stereo, removed the cassette, put it into its box, and placed the box on the bookcase, square with the edge. Paul watched him move around the room.

The man moved the edge of the blackout curtain and looked out. It was almost sunset, and the light that spilled onto his face through the opening was warm and amber.

"How do you know," he said, without looking away from the window.

"I was careful."

The man made an amused and patronizing sound in his throat.

"Look," Paul said. "I was careful, okay? Nobody followed me."

"All right. We'll say you weren't followed. So. What to do next."

"I know what to do next. I don't need your help figuring things out. I just thought you wanted to be kept up to date."

The man glanced at him. "Everything's fine, you're covered, it's all under control."

"Definitely."

The man closed the blackout curtain and tucked its edge against the frame so no sliver of light came through. He crossed the small room and sat again at the table. "What's your plan for retrieving it?"

"Don't worry about that," Paul said. "I'll have it tonight, no problem."

"Good," the man said. "If you're sure there won't be any problems."

Paul nodded. A moment passed in silence.

The man said, "Your being here compromises both of us."

"No problem," Paul said, standing. "I'll contact you tonight when I have it." He extended his hand for Jeffrey's ugly handgun.

The man said, "It's called a Desert Eagle." He picked the gun up and regarded it. "I'll be keeping it."

Paul hesitated with his hand still out.

The man looked up from the gun and said, "Nothing comes free in this world, Mr. Reno. Consider it a late fee."

Paul hesitated again, and then said, "Okay." The man got up to tap a six-digit code into a wall-mounted keypad. He opened the door, and Paul went out into the musty hallway.

12

Playing music onstage in a crowded nightclub is like being in a strange aquarium where the fish are on the outside. With experience comes recognition of predatory markings and the knowledge that the most fearsome predators disguise themselves as prey. Patterns of acceptance and rejection, camouflage and display, all flow and move in probabilistic predictability. The dedicated observer learns to differentiate species, learns which are mutually compatible and which require parasitic or symbiotic relationships.

Classifications become clear:

Actor, Jason thought as he surveyed the room over a tier of keyboards. *Guy who calls himself a producer. . . . Construction workers who would rather hear "Freebird." . . . Rich USC cinema students feeling culturally open-minded for being here. . . . The usual flock of girls with practiced wiggles, revealing necklines, and all the genuine charm of an air crash. Same same*

same. Trashy office ladies on a girls' night out, making crude com-
ments. . . . Semi-witty office men trying to dull the desperation of
the six-by-six cubicle by drinking deeply and laughing loudly, as
they've heard men should do. Same same same same same.

For this gig, he'd torn down most of his home studio
and brought nearly all his stuff. He was wearing his only
African clothing, a Nigerian mudcloth tunic, over jeans.
All the performers wore an Afro-American panoply: colorful shirts over corduroys, pillbox hats and mirror shades,
old sandals and new Polo shirts.

He who would be a man, Jason thought, looking at the
audience and suddenly in a vile mood, *must first be a non-*
conformist. At the same moment, the conga rhythm took a
certain subtle turn, and with it came the immediate, un-
conscious sense of a vacancy appearing, a fraction-of-a-
second opportunity that would pass before he could finish
noticing it. Without pausing to consider, he played the cadence of his thought on his keyboard: *da* dadadada *da*, da
da dada dada*da*da. He noticed distantly that he'd done it
right; the vacancy accepted the cadence.

None of the clubgoers seemed to receive enlighten-
ment, but all the musicians opened their eyes and looked at
him. The talking drum player answered the cadence with
a variation, and the rest of the band changed direction
with it, playing interlacing parts that supported the new
rhythm.

Da dadadada *da*, Jason found himself playing again, da
da dada dada*da*da. The talking drum answered it again. Jason carefully and carelessly did not think about what he
was doing.

Da *da* da da da da*da*dada, da da *da*, he played: My *life* is
not an a*pol*ogy, but a *life*. The talking drum player repeated
it, striking the conga heads more sharply to catch the

accents. He grinned at Jason. Jason saw it but couldn't acknowledge it; allowing it to register would break the focus.

The talking drum played an eight-bar phrase and stopped, and Jason was aware of his hands moving and his keyboard answering it.

Again, the talking drum spoke an eight-bar phrase, and Jason's keyboard pretty much repeated the same thing it had just said in its last answer, adding a few notes to clarify.

The talking drum repeated what the keyboard had said, and Jason thought the keyboard seemed a little impatient when it isolated just one part of the phrase and harped on it for a few bars.

The talking drum paused. *Oh yes?* it questioned presently.

Yes, yes, yes, said the keyboard. *I'm saying to you yes.*

Then it was clear that the two instruments were done talking to each other. The lead conga player signaled for a percussion break. Everyone but the percussionists stopped playing, and the percussionists built their rhythms into *crescendo* and *accelerando*, playing with and around the patterns Jason had introduced. The audience became more attentive, and some of the office men and cinema students yelled and whistled and sloshed their beers. Jason listened, feeling the spell depart and the energy build. The rhythms shook and thundered until the lead conga player played a pattern that readied the other players for the ending, which Jason joined in on four bars later in a crash of hands and sticks on drumheads, strings, and keys. The audience hooted and stomped. The percussionists grinned and gave each other high fives. Jason awarded himself five originality points for working Ralph Waldo Emerson into an Afrobeat percussion jam.

The lead conga player leaned forward and said into the microphone suspended over his drums, with his head upside-down, "Thank you very much. We'll be back in fifteen minutes."

The house PA system began playing Bob Marley. Some of the nightclub patrons began to leave, and as a few couples started to dance, the band unstrapped and disentangled itself from its instruments and various cables and stepped off the stage.

The talking drum player clapped Jason on the shoulder.

"You got it tonight, man."

Jason raised his eyebrows in acknowledgment of the praise. "Nice eights," he said. The talking drum player dropped off the edge of the stage and headed for the bar. Jason reached into his gig bag and pulled out a paperback copy of *Spotted Horses* by William Faulkner that he'd been trying to get through during band breaks for several years.

He carried *Spotted Horses* across the stage, stepped down onto the dance floor, and went out the front door.

The Bay City night air was cool. It chilled the perspiration on Jason's forehead and filtered through his shirt. A man and a woman had stepped out of the club, and they were standing on the sidewalk, discussing how best to spend the remainder of the evening. The man had a mustache and a gut, and his T-shirt said, "Cowgirl Butts Drive Me Nuts." Sometimes Jason found it astonishing that there were people who found men attractive.

"I don't care," the woman said. She was blonde and not unpretty. "We'll do whatever you want." Her tone of voice was at odds with her words. Jason wondered if her date would catch the discrepancy.

"You sure?" her date said.

Wrong! Jason thought. *Bzzzt! You do not continue to the bonus round!* He leaned against a vertical element of the aluminum windowframe and opened *Spotted Horses*, found the place where he'd stopped reading last time, and backed up a few pages. Before he started to read it again, he looked up to watch the man and woman heading off in two different moods to do what the man wanted.

If I'm so good at reading women, he thought, *how come he's the one with a date?*

He didn't have an answer.

Faulkner was not a good author to read in noisy fifteen-minute increments several months apart. Who was? Burroughs, maybe. William S. or Edgar Rice; either would do. A character in *Spotted Horses* was eating gingersnaps, but Jason couldn't remember who the character was. He remembered the gingersnaps, though.

After half a page, he closed the book and walked uphill to check on his car. He'd parked in a small lot over a rise, down the hill, and across a street. There were enough streetlights to see clearly as he crested the hill that someone was standing next to the Plymouth. It looked like it might be Paul Reno, but the streetlights cast its face in the sharp contrast of shadow.

Jason stopped. The figure that might be Paul walked to the front of the Plymouth and crouched in front of it, running its hands over the grille. Jason strolled slowly down the hill toward the parking lot.

The figure bent sideways and got its face up close to the grille, still searching with its hands. After a few seconds, it found the hood latch and pulled it forward. Nothing happened. Jason got a little closer.

The figure straightened somewhat and the light hit its face. It was, indeed, Paul Reno. Jason opened *Spotted Horses* and pretended to read it as he walked down the hill, trying to watch Paul with his peripheral vision. About fifty feet from the lot, he scuffed his right shoe against the side-

walk. Paul moved lightly away from the front of the Plymouth and took a few quick, dancing steps to the sidewalk, where he started walking toward Jason.

Jason glanced up offhandedly from his book, started to
look back down, and then looked up again, trying to appear as though he'd just then recognized Paul.

Paul said, "Hey, Jason!" in a pleased voice.

"Hey, Paul," Jason said, matching Paul's tone. "What
are you doing out here?"

"Came to see you play," Paul said. "You told me you
had a gig tonight, so I looked through the *L.A. Weekly* list-
ings until I found it."

"Well, you found it," Jason said. "I was just coming out
to make sure nobody was messing with my car."

Paul looked at the Plymouth. "Looks okay to me."

Jason followed his gaze and nodded. "Yup. I'm glad
you're okay. I was worried about you. Come on inside;
we're playing one more set."

A small school of Trashy Office Ladies was vacating its
table near the stage when Jason and Paul came in, so Paul
sat there, and Jason stepped onto the stage and put his book
back into his gig bag.

The bass player was leaning against the bar and talking
with a Deep-Clefted Wiggler. When he saw Jason onstage,
he gave his business card to the Wiggler and rousted the
rest of the band from the table they were sitting at. Everyone got up and began to re-entangle themselves in instruments and cables.

The house music faded. "Thank you," the conga player
said into his microphone, in response to nothing. Somebody applauded. Only a third of the audience had stayed
through the break.

The conga player moved his chair, adjusted his body's

position in relation to his congas, and started to play. The rest of the band trickled into the rhythm one by one until everyone was playing.

The second set wasn't as good as the first. Everyone played well, but Jason didn't have another in-the-music experience. He was too busy keeping an eye on Paul, who sat at a table and read the free weekly newspapers from a stack near the door. There weren't enough people in the place to feed the band toward the threshold of any kind of mutual chemical reaction anyway. After a while, the conga player drummed out a two-bar pattern and they finished the piece and ended the gig.

The house PA system played Bob Marley again, only more softly, while the bartender and waitresses cleaned the bar and tallied figures. The clock across the club on the cash register said it was a little after one in the morning. Jason dragged his instrument cases onto the stage, disconnected all the cables, and slipped the keyboards into their tight foam cutouts. When he looked up, Paul was coiling a cable wrist-to-elbow.

"I'll get those," Jason said.

"It's no problem," Paul said, and continued coiling.

"That's not how I want them coiled," Jason said. "How about you just help me carry?"

"Okay," Paul said, and dropped the cable on the floor. Jason picked it up and re-coiled it in loops that alternated coil directions.

"This way keeps the shielding from getting messed up and prevents it from tangling," he said.

"Hey, whatever."

The bag, his rack case, and the wheeled amplifier joined his road cases at the door. Keyboardists were always the last to finish loading out.

"Think you got enough stuff?" Paul said.

Jason hoisted the bag over his shoulder and gripped the handle of a keyboard case. "Next life, I'll play nose flute. Ready to carry?"

The lead conga player came over, proffered one hand, and said, "You got the fever or somethin' tonight, bro." Jason clasped his hand and came away with the folded bills the conga player had palmed.

"Thanks," he said, putting the bills in his pocket without looking at them. "Good first set."

"Yeah, yeah. Man, you got the fever or somethin'. I think your great-granddaddy mus' be Nigeriaman, bro; they go nuts for you in Lagos. You don't play like no white boy."

"Thanks," Jason said, flattered.

The conga player said, "Big gig next month, man. Big money, Ghanaians got big, big money. You call me."

Jason said he would and the conga player left. Paul bumped the amplifier over the doorsill.

"Where's your car?" Jason said outside. The casters under the amplifier clattered as they rolled on the sidewalk, catching and scraping occasional bits of gravel.

"Around the corner from yours."

At the Plymouth, Jason stacked the two keyboard cases on the back seat and put the rack case on top of them. He heaved the amplifier up onto the front bench seat and buckled it in. The amplifier weighed about sixty pounds, and its casters sank into the vinyl seat.

"I'll watch this stuff while you get the rest," Paul said.

Jason pretended to consider the offer. "Nah," he said. "It'll be fine. Let's just hump all the stuff down here and skedaddle. You feel like getting something to eat?"

Paul shrugged. "Sure."

As they walked back toward the club, Jason looked at the folded bills. Two twenties. He'd just gotten a raise.

They carted the rest of his equipment out to the parking lot, and Jason packed it carefully in the Plymouth. Every time he bought another piece of gear, he had to find a new way of packing everything. It was like a Chinese woodblock puzzle.

"You want to get your car and follow me?" he said to Paul when the last of it was stowed. He didn't want to let Paul out of his sight, but there was no room in the Plymouth for a passenger.

"Sure," Paul said. "I'll bring it around and meet you at the driveway." He walked out of the lot and around the corner of a building. Hoping Paul wouldn't disappear, Jason got into the Plymouth and nursed the engine until it almost sounded like it had a rhythm. He put it into reverse to back out of the parking space and the engine died. Stomping on the accelerator resulted in a widening of the crumbly hole in the floorboard. The hole looked as though it might not take many more stompings. Maybe the Plymouth wasn't going to make it to antique status.

The Plymouth joggled in the driveway like a washing machine with a lopsided load of tennis shoes. Maybe if he took it to the right garage, some brilliant mechanic would say, "Well, no wonder it runs like shit! Your auxiliary 340 hemi came loose. Most people don't even know these babies are in the trunk. I'll just torque down this little hex nut here—"

Jason wondered what Paul had been after. He decided that it would be a good idea to open the Plymouth's hood and look under it.

Good. He nodded once, decisively. *Jase have plan*.

Paul's little beige hatchback came around the corner

and slowed before the driveway, and Jason persuaded the Plymouth out in front of it.

He was careful to stay immediately in front of Paul, which meant checking the rearview mirror every few seconds. They were almost two miles east before he noticed the other car behind them.

13

The other car crossed an intersection against the red light after he and Paul beat the amber, but Jason didn't really pick up on it until it followed them onto a side street. He was in the process of pulling it to the curb so he could roll down his window and suggest to Paul that they eat in Pasadena when the other car came around the corner behind them. He edged back into the street instead of pulling to a stop and turned left at the next corner. Paul followed him. A few seconds later, so did the other car. Judging from the look of its headlights, it was a mid-sized American domestic, staying about a block back.

"Hello," he said to its reflection in the rearview mirror. "Who are you?" Slipping his left hand between his seat and the door, he located the old iron jack-handle with his fingertips. It was original equipment on the Plymouth, and would win no Most Sanitary Jack-Handle contests. He inched it forward so its grimy ninety-degree elbow stuck out in front of the seat, easy to grab, if necessary.

He pulled to the curb, waved for Paul to draw up next to him, and rolled down his window. Behind them, the third car turned its lights off and hung back.

The beige hatchback drew up next to him, and Paul leaned across and rolled the window down. "What's up?" he said loudly across the gap between them.

Jason shouted, "We're being followed by somebody un-subtle in an American car. Let's split up and regroup at the Pantry, on Figueroa. Got it?"

Instead of doing what Jason said, Paul said, "Fol-lowed?" and lurched around in his seat to peer back. After a second, the other car started toward them and its head-lights came on.

Who were they after?

"Go!" Jason said. *You bozo!* Paul looked at him for a second. "Go!" Jason said again. He waved his hand impa-tiently toward the street, as though to whisk Paul onto it. Still looking at him, Paul put the hatchback in gear and floored it. Jason wiggled his accelerator gingerly and tried to get moving, but the Plymouth's engine coughed and died. The Plymouth drifted sluggishly into the middle of the street, blocking it diagonally as Jason tried to start the engine in neutral. Tires squealed to his left and then chirped as a shiny, new-looking Taurus station wagon with smooth white paint stopped a few feet from his door.

Then it backed away. Apparently, they were after Paul.

Jason got the engine going and took as tight a U-turn as the Plymouth could do, bumping into and over the oppos-ing curb. Something on the passenger's side banged down onto the curb and scraped loudly when he moved back into the street.

The Taurus wagon had stopped in the empty intersection, but it was moving forward again, bearing into a left turn onto a side street. Jason got the Plymouth's speed up to about ten miles per hour and gently put the accelerator pedal to the floorboard. The engine hesitated. Then it caught and surged, and the Plymouth moved forward quickly and took the turn going thirty, skipping sideways a little as the mismatched tires temporarily lost traction, following the Taurus past dark, broken-windowed warehouses.

The Taurus cut a tight right turn at the next cross street, and Jason followed, not as tightly. His music equipment slid to the left and the heavy amplifier on the seat next to him toppled toward him. He caught it with his right forearm and shoved it upright on the seat. It had a nubbly black finish that scraped his arm a little when he shoved it.

The person in the Taurus was probably trying to head Paul off, but Jason figured Paul was probably already gone.

What was he into?

The Taurus arced into a wide left turn and he steered to follow it. The music equipment on the back seat all slid to the right, and the heavy amplifier banged against the passenger window. The street was a secondary artery that supported small businesses and liquor stores, and there were no other cars on it. Paul had either doubled back or taken a less direct route.

Jason jammed his hand back into the crack between seatback and cushion and yanked a black ballpoint out from among the hardened crumbs and loose change. He pulled the cap off with his teeth, blew it out of his mouth onto the floorboard, and wrote the Taurus' license plate number by feel on the knee of his jeans. He glanced down.

There was no ink on his jeans. He shook the pen violently and recited the license plate number aloud three times.

The driver of the Taurus suddenly braked hard in preparation for a right turn onto a side street. Jason decided the Plymouth wasn't going to be an antique after all and aimed for the Taurus' right rear quarter panel, feeling his seat belt to ensure that it was engaged. The Taurus curved into its turn faster than he anticipated, but he still managed to clip it near the rear, hard enough to bang it sideways and revise its trajectory. The impact sent his amplifier crashing into the dashboard. Something in the pile on the back seat hit Jason in the back of the head and the jack-handle shot forward and hit the back of his left foot. He smacked the jack-handle sharply back with the heel of his shoe and pushed back with his head against whatever it was that had slid into him. It slid back.

The Taurus corrected its bearing and headed up the side street with a bashed-in rear corner. Jason hit his brakes to follow it into the turn. They didn't work. The corner came up fast, and he pulled the wheel to the right. The ballpoint pen caught the spoke of the wheel and hurt his middle finger, and as he let go of it and tried to bring the turn back under control, the Plymouth slewed heavily and shook as though it were going to come apart, the old tires trembling and skidding sideways on the pavement, threatening to lose their grip completely, the driver's side dipping toward the street. The pen rolled on the floorboard and caught at the edge of the hole in the floorboard, and all the equipment on the back seat slid to the left. He disregarded the impulse to try to save his pen and tried to keep his steering smooth so the Plymouth wouldn't spin out, but the amplifier scraped along the dashboard and toppled onto his right arm, jogging the steering wheel and making the Plymouth shudder. He let it lie on his arm and steered slightly into a potential skid with the fallen amplifier blocking his view of where he was steering.

The tires held a brief, intense debate with the street about momentum and coefficients of friction, wobbled, found traction, and held. The engine hesitated and almost died but then recovered as gasoline that had sloshed away from the gas line intake sloshed back to it. The ballpoint pen dropped neatly through the hole in the floorboard.

The curb was suddenly very close on the passenger's side, and Jason cut the wheel sharply to the left. Inertia lifted the amplifier slightly away from him, and he helped it on its way with a shove of his shoulder and a sharp yank of the wheel. The amplifier rocked to the right and its metal-reinforced corner shattered the passenger's window.

Picking up speed on the side street, the Taurus shot through a series of intersections and past several stop signs. Behind it, the Plymouth bottomed out joltingly in the concrete drainage swales that ran across the street at each intersection. The Taurus hung a fast left and shot onto an onramp to the westbound 10, and Jason followed it. On the way up the ramp over the white-painted diamonds that indicated the carpool lane, he could make out in the flowing rhythm of passing streetlights that there were two people in the front seat. That meant they were using the carpool lane legally. Jason wasn't. He felt vaguely guilty. As they left the onramp, the Taurus pulled away and headed for the fast lane.

"Nuts," he muttered under his breath. He kept the accelerator floored, and the Plymouth picked up speed and sailed forward. The engine rhythm smoothed out when it hit sixty-five, but the cable behind the speedometer went *clikliklikliklik*, and its needle shuddered jerkily.

Going eighty miles per hour, the engine started to

complain a little, and by ninety-five, it was hollering. The Taurus was still ahead by a good ten carlengths, but the gap wasn't increasing. Another five seconds would put both of them in the middle of a pack of cars ahead, going about sixty-five. Jason glanced in his rearview mirror, and his eye was caught by something half a mile back, coming up fast in the next lane over. He looked ahead, saw a hole to the right of the pack of cars, and swooped across three lanes to enter it before it closed up. The swoop let the Taurus gain distance and put the Plymouth in the slow lane.

He passed a Hyundai and an Acura and cut left two lanes. The fast thing he'd seen in his rearview mirror was a black Corvette, and it passed him on his left, going about one-ten with the light from the streetlamps oozing over it like corn syrup. Immediately, Jason moved behind it and watched it accelerate, hoping it would get into the fast lane in front of the Taurus.

As it sliced left in front of the Taurus, the Taurus braked and moved to change lanes to the right, but Jason was there in the Plymouth. He looked to his left, expecting to see Jeffrey and Lowell in the Taurus, with Lowell driving, but he didn't know the two men who looked back at him. The passenger was blond and young-looking. Jason couldn't see the driver.

The Taurus lunged quickly toward the Plymouth and just as quickly lunged away. Jason hit the brakes, but they didn't work. He put the accelerator pedal to the floorboard, but the engine already sounded as though it was going to tear itself apart, and the Plymouth did not move away from the Taurus. The *clik* of the speedometer rattled more loudly and then it went *ping!* and broke, and the little orange needle spun counterclockwise, hit the little ledge below the dial, and stayed there.

He wanted to change lanes to the right to get away from the Taurus, but a pink Suzuki Sidekick was there, so before the Taurus could lunge at him again, he clenched his teeth and steered left, into the Taurus, and heard metal crumple as the steering wheel tried to shudder out of his grip. The impact moved the Taurus over in its lane, but it wasn't as violent as Jason had feared, so he was able to keep his hold on the wheel.

Now the Corvette was gone, and the Taurus pulled ahead of the Plymouth. Its rear passenger door was mashed in, and the bent edge of the front door stuck out over it. Part of a green maintenance sticker was visible on the part of the door that showed in the Plymouth's one working headlight.

The Taurus pulled a little farther forward and changed lanes to the right, in front of Jason. He braked, and felt the brakes grab, but the car didn't slow. Disconcertingly, he experienced a floating sense of panic and disorientation. He let up on the brakes, and the car sped up by itself. He shifted into neutral and the engine revved up sharply, as though the accelerator had been floored. He shifted back into drive, startled, and the reengagement of the transmission with the howling engine shook the entire car. The Taurus moved farther away.

Whatever was wrong, it would get worse if he kept trying to follow the Taurus.

Chase over. He realized that his teeth were still clenched, so he opened his mouth and worked his jaw around. Signaling right and braking against the straining engine, he headed for the next offramp, wondering what was wrong, how he was going to come to a stop without making it worse, and how much it was going to cost. He could no longer differentiate the Taurus in the taillights ahead. He tried to remember its license plate and thought it had a *B* in it, and maybe an *M*. Or an *N*. Maybe the *B* was a *3*.

At the entrance to the offramp, he shifted into neutral. The engine roared as though enraged. He killed it by taking the key out of the ignition and coasted down the ramp. The Plymouth didn't have power steering or power brakes or power anything, so as the light at the bottom of the offramp turned green, he was able to turn right and steer for half a block before rolling to a stop fifty feet short of a lighted gas station.

The driver's door was jammed shut, so he pushed and wrestled the amplifier out the passenger's side onto the pavement. The old dashboard was knocked out of true where the amplifier had hit it, and its surface was bashed and broken. He scooted across the front seat and got out.

The front passenger's window was shattered, and the bang and scrape when he'd come off the curb in Santa Monica had been the rear quarter panel, which was squashed upward and pulled out. The rear bumper was gone. The face of his amplifier was dented, and two of its knobs were bent at forty-five-degree angles.

He walked around to the driver's side. The door and the front quarter panel were bashed in, and there were two bare screw holes to which the side-view mirror had once been mounted.

The driver's window was jammed in its track, so he got back in, lay on his back on the front bench seat, and kicked the glass out. Then he hoisted the amplifier back in on the passenger's side, went around to the driver's side, put his right arm through the broken window to steer, and started pushing toward the gas station.

The gas station driveway took five attempts, rocking the car back and forth and then heaving forward, up the shallow ramp. Finally, the Plymouth rolled into the lighted gas bay. The guy in the self-service kiosk watched with mild interest.

The hood latch had been knocked out of alignment and wouldn't open. Jason's right thumb slipped sharply off the latch and received a blood blister on its tip, and he sliced his left forefinger on a loose edge of the front grille. Eventually, he raised the hood and looked into the engine compartment.

It was hard to see well in the dim light, but he finally found the problem. A bolt had come free from the carburetor linkage, and the linkage had disintegrated, with the result that the throttle was permanently open. He looked halfheartedly for the bolt. Chances were it was lying somewhere on the 10 freeway.

One of the spark plug wires was dangling, disconnected, so he pushed it back in, but it wouldn't seat. He tipped sideways on one foot to get a better view. There was something where the number four spark plug was supposed to be, but his hair fell in front of his eyes. Holding his hair back with his left hand, he probed gingerly with the fingertips of his right, and felt fabric. Frowning, he pulled at it with thumb and forefinger, and it slid out of the socket and lay in his hand. What he'd thought had been fabric was paper towels, the light brown kind from public rest room dispensers, wrapped tightly around something the size and heft of a 35-millimeter film container.

He unwrapped it. It was a 35-millimeter film container, a plastic one with a black cylindrical body and a gray plastic snap top. The snap top had small holes in it from which ran a pair of putty-colored wires, ending in small plugs that he recognized as standard Macintosh connectors. He had no idea what the thing was, but it wasn't standard equipment on a mid-1960s 170-cubic-inch internal combustion engine.

The innermost paper towels were slightly damp. Several minutes of examining the thing under the stark light of the gas station yielded no answers, and he was reluctant to pry the cap off, so he rewrapped it and put it in the glove box. He rummaged around in his trunk until he found pliers and a wire coat hanger and turned the coat hanger into a crude fastener for the linkage. He wasn't at all sure that he was fastening things correctly, but he tried to be logical about it, and when he started the engine, it seemed to work. He threw the pliers and the coat hanger remains into the cluttered trunk, wrenched the driver's door violently until it screeched open for him, and thought murderous thoughts as he nursed the Plymouth toward downtown Los Angeles on surface streets. The accelerator pedal felt loose and sloppy from its homemade linkage.

A few blocks later, he stopped the car, pulled out the dashboard cigarette lighter, wrapped it in the paper towels, popped the hood, pulled the spark plug wire, and jammed the wrapped lighter where the film container had been.

14

The Pantry was always open. It was the only place downtown on Figueroa where you could get a meal at two in the morning unless you were cloistered within one of the nearby mirror-finished hotels, and it was almost always busy. A plaque near the front described how it had never closed since the Depression. The unceasing flow of customers continued to erode glacially through linoleum strata, deepening the multicolored, bevel-edged streambeds that ran to an ovoid pond in front of the old-fashioned cashier's cage.

Large gilt-framed paintings hung over the tables, but it was difficult to discern their subjects through fifty years' accumulated gunk. The menu was chalked on a chipped blackboard halfway down the narrow aisle. As customers were seated, relish plates of okay raw vegetables were delivered by a population of waiters that took pride in its work and had an average age of six hundred.

Paul was sitting all the way back under a big, dark oil painting of something, drinking coffee and munching on a carrot from the half-empty relish plate. He raised his eyebrows and said, "Your hands are all greasy. Where you been?"

Dropping onto one of four wooden chairs at the table, Jason said, "I delivered a baby gas engine. The miracles of birth and internal combustion, combined. Tell me what the hell is going on."

Paul's expression became vague and confused. "What do you mean?"

Jason had not previously noticed that between Paul's Adam's apple and collarbone was a little hollow that seemed ideally suited to have a relish plate rammed through it.

He nodded patiently and picked up a radish.

"Radish?"

Paul looked confused. "Uh, no, thanks."

Twirling the radish by its thin root, Jason said, "You were tampering with my car at the club tonight, and the goons in the Taurus were after you, not me. Are you going to tell me what's going on, or do I now get the innocent expression, maybe with just a tinge of injured trust?"

The innocent expression and the tinge of injured trust had already begun to make their way onstage, but *exeunt*ed quickly upon hearing their names. A certain facial hardening indicative of impugned honor trooped forward and took their place.

"What are you inferring?"

"Implying. I imply, you infer."

"Whatever. What are you saying, Jason?"

"You were tampering with my car, and the Taurus was after you."

"What are you saying?"

"Egad!" Jason exclaimed, tossing the radish into the air. "Time is rent asunder, trapping our heroes in a mysterious and fiendish temporal loop!" The radish went *thok!* on the floor. He picked it up and put it on the table. It rolled once and stopped against his plate.

"Look," Paul said. "I just want to know what you're *implying*."

"Okay, how about I'm *implying* that you were tampering with my car, and that the Taurus was after you?"

"What do you mean?"

Jason threw his hands up in exasperation and let them fall heavily on the table, rattling the relish plate and condiment bottles. "Jesus Christ, Paul, give me a goddamn break! Whatever you're into, you've got me into it now too, and I want to fucking well know what it is. Don't bother trying to snow me on this, because I already know you're doing something big and stupid, and I'm not going to settle for your usual bullshit."

He glared at Paul and docked himself ten originality points for "fucking" and "bullshit."

Paul tried to say something.

Jason cut him off. "My car's trashed, I'm fed up, my amp is probably broken, and my steering wheel's all greasy, I'm in a truly vile mood, and you are not going anywhere until I get some answers that don't sound like that maybe-could-be eighty-percent-possible kernel-of-truth I-can't-reveal-my-sources pokerface crap you usually spout."

Paul picked up a carrot and said, "This hurts me, you know? It does. I thought you were pretty cool lately, wanting me to live with you and all, but you know, this really hurts my feelings. Maybe I was wrong about you."

Jason said, "Oh, for god's sake."

"Hey," Paul said, "I'm trying to talk to you here, okay?

Maybe we ought to just do it some other time, when you're feeling a little more reasonable."

"Maybe we ought to stay right here and finish our conversation."

"Or what?"

" 'Or what'? What do you mean, 'or what'? Or nothing, Paul. I'm not going to get into a penis-size contest with you."

Paul shrugged. "You'd lose."

Jason said, "Tell you what maybe I'll do. I banged up the Plymouth real good tonight chasing those guys you've never seen before. I'm pretty well ready to write it off and figure out what else to do for transportation. I think whatever you were looking for is still in it. Maybe I'll drive it out someplace and burn it just to piss you off. It was already on its last legs—maybe a nice automotive funeral pyre, send it off to the big auto show in the sky, where all the good cars get fuel-injection and unborn calfskin seats, and nobody ever slams the door on their seat belts."

"Let me get this straight," Paul said, frowning. "You're saying that if I don't talk to you, you'll torch your own car?"

"There's a good half-gallon in the gas can in the trunk. Come on, *mí amigo*, let's go do something together." He stood up. "You coming?"

"I think you're crazy."

"You coming or not?"

"I don't get you."

"Okay, then. Once more at an eighth-grade level for the thinking-impaired: There's something you want in my car, and you're stonewalling me about it. I have no idea what it is, but I'm royally annoyed with you, and I'm ready to throw cunning and guile to the winds and just torch the damn car to put an end to this clever-clever secret-secret stuff. Maybe I'll just get the fire going and watch your secret whatever-it-is turn to ash. Maybe I'll look for it before I toss the match in. Maybe I won't. Maybe I'll get some hot dogs first and have a weenie roast over Paul's little secret. That has a nice kind of pointless symmetry to it."

Paul bit off a third of his carrot and chomped on it without saying anything. Jason shrugged and moved to leave.

"*You're* annoyed with *me*?" Paul said through his carrot. Jason waited. Paul swallowed. "Who was going to stand there and watch me get my head blown off yesterday?"

"Try actually firing up some neurons, Paul. My other option was to leave me, Robert, and Martin exposed and unarmed. What do you think might have happened if I'd done that? Instead of just one dead Paul, we could have had one dead Paul, one dead Jason, one dead Robert, and one dead Martin." He ticked the corpses off on his fingers. "That's four, which is more than one by approximately three hundred percent. You tell me what I should have done."

"Well, whatever. I just think you've got some nerve being the one who's annoyed with *me*."

"Another trenchant commentary from Paul Reno, ladies and logicians! Note the uncompromising rigor with which he wavers not from the serpentine path of reason!"

Paul threw his partial carrot onto the relish plate. "Fine. You want to go make a big statement? Make the big fucking gesture? Fine. Let's go. I think you're full of shit, and I'm going to come along just to make sure you do it. 'Cause if you don't, I'll never believe anything you say anymore."

"Oh happy," Jason said. "We'll be even."

Paul looked at him without expression, stood, and put two dollars on the table.

"Okay, smart man," he said. "Let's go."

They left the Pantry and crossed the street toward the parking lot. The Plymouth was parked next to Paul's hatchback.

Paul said, "Wow, you really messed it up, didn't you?"

"We're going east on the 10 until someplace barren shows up."

"Whatever."

Jason got into the Plymouth and started it, and Paul went around to the driver's door of the hatchback. In his rearview mirror, Jason saw an old white Corvair in excellent shape draw up behind the Plymouth, blocking it in. A stocky, bearded man got out.

Jason glanced at Paul. He wasn't getting into his hatchback.

He slammed the Plymouth into drive and wiggled the loose accelerator pedal, wanting to go over the concrete parking stop and across the sidewalk into the street, but he couldn't get any power to the wheels before the man was at the driver's window, aiming Jeffrey's monster gun at him in a two-handed grip.

The man said, "Turn off the engine," through the broken window glass. He had blue eyes, and the beard was neatly trimmed. Nobody else was in the parking lot. Jason reached for the key and turned it off.

"Paul," the bearded man said, "get the hood up and get it."

Paul didn't look at Jason as he went to the front of the Plymouth, fumbled with the hood latch, and managed to open the hood. Jason could see his waist moving around through the gap at the hinge.

Paul closed the hood. He was holding the little paper towel bundle. The bearded man said, "Move my car back."

Still without looking at Jason, Paul walked behind the stocky man, got into the driver's side of the Corvair, and pulled forward to allow Jason to exit. The bearded man jerked his head toward the driveway without wobbling the gun. Jason started the engine, put it into reverse, and backed out of the parking lot into the street. He glanced through the shattered passenger window at the Corvair as he shifted into drive. Paul was on the passenger's side, with the bearded man behind the wheel, and the backup lights were on. Paul was probably unwrapping Jason's cigarette lighter. Jason accelerated as smoothly as he could and got the hell out of there.

15

He thought about doubling back, decided it would be too obvious, got onto the 110 freeway to the northbound interstate, and headed into Glendale. At the back of the Denny's where he'd met Norton Platt previously, he called Light Wizards from a pay phone. A woman told him that Platt was not expected for another two hours, at 6:00 A.M., but that he often arrived an hour early. Jason thanked her and hung up and Platt walked through the front door of the restaurant carrying a worn brown leather shoulder bag and an unread newspaper. He spotted Jason.

Walking from the telephone, Jason said, "I just tried you at Light Wizards. I need to talk to you."

"I usually have lunch here before I go to work," Platt said.

"Four in the morning is a weird lunchtime even for musicians."

"I haven't had any kind of predictable schedule in twenty years," Platt said. "It's easier just to call everything lunch."

A tall woman with thick black hair picked two menus out of a holder and led them back to a booth. Jason noticed her hips moving as she walked. He'd forgotten that women's hips did that thing that men's hips didn't.

"I assume," Platt said when they were seated with their menus, "that you're here to talk to me."

"Yeah, and we're way overdue for it. I've got several things for you, but this is first." Jason took the film container out of his jeans pocket and put it on the table. He hadn't seen in the harsh light of the gas station that it was partially melted. Platt picked it up and examined it.

"Homegrown device," he said. "What is it?"

"A half-melted film container with two wires sticking out of it."

Platt looked at him patiently. "Really," he said.

"Yes," Jason said. "Honestly, you could have figured that out by yourself."

Platt turned it over. "ADB connectors," he said. He tried the edge of the snap cap and then pried one side up and peered in, repositioning the item to cast light into it.

The seating person came back and took their orders. Platt asked for waffles, and Jason ordered a Monte Cristo. She smiled and took their menus. Jason watched her leave, and quickly looked away, embarrassed, when she glanced back at him.

Platt examined the thing again. After a minute, he pried up the other side so the snap cap hung on the wires like a button on a thread, and looked inside again. Then he tipped it so Jason could see inside. Jason looked. Inside was a compact bundle of electronics.

"What is it?" he said.

Platt said, "A half-melted film container with two wires sticking out and some electronic stuff inside."

"Gosh, I knew you'd help."

"I want you to tell me all about where you got this, but one thing at a time." Platt put his brown shoulder bag on the table, unzipped it, and took out a little electrical testing device about the size of a man's wallet. It had two thin probe wires, one red and one black, which terminated in small, blunt needles. "How good are your hands?"

"Been doing my Hanon," Jason said. "So they're above average."

"Good. Hold the connectors so they face me."

Jason did. Platt repositioned them a little and said, "This test is kind of pointless, but the multimeter is the only diagnostic equipment I have here."

Each of the item's connectors consisted of several tiny pins inside a single terminator, and Platt touched the probe needles to them in different combinations.

"It could be anything," he said presently. "But my guess is that it's Huey Benton's homemade scrambler/descrambler." He coiled the probe wires neatly and put the device back in his shoulder bag.

"My thoughts exactly," Jason said. "Paul knew where it was in my car. The obvious conclusion is that he put it there."

"He was with you the night Benton died."

"Yeah."

"He probably got it then."

"And then hid it in my engine when he went to get my car. I thought he was just being considerate because I was so out of it."

Platt nodded.

Jason shook his head. "He must have missed the meeting about how plastic melts."

Platt said, "Be right back." He got up and went back to the pay phone, leaving the thing on the table. Jason fiddled with it idly and tried not to watch the seating person's hips because staring was rude.

Platt came back and said, "They can do without me until later. We'll head out to my place after we eat and put this gadget on the bench."

"Okay. Hey, wait a minute. I remember telling Paul to back off a little when I was doing CPR on Huey Benton. I thought he was trying to help. That's when he must have gotten it."

"Could be."

"And then the Plymouth seemed to have gotten worse when I drove it away from there."

Platt nodded. "This little thing was keeping a plug wire from connecting with its spark plug."

Jason shook his head. "I'm trying to keep the guy alive and Paul's rolling him. That's just charming as all hell."

Platt watched him.

"In fact," Jason said, "it's pretty much despicable."

Platt nodded. "What's the next thing you want to tell me?"

"Someone in a white Taurus is after Paul."

"Get a license number?"

"Yeah, but now I can't remember it."

"You didn't write it down?"

"My pen fell through the floorboard during the car chase."

"You had a car chase?"

"Yeah."

"In your Plymouth?"

"Yeah."

"That must have been interesting. What else?"

"After that, I met up with Paul at the Pantry. I told him I was going to torch my car if he didn't tell me what was in it. When we went back out to do it, this other guy ambushed me. Paul was cooperating with him."

"Who was the other guy?"

"I don't know. He had a beard. Blue eyes. Maybe five-nine, one-sixty. Maybe in his forties. Drove an old white Corvair."

"A Corvair?"

"Yeah. Why, you know this car?"

Platt didn't respond at first but when Jason didn't break the silence, he nodded slowly and said, "I might."

There was nothing else forthcoming.

Jason said, "He had Jeffrey's gun."

"And Jeffrey is—?"

"Hibbit's pet gargoyle. Oh yeah, you don't know this, either." He told Platt about the standoff in the Manor parking lot.

"How do you know the gun he had was Jeffrey's?"

"It's kind of hard to miss. It's all different colors. It's got a blue barrel, a shiny metal grip, and a gold trigger. And a black sight or something on top."

"He's customized it."

"More like Frankensteined it. You can almost see the stitch marks. And it's huge."

"How huge?"

"Huge." Jason made dimensions with his hands.

"That could be a Desert Eagle. Navy men call it the world's only crew-operated handgun. Is there anything else I don't know about?"

"I don't think so. I would have e-mailed you, but you

said not to with anything important, and I couldn't reach you on the phone."

Platt nodded. After lunch, in the overhead lighting of the parking lot, Platt looked at the mashed Plymouth and said, "You weren't kidding." He walked all the way around it and chuckled. "You don't do things halfway, I'll give you that."

"A post–modernist expression of man's struggle with his place in the universe," Jason said, indicating the Plymouth with one hand, like a museum docent. "Note the complex interplay of light and angle."

"Sure," Platt said. He fished a key ring from his shoulder bag. "I'll drive. I'm headed to Light Wizards after we're done, so I'll bring you back to man's struggle on the way back."

"You think it'll be safe here?"

Platt said, "As long as it's not trash day." He walked toward a light blue minivan with no side windows and dark blue swashes across its flanks.

"Oh, right," Jason said. "Like I'm going to listen to my vintage automobile be insulted by a guy in a minivan."

Platt smiled, chirped the minivan's alarm, and unlocked the doors. "You can load your music stuff into the back."

He pulled around to the Plymouth, and Jason transferred his road cases and amplifier into the back of the minivan and got into the passenger's seat. It was comfortable and completely barren of duct tape, and no pointy metal things poked through the fabric. There were not holes in the floor. Platt turned the key and the engine started smoothly. The tape player whirred and clicked neatly, and Ray Charles started his electric piano solo in the middle of "One Mint Julep." All four speakers worked. There were no unseemly odors. It was clean.

A metal wall with a single smoked window separated the cab from the cargo area where Jason's music equipment was. Platt put it in gear and they left the parking lot.

RAY CHARLES WAS in the middle of singing "Your Cheating Heart" when Platt pulled of Cahuenga into a driveway on the Valley side of Hollywood, took a remote control from the minivan's visor, buzzed open the garage door, and parked. They rode a small freight elevator in the corner of the garage up one floor to a small, enclosed entryway with a single door, which Platt unlocked and opened. Jason followed him in.

The Realtor, when showing Platt the place, had probably called attention to the room's airy spaciousness, its southern exposure and big picture windows, its 2,500 square feet of glowingly beautiful wooden floor, and its massive, ornate ceiling fan. "Gracious living," she'd probably emoted, pointing out the brass switchplates and doorknobs and the molding around the high ceiling. "Elegant; plenty of room for entertaining," she'd probably suggested. "A real dream pad," she might have ventured, daring to bandy the lingo with her long-haired client.

Jason pictured Platt giving it a cursory once-over, checking the circuitry for load capacity and proper grounding, handing the Realtor a wad of cash, and then backing up the trucks.

It was that bad.

Perhaps 10 of the 2,500 square feet of beautiful wooden floor were visible. The other 2,490 were protected from the deleterious effects of natural light by a seemingly uniform mass of electronic equipment that varied only in height, color, and decade of origin. Chains and sturdy black straps ran from the tops of the taller items to thick silver bolts in the ceiling. A narrow trail wound through the chaos, and Platt followed it to a beige secretary's chair in front of a workbench against the east wall. Jason followed gingerly, glancing at the individual pieces that made up the great mass of *stuff* as Platt sat and put the item on the workbench.

Within immediate eyesight were a gray thirty-two-channel audio mixing console, a short stack of small cardboard boxes with white labels that said "Transport Assembly," a Ziploc baggie full of small black screws and washers, a leather-bound copy of the Qur'an with a pink ribbon bookmark in it, a pistol-sized crossbow, several large blue totes full of bulk-packed digital audio and Hi-8 videocassettes, a six-foot-tall orange flight case standing open with video gear bolted into it, half a dozen dark video monitors on a steel wall unit, three laptop computers atop a narrow counter with text flowing up their screens, eight recent catalogues from different electronic supply companies, four pink sticky notepads, a floor-to-ceiling beige carpeted thing intended for cats, a closed black flight case with the words DANGER: INFECTIOUS HUMAN WASTE stenciled on it in white paint, a hassock-sized spool of thick blue cabling, and a kayak.

"You're not married," Jason said.

Platt said, "The interesting things start about two feet down from clutter surface."

"Such as?"

Platt worked with the mystery gadget as he talked, clamping it gently to the bench in a small vise. "Well, there's a voltage-controlled oboe in the corner under the other workbench behind the video monitors, and the coffin to the east of the cat tree is rigged to protect someone with a weight of up to 120 pounds from a forty-foot drop."

"Uh huh."

"I think the internal structure is close to being sound, but the coffin itself would shatter on impact. I have to find something better for the outer shell, preferably something without hinges." He moved a light on a flexible stalk to the front of the workbench. Switching it on, he said, "Of course, then I'll have to deal with the additional energy that's currently being dissipated mechanically through shell disintegration."

"Of course."

Platt pulled on a black articulating arm to position a rectangular magnifying glass before him. Without looking, he flipped a little toggle switch above the workbench, and Bryan Lee and the Jump Street Five started playing "Memphis Bound" over two large speakers at different ends of the room. His voice became distracted. "Which shouldn't be . . . all that tricky . . . you want to look at this?"

Jason picked his way carefully to the workbench and said, "Okay, what am I looking at?"

"I don't know yet," Platt said. He moved to one side so Jason could see through the magnifier. Pointing with a pair of rubber-tipped tweezers, he said, "This is a battery. This is an EEPROM. These are ADB connectors for a Macintosh. This big silvery glob here is heat damage, most likely from your engine. I don't know how much I can do about that. It all depends on what melted and what the glob is covering. Huey Benton made this thing."

"How do you know?"

"See this right here?"

Platt pointed with the rubber-tipped tweezers. On one corner of a circuit board were the letters *HB* in fine black ink.

Jason said, "And here I was about to be impressed with

your preternatural powers of deductive reasoning." He looked up. "Wait; it could be Humphrey Bogart."

"I was thinking Hildegard of Bingen, but cryptography's not in her dossier. No, I'm relatively certain this is Huey Benton's mysterious dongle."

"Dongle?"

"Yes. You've never heard the term? Little devices like this are called dongles. Their most common function is to prevent people from using pirated software. Some software will run only if it detects a certain dongle connected to the computer. But there's nothing that says you can't make dongles that do other things." He gestured at the little gadget. "Encryption and decryption, for instance."

Jason's face must have showed something. Platt's raised eyebrows said, Yes?

Jason said, "The conversation with Ian Hibbit at Chuck E. Cheese went off on its tangent when Robert used the word *dongle* in a somewhat earthier context. This must be what Hibbit was looking for at the Manor. He showed up the morning after Benton died, so Paul must have told someone pretty quickly."

"That is reasonable."

"I can't see that Paul has any use for a 'dongle,' so probably he's just trying to sell it."

"You don't know where Paul is."

"No."

"And you don't know where Hibbit is."

"No, and I don't know who any of these other people like Jeffrey or Lowell or the Taurus guys were, I don't know who Paul is dealing with, I don't know seventeen what, and I don't know what to do next."

Platt grinned. "Swofford's First Rule of Spying: When

no clear course of action suggests itself, pick something at random."

Jason said, "That's much more coolly enigmatic than Keltner's First Rule of Computer Music."

Platt looked expectant and said, "Which is?"

"Don't put your coffee on your keyboard."

"Uh, right."

"What's a Swofford?"

"Carl Swofford. He taught me most of what I know."

"How'd you meet him?"

"He had a habit of taking in strays and turning out protégés." Platt swiveled a little in his chair. "One advantage to choosing a random course of action is that people tend to interpret it based upon their own agendas, which means that if you're observant, it's often possible to deduce their agendas from their reactions to you. The other advantage is that anything you do is a surprise."

"Okay, makes sense."

"The disadvantage is that since people do interpret it based upon their own agendas, you run a big risk of being pulled very quickly into situations you had no idea existed and for which you are unprepared."

"Why stop now?"

Platt nodded. "You seem to have some talent for this stuff. I wouldn't have hired you if you hadn't demonstrated back with that Monica Gleason thing that you've got instincts. But you don't have any kind of firm grounding. Your letting Paul walk away from you tonight, for instance. Sometimes, that turns out okay. Other times . . .'"

"Kind of like how being naturally musical doesn't mean you can hold your own with trained session musicians."

"Exactly."

"But it also means that you might have a better chance of coming up with something unexpected."

"Maybe."

"Until someone shows up who is both trained and unexpected."

"It happens."

Jason nodded.

Platt said, "You've done fine, but I'm not sure I want you in this anymore."

A large orange tiger-stripe tomcat wandered in from another room through a door next to the computer counter and froze when it saw Jason.

"Who's this?" Jason said, squatting with one hand at cat-level in front of him. The cat walked toward him, stopped just out of reach, and regarded him suspiciously, sniffing the air in his general direction.

"That's Brother Ray," Platt said. "He was the studio cat over at Big Cheese before it closed. You know the place?"

"No."

"They did mostly soul, R&B, some hiphop. When they closed, I took their Bösendorfer. Brother Ray was in it."

Jason said, "Their Bösendorfer?" He stood up. Brother Ray shied back and held himself ready to bolt. Jason looked around the room again and spotted the Bösendorfer, a long black grand piano on a wheeled platform, lid down, under a blue quilted packing blanket and the kayak. The blanket edge hung at an angle, revealing the left side of the exposed keyboard, where a small black cover lay closed over a few extra bass keys.

"Yes," he said. "That's a Bösendorfer, all right."

"They owed me a lot of money," Platt said. "When they pay up, they can have it back."

"Wouldn't it have been easier just to take a couple of expensive microphones?"

Platt grinned. "Swofford's Second Rule of Spying," he said. "Style counts."

"Why'd they go out of business?"

"The usual reasons. Lousy management and the owner's cocaine habit."

Brother Ray leaped nimbly over the blue totes and up onto the first tier of the carpeted cat tree.

"Hey," Jason said. "The cat actually uses the cat tree. How'd you accomplish that?"

"Cat psychology," Platt said. "I chase him off it every so often."

Brother Ray sharpened his claws on the center pole of the cat tree and then climbed to the second tier and began to groom himself.

Platt removed the dongle from the vise and waited.

"Okay," Jason said. "I guess I'm out."

SITTING IN THE minivan with the motor running, Platt said, "Now would be a good time to leave town for a little while." They were in the parking lot at Denny's, and Jason was standing next to the minivan after having transferred his music equipment back into the Plymouth.

"Okay," Jason said. "Well, uh, thanks for the work."

"You did fine," Platt said. He nodded toward the Plymouth. "Take the repairs out of the discretionary fund. Or it might be cheaper just to buy another car."

The extra two thousand dollars in Platt's initial check had slipped Jason's mind. It wasn't charity. He said, "Thanks."

"Take care," Platt said. Jason closed the minivan door and got into the Plymouth. He started the engine.

Which left the question of what to do next. Jason didn't

feel like leaving town. He flirted briefly with the notion of going back into Denny's and asking the seating person to go somewhere, but there was nowhere to go, she was probably not there anymore, it was getting light out, and—the most compelling reason—there was no way in hell he could ever actually bring himself to do that.

He glanced at the minivan as he put it in drive. Platt waved.

He pulled out of the driveway. Going back to the Manor was probably a bad idea. He had a car full of all his music gear, nine hundred dollars newly nestled in his pocket, a couple of thousand in the bank, no expenses, and nowhere he had to be. He'd been complaining about wanting to leave town for a few weeks, but now that a real opportunity existed, it held no charm.

Something flared in his rearview mirror as the Denny's went out of sight behind him. He turned onto an empty side street and watched for cars that might be following him, but none came. He left Glendale with a couple of days to kill, a vague feeling of paranoia, and no idea where he was going.

16

"Uh huh," Martin's voice said on the pay telephone. "And what exactly are you doing in Death Valley?"

"I told you," Jason said. "Driving around."

The telephone was on a creaking porch in front of a gas station and general store on a narrow, shimmering highway so bright that Jason had to squint through his Wayfarers. The Plymouth, coated with reddish-beige dust, sat nearby with the driver's door open and joggling on its hinges in sympathy with the irregular beat of the ill-tuned engine. Two motor homes sat stolidly next to the store, at careless angles to it.

The telephone handpiece was too hot to hold, so Jason had it cocked on the shoulder of his shirt with a lot of hair between his ear and the earpiece. The tip of his index finger was mildly blistered from pressing the metal push buttons on the face of the telephone, and he was careful not to touch his face to the mouthpiece, which radiated heat he could feel on his lips.

"I walked up this long dirt path to an old borax processing plant today," he said. "Out there in the flats, in this incredible heat. The historical plaque said Chinese people used to mine borax and haul it from the flats in the middle of summer. I can't imagine. I mean, when they call it 'furnace-like' out here, they're not kidding. I couldn't even stand there and read the plaque without my head burning."

"So Chinese people, huh?"

"Yeah. Next time someone tells you that white people built America, tell them to go screw themselves."

"How hot is it there?"

"About one-thirty."

"You are drinking a lot of water, right?"

"Yes, Mom."

"I'm not kidding, Jase. You don't have air conditioning in that car."

"I have four-sixty air conditioning," Jason said. "Open all four windows—"

"—go sixty miles an hour," they said in unison.

Martin said, "Yeah, all that hundred-and-thirty-degree air blowing into the car really cools a guy down. By the time you feel thirsty, it can already be too late. You know that, right?"

Jason made whooshy static noises with his mouth. "Mom? You there? I can't hear you over this bad connection."

"Look, just be careful, okay?" Martin's voice said.

"Okay?" he repeated when Jason didn't answer.

"Okay, okay, okay, yeah, yeah, yeah," Jason said.

"So is this some kind of symbolic purifying journey or something, or are you really just driving around?"

"Got me," Jason said. "I just kind of ended up here."

"How's the car running?"

"*Dee*troit steel, son," Jason said. "Hunnert-seventy-cubic-inch slant-six engine. Runs forever. Until the rest of the car falls apart around it. Which could be any time now."

The Plymouth's engine died momentarily, teetered at the brink of expiration, sputtered, and heaved itself pessimistically toward a vague approximation of an uneven idle. The open door shuddered on its hinge.

Jason said, "I spend a lot of time watching the temperature gauge."

"Well," Martin's voice said, "I'll tell Robert. How long are you going to be gone?"

"I don't know. At least a few days."

"Okay, man." Martin coughed away from the phone receiver momentarily. "Well, say hello to the cactuses for me."

Jason said, "Hold on." He put the phone to his chest to muffle it and bellowed, "Martin says hi!" at the unmoving cholla cactuses across the highway. His voice disappeared in the flat desert air. The cactuses showed no sign of pleasure.

After a moment, he put the phone to his ear again. "They say hi back."

"Where can I reach you?"

"Don't know. There's probably a town around here somewhere with a motel for tonight. If not, I'll sleep at a turnoff."

Martin coughed again. " 'Scuse me," he said when the cough subsided. "Okay, man. You going to drink lots of water?"

"You going to quit smoking?"

A recorded female voice demanded more money.

Jason said, "Bye, I'm out of change." He hung up and rubbed his ear. In the store, he bought two one-gallon containers of water, a blue bandanna, and a cold, prepackaged ham sandwich, and paid for twenty gallons of gasoline. He discarded the two empty plastic jugs that were sitting on the front passenger-side floorboard and put the new two in their place, tied the bandanna around his forehead to keep sweat out of his eyes, pumped fifteen gallons of gas into the Plymouth and the other five into his gas can, sealed the can tightly and put it in the back, and got back on the highway.

For sixty miles, he didn't think about anything and just watched the rocks and scrub and cholla cactuses go by, kept an eye on the temperature gauge, and avoided cooperating in the suicide of a despondent rabbit. Then he ate his warm sandwich, which was good for killing another fifteen miles. Then he spent eighty miles assembling God's Own Rhythm Section and couldn't decide between Tony Levin and Aston "Familyman" Barrett on bass. Then he wondered what Sting's music would be like if Stewart Copeland were still around and breaking his ribs from time to time and thought that it was a good thing that someone had put Bob Marley's live version of "No Woman No Cry" onto the *Legend* album despite feedback in the mix. Then he remembered that Manu Katché was a contender for God's Own Rhythm Section, but it was too much trouble to start over, so instead he wondered why the Los Angeles Music Center Opera insisted on modernizing old operas strangely instead of just performing new ones. He decided that it was because he was not in charge. Then he decided that it was the cause of most of the world's problems. Then he drank some water.

THE SUN WAS lower and shadows were longer. Jason pulled off to the left without thinking about it and stopped the Plymouth at the end of a deep, flat turnout, its front tires up on a short, sandy rise that precipitated a canyon dropoff.

His shoes crunched lightly as he walked to the unrailed edge. The infinite blue of the sky met the reds and rusts in a vivid line. Below the line, short ledges and small, blunt outcrops cast knife-straight black shadows against the red canyon face. A hawk hung in the arid sky, tilting itself subtly against updrafts, solitary and perfect.

Hot wind whuffed in his ears, and he squinted behind his Wayfarers, watching the hawk find and ride lift far above two big crows that raced across the canyon to veer up sharply at the far face, cawing raucously. The hot wind lifted his hair and briefly cooled the back of his neck where there was sweat.

The shimmering of the horizon was completely, deeply silent. It was a good thing Jason wasn't God, because he would have given the shimmer a soft fizzing noise. That was all the world needed, a fizzing horizon.

He took it as a lesson: Restraint in art is good.

He listened:

A motor home on the highway hissed softly behind him, whirring past the turnoff entrance toward somewhere.

The stilled engine under the hood of the Plymouth clinked as it gave up its heat.

The earth under his shoes shifted coarsely with his weight.

Something quick, small, and dry scuttled through the leaves in the crackly underbrush to his right.

A vehicle entered the turnoff behind him, crushing

sand under its tires. Jason turned and watched a burgundy minivan roll up and park a few feet from the Plymouth. Its driver's door opened, releasing what sounded like muted polka music into the hot, dry air. A sweating man in his late sixties got out and stretched. Green checked shorts, brown sandals, black socks, shapeless fishing hat, and aviator sunglasses.

He nodded to Jason, fanning himself. Jason nodded. The man pulled a cellophane-wrapped junk food snack out of the minivan's passenger seat and began unwrapping it noisily and clearing his throat while he looked around the turnout. Jason went to the Plymouth and popped the hood. From one of the one-gallon drinking jugs, he topped up the ancient bleach bottle that served as his radiator reservoir.

The engine started without incident and he backed the Plymouth through the turnout, angled it rear-first onto the highway, clunked the brakes, and shifted into drive. As the turnout rolled past the edge of his rearview mirror, the man was momentarily visible, his hand up to block the sun from his eyes, looking at the hawk.

IT WAS ABOUT half an hour before sundown when Jason steered around a curve, passing the entry and parking lot of a resort and a small court of shops in the middle of the desert. The cars in the parking lot had rental stickers and out-of-state license plates. He pumped the brakes, made a U-turn, and parked in the lot next to a rented sedan with a baby seat in it and walked past three new Harley-Davidson motorcycles. The Harley riders were smoking cigarettes and sitting on a short brick wall. They were appropriately dusty and scruffy, but all their leather looked new and they were speaking French, so Jason figured the bikes for rentals.

The man behind the counter at the Furnace Creek hotel seemed genuinely sad as he told Jason that a night in the least expensive room would cost more than half Jason's monthly rent. Jason asked if that included a foot rub, and the man said he was sorry but no, it didn't. Jason suggested that it should, and the man said he would pass the suggestion on to management. Jason also suggested that the parking lot should be carpeted so people didn't burn their feet when they walked on it. The man thought that was an excellent suggestion and suggested a less expensive hotel half an hour away. Jason said that people should care more for their feet. The man agreed, and emphasized that the less expensive hotel was certainly what Jason was looking for. Jason inquired as to whether the other hotel would greet him with camels bearing apes, ivory, and peacocks. The man said he wasn't familiar with the other hotel's greeting arrangements, but reiterated that he was absolutely certain that it would be absolutely perfect for Jason. He smiled when he was done.

Jason thought the smile looked a little forced.

He wandered through the courtyard of shops, listened to pale, sunburned people in shorts speaking German and French, didn't buy anything, and got back in the Plymouth. The burgundy minivan was parked across the lot.

He set out in early dusk for the hotel at Death Valley Junction. Now that he was out of town—really, thoroughly, properly, unambiguously, utterly, inarguably out of town—he would get a cheap room, set his music stuff up in it, and finish "Untitled #23." And at some point, he mostly believed, the desert would tell him a name for it.

17

Jason's room at the Amargosa Motor Hotel in Death Valley Junction had no telephone and no television. It had a bed, a table with a lamp, a dresser, an air conditioner, and a bathroom. There was nothing to do and nowhere to go without driving twenty-three discontiguously paved miles up State Line Road and across the flats to Pahrump, where they had a small casino and some bad food in Quonset huts and an ATM machine.

The Amargosa Opera House adjoined the Motor Hotel, completing an L-shaped structure that surrounded a hundred-foot dirt parking lot. A woman named Marta Becket had been producing musical theater in the Opera House by herself for over thirty years. She wrote the shows, made the scenery, sewed the costumes, and danced all the roles, going up en pointe and doing kicks higher than her head.

To the left of the Hotel and Opera House was highway, to its right was highway and a few decrepit buildings, behind it was the remains of a borax processing plant and what had once been the hotel laundry, in front of it was State Line Road, above it was sky, and below it was dirt. It boasted a self-service refrigerator with cold drinks, an abandoned wing—said to be haunted—and a resident peahen named Esmerelda. That and a small herd of wild horses was all there was in Death Valley Junction. The only other person at the hotel was a desk clerk in khakis with whom Jason discussed the fine points of concocting fake UFOs in order to mess with Japanese tourists.

In her spare time, Marta Becket painted faces and scenes on the interior walls of the hotel. Jason was in the Jezebel Room. One wall bore a painting of an open boudoir containing frilly underthings and a feather boa. Depicted on the opposing wall were a Victrola and a hatstand with a woman's hat and another boa. Jason's music stuff was laid out on the bed and dresser, with cables roped in sagging runs from one black plastic and metal thing to another. His laptop computer sat open on the table. "Untitled #23" was onscreen awaiting Jason, who was sitting outside his door on the colonnade in the heat, sharing an iron bench with a roadrunner that wanted his sandwich. Jason still had no name for "Untitled #23," but he had decided that Flipper was a good name for the roadrunner. The Plymouth was parked neat against the colonnade.

In the three days he'd been there, he'd done nothing but eat, sleep, look at the sky, listen to UFO stories, name Flipper, watch Esmerelda the peahen intentionally and repeatedly scare the bejesus out of the feral cats that snoozed on the thick, low branches of the salt cedars next to the hotel, and work on music.

The music wasn't what it had to be yet, but it was less what it shouldn't be. One of the sections had a bass part that was a subtle kind of spooky, something he wouldn't have noticed outside the stillness of the desert. His new awareness of the spookiness was beginning to shape the rest of the piece.

But always, there was something that made a piece of music more than the sum of its notes, and that something hadn't yet broken the surface of "Untitled #23." There was no telling how much devotion was required before the thing would agree to reveal itself.

Flipper looked attentive and then scooted off the bench and zipped across the parking lot and behind the Opera House. A burgundy minivan and a trailing dust plume pulled in from the right and stopped in front of the main entrance, fifty feet down the colonnade from Jason's bench. The plume overtook the van briefly before dissipating. The man in the squashed fishing hat got out, looked around, recognized Jason and saluted at him, and went through he doors into the hotel office. A few minutes later, he came back out, got a new-looking purple duffel bag out of the minivan, and walked up the colonnade to Jason.

"Hot day," he said.

Jason agreed.

"Bill Thurlow," the man said, extending his hand. "Newhall, California. Used to be in vending machines, but now I'm retired."

"Pete," Jason said, shaking his hand. "Pete Whitley. Burbank, California. What brings you out here?"

"Just driving around," Thurlow said. "Came into a little money last year when I sold my vending machine business, and I like to see things. So here I am."

"Here you are," Jason said. "Plenty of things to see."

Thurlow looked around, taking his own assessment of how many things there were to see.

"So," he said. "What's to do around here?"

"Not a single damn thing unless you're into bats, ghosts, UFOs, or brothels."

"Brothels," Thurlow said. "I forgot they were legal out here."

"They're not legal here," Jason said. "This is still California. But there's one maybe thirty miles out, in Nevada. There's a place for dinner there, too, next to the brothel. It's not very good. The dinner, I mean. Not the brothel. I don't know how the brothel is."

"I'll keep that in mind. About dinner." Thurlow winked, unlocked a room halfway between Jason's and the front office, and went in. Flipper emerged from behind the opera house, skittered across the dirt lot, and disappeared behind the hotel.

"Meep meep," Jason said.

"Bill Thurlow," my ass, he thought.

18

The outer parts of Jason's ears hurt. He took the padded headphones off and massaged his ears and temples. No noise or light entered through the window. He put on a denim jacket and went out onto the dark colonnade and bent forward with his hands down toward his feet, stretching his back muscles. He couldn't tell what time it was, but the lobby was closed and dark.

Above the horizon, a silent dazzle of stars and galaxies overlaid utter blackness. Below it, generalities of terrain were almost intangible in the distant starlight.

Dim, dark rushing things whisked by above head level, and Jason ducked away felt dumb for flinching. Bats were harmless.

He crunched out into the middle of the dirt lot and lay on his back with his feet toward the building. He found Orion's belt and something that might have been some variety of Dipper. Those were the only conventional constellations he could ever recognize.

He looked for the Keltner-Goldstein constellations, superior to conventional constellations in that they didn't require specific stars, so no actual understanding of the night sky was necessary. He found three pinpoints of equal magnitude for The Last Piece of Pie and then searched for two, one brighter and one dimmer, to be The Little Sister Who Does Everything You Do. Then he found four in a trapezoid for Einstein's Tongue, and five clustered together for Robert's Five-Star Review.

A silent white pen stroke dashed through Einstein's Tongue.

"Marvin," Jason acknowledged. Martin's contribution to the Keltner-Goldstein stellar pantheon was that all meteors were named Marvin Gaye. Martin's justification for this was, "Because that's just how it should be."

Movie meteors always had whooshing sounds. They were better silent.

Robert and Martin had both been as immediately, deeply affected as Jason by the news of evidence of life in Mars rocks. It was good to have friends who got why that was amazing.

He realized he hadn't added a new constellation in a while. He looked until he found a cluster he named The Monster Chicken Heart and a fuzzy brightish patch near it, which he christened Smoke And Fire And Jell-O.

He listened carefully to insects and occasional breezes. Bats fluttered like washcloths as he got up and went to the bench on the colonnade.

As he sat, a door opened at the far end of the walkway, past Jason's room, near the opera house. A figure came out. Although Jason's eyes had adjusted to the dark, there was only enough light to see dark figure against dark ground, not enough to determine whether the person had a face.

He could have scuffed a shoe or cleared his throat to make himself known, but he didn't. The moment passed, and he knew the figure thought itself alone.

Something long, off which starlight glinted dimly, swung in the figure's hand as it stepped off the colonnade and crunched out toward the road. Something metallic knocked against its legs rhythmically as it walked, and its gait was a little uneven, as though it carried an awkward burden.

It stopped about fifty feet away, directly across from the door to Jason's room near the edge of the road, and unencumbered itself. The metal creak of an oven door pierced the silence.

Not an oven door; an unfolding lawn chair.

The chair issued smaller creaks as the figure sat in it and fiddled with other objects it had been carrying.

It struck him as deceptive to let on that he was there watching, even though it was really more deceptive not to. The figure settled into the chair, apparently finished and waiting.

Jason waited, too. The air was cool, and his denim jacket was comfortable. Because he didn't want the other person to know he was there, he couldn't do more than contract and relax his muscles to keep them from going to sleep. He went through his whole body that way, starting with the little toe of his left foot and going systematically up to his forehead. The dark figure occasionally shifted in its creaky lawn chair.

Some uncertain time later, distant headlights, probably a mile away, made the black air gray as the car turned onto some other highway, and Jason made out that something longish was mounted near the figure on a stand or brace, pointed toward the building, with a smaller something, like a scope or sight, mounted to it.

A little shudder like a chill sent small convulsions through him, and his breath drew in. *Thurlow.* It bothered him that he'd had no sense of danger when he first saw the figure.

If he moved, he'd be spotted. If he didn't move, the dawn would reveal him. Maybe the desk clerk would show up as it started getting light, and then there would be too many people around for Thurlow to shoot him.

Wouldn't someone waiting to shoot him have a night sight on their gun, and just shoot him now?

Yes, they probably would.

Logic wasn't comforting. He was just going to have to sit there scared.

NIGHT STOPPED BEING quite as black, and the figure became gradually distinct from the darkness. Jason tried to keep his muscles relaxed, which left nowhere for his tension to go. There was no motion apparent from the figure.

With the gradual, inevitable dawn, coarse details resolved: There was indeed something long and shiny set beside the figure on a mounting of some sort.

Most of his muscles were slightly contracted. He relaxed them.

Darkness continued to dissolve. Weak hints of light and uncertain promises of color coaxed a return of the landscape. The bats weren't there anymore. He hadn't seen or heard them leave. He was poised to throw himself off the walkway and behind the building, his gaze locked on the unmoving figure.

Dawn pressed on in preparation of sunrise. Jason squinted, concentrating his focus on the long thing with the scope or sight. In the thin beginnings of daylight, the image suddenly resolved with a *thump* of such viscerality that it seemed as though it should have been audible.

The figure was dark-haired and wore an orange down jacket. The small attached object was indeed a scope or sight. The thing to which it was attached was a long, black telescope, mounted on a metal tripod, aimed above the building at the region of the sky where Jason had seen the meteors. A green cloth backpack sat casually on the dirt next to it.

The figure in the chair was unmoving because she was asleep. Her name was Bonnie, he learned over breakfast. She was a former lawyer from Michigan, writing a screenplay about the Chinese laborers in the borax mines. She had brown eyes.

19

The morning after she left, on what might have been a Tuesday, he rose when the sunlight was still early, dressed in blue jeans, old shirt, and boots, transferred the pretty rock she'd given him from yesterday's shirt pocket to today's, and went outside to take the Plymouth to Pahrump for a last breakfast by himself before heading home. Or maybe to Michigan; he'd decide which over breakfast.

He'd dreamed an ending to "Untitled #23." It was chillingly perfect, and he remembered the sensation of the hair on his forearms prickling and the conviction that he had finished the piece and ended his stay in the desert. He couldn't remember the ending, but his trip was still over.

It was already approaching ninety degrees. Bill Thurlow was standing in the colonnade in the unromantic light of post-dawn, leaning against a column, his shapeless fishing hat on his head and his hands in the pockets of a red windbreaker. His minivan was parked along the colonnade in front of the Plymouth. He nodded at Jason.

Jason nodded back, got into the Plymouth, and turned the ignition. The engine cranked a lot without starting. He got out and opened the hood. Thurlow watched him.

He didn't see anything obviously wrong.

"Time to call Triple-A, Pete?" Thurlow said.

"Looks that way."

"If you were headed into Pahrump," Thurlow said. "I'm going that way."

Jason looked at the Plymouth and then at Thurlow, and thought before he answered. His thought was: *Might as well find out what the guy wants.*

He slammed the hood. "Sure."

"Jump in," Thurlow said.

"SO YOU'RE IN vending machines," Jason conversed, partway to Pahrump on State Line Road. The floor of the Amargosa Valley drifted very slowly past the road that carried the burgundy minivan, wide flats of dirt and salt and then sparse stretches of half-scorched, scrubby plants. The road wasn't all smooth, and the minivan's right front shock absorber went *squonk* when it bumped irregularly.

"Used to be," Thurlow said.

"What kind?"

"Just about every kind," Thurlow said. "Soft drinks, snacks, sandwiches, candy. You name it, someone's put it in a vending machine. You'd be surprised."

He slalomed the minivan smoothly around bad asphalt.

"So how come those things always reject my dollar bills?" Jason said.

"Maybe they're forged." Thurlow chortled at his joke. The flats eased by, salt clay and scattered, foot-tall scrub and a homemade wooden cross that drifted past on the left, its whitewash brilliant against the baked landscape.

Thurlow said, "What kind of work are you in, Pete?"

"Water quality," Jason said.

"That so?"

"Yup."

"You work for the city?"

"Yeah."

"Burbank?"

"Yeah."

"Good job?"

Jason shrugged. "Good benefits once you've vested."

"What brings you out here?"

"Just like you: driving around. Got some comp time I got to use or lose."

"Guy your age, you ought to take your vacations someplace more co-ed. If I were a few years younger, I'd be out in Club Med, soaking up some rays and trying to make a little time."

Jason nodded.

Thurlow said, "No ring through your nose, far as I can see."

"No," Jason said. "That's true. No nose ring," He was conscious of the pretty rock in his shirt pocket.

"That was one pretty little thing back at the hotel, there."

Jason didn't comment.

The sign that welcomed them to Nevada had taken so many bullets that it was more hole than sign. When they passed it, the road smoothed out and a broken yellow line divided it.

"I used to be married," Thurlow said. "Not now, though."

"What was her name?"

"Louise."

"Kids?"

"Two, Rose and Robby."

"Louise, Rose, and Robby. And what's your name, Bill?"

Thurlow glanced away from the road to give him an interested look. The minivan bumped over a stretch of uneven pavement and the shock absorber went *squa-squonk-onk*.

"Thurlow," he said. "Thought I told you that, Pete."

"Right, sorry," Jason said. "I forgot."

A little while later, Jason said, "You're a lousy actor, Bill. What do you want?"

"Just a little conversation."

"About what?"

"What brings you out here?"

Jason sat on that one for a little while.

"Why don't you tell me what brings *you* out here," he said when he was done thinking.

"You."

"Then let me set something straight," Jason said. "I don't know who you are, but you should know I'm out of the loop. I have nothing for you. No information, no little gadget, nothing. I'm out. Gone. Poof. Vapor. Sorry to send you home empty-handed, but you're arfing up the wrong sequoia."

"Where's the little gadget?"

"Spain."

"Spain?"

"You don't like Spain? How about Narnia, you like that better?"

Thurlow's expression turned from confusion to blank irritation.

"Sri Lanka," Jason said. "Baltimore, Ivory Coast. The Islets of Langerhans. Mare Nostrum. The Emerald City."

After a pause during which Thurlow said nothing, Jason said, "Translation: Why should I tell you?"

"What difference does it make to you? You told me you were out of the loop."

"Who are you, Bill?"

"Where's the little gadget?"

"Are you going to show me a weapon? Because if you're not, I'm done talking."

"Oo, tough," Thurlow said. He made little I'm-scared gestures, wiggles his fingers momentarily off the steering wheel.

Jason had said he was done talking, so he didn't say anything.

Thurlow said, "You strike me as a guy who needs convincing." He looked sharply at Jason.

Jason looked back at him. "And you strike me as a guy who needs a boot to the head while he's going sixty-five."

"Kind of a violent type, aren't you?"

"You're the one who started the fake name BS. If I'm jittery about it, whose fault is that?"

Thurlow nodded thoughtfully.

"I see your point," he said. The heel of his right hand whipped toward Jason too fast to be avoided and crashed solidly into Jason's jaw. The minivan didn't seem to waver in its trajectory, and Jason had a brand-new splitting headache.

"I'm through fucking around," Thurlow said. He reached into his windbreaker.

Jason released his seat belt latch.

"I'm not," he said. He lunged at Thurlow.

His right forearm knocked Thurlow's head against the

driver's side window, and the minivan swerved. Thurlow overcorrected the minivan's trajectory to try to throw Jason away from him, but Jason had his left arm around Thurlow's seat. Thurlow's hat was mostly off his head, and Jason tried to grab a bunch of hair and yank it back, but Thurlow didn't have enough hair, so it didn't work.

The minivan began to decelerate. Thurlow's hand was almost out of his red windbreaker, and Jason didn't think he could stop it, so as the gun came out and up to bear, he pushed his feet hard against the dashboard and shoved himself onto the bench seat behind Thurlow. As the gun followed him, he grabbed Thurlow's arm and pulled it toward himself. When it was as far as it would go, he wrenched it farther.

Thurlow cried out and locked the minivan brakes, and Jason lost his grip on Thurlow's seat. The minivan went off the pavement and slid to a stop on the dirt shoulder, dislodging so much dust that the valley around them disappeared in a swirl of dirty brown. The gun didn't fall from Thurlow's hand. With his rump planted in his seat, Jason grabbed the wavering right wrist tightly with both hands and kicked brutally up against the gun hand with his right boot. The fifth kick sent the pistol bouncing against the headliner and onto the floor of the minivan in front of him. Jason picked it up with his right hand.

"I hate guns!" he shouted. He hadn't previously realized that. He didn't seem to be pronouncing consonants clearly: "They're . . . not . . . fair!"

The dust cloaking the minivan cleared.

"Let go of my arm," Thurlow said. Jason still had a grip on it with his left hand, and it was still forced backward, obviously painfully.

"No," he yelled. He gave it a yank backward and Thurlow's jaw muscles clenched.

"*Now* you're just getting goddamn *sadistic*!" Thurlow ground out through gritted teeth.

Jason shouted, "Who are ya, Bill? Straight goddamn answer or I'll show you sadistic." He braced for another yank on Thurlow's hurt arm but didn't do it yet.

Thurlow's head angled back to see Jason better, and his left hand came around his body with another pistol in it. It leveled at Jason's forehead.

"Ease it off, tough boy," he gasped. "You don't hurt people when you don't have to. Norton must have taught you better than that." Sweat gleamed slick on his reddened face.

Maintaining the pressure on Thurlow's arm, Jason aimed the gun he'd picked up at Thurlow and said, "Answers!"

"Not until you ease the fuck *off*!"

Jason gave the arm an inch, relieving strain on the shoulder. Thurlow moved a little in his seat to adjust to the small increase in freedom, but his jaw was still clenched in pain.

"What do you want me to answer?" Thurlow grated.

"Who are you? What's your real name?"

"Carl Swofford."

Jason didn't have anything to say for a few moments. Then he said, "ID?"

"Pants pocket."

"Don't reach for it."

Thurlow grimaced. "Let the arm up a little more, please."

"Why should I?"

Thurlow's face twitched in pain and hatred. "Let the arm up, *please*," he spat angrily. His neck muscles corded.

"What's Swofford's First Rule of Spying?"

"I don't have one. That's just how Norton talks."

"What do you want with me?"

Thurlow lurched around clumsily but quickly, banging the end of his pistol's barrel up against Jason's forehead, and narrowed his eyes. "Look, shit-for-brains, I'm almost tired enough of this to shoot you. Make a decision. Enough of this halfway crap; either let go of my arm or try to kill me. You got maybe ten seconds at the outside before I put a round through your head."

Jason hesitated.

"That gun you got there isn't loaded," Thurlow said. "That's why it didn't fire when you were kicking it."

Jason let go of the arm but kept the possibly unloaded pistol aimed where it was.

"*Thank* you." Thurlow moved his arm gingerly in front of his body.

"Okay," Jason said suspiciously. "What the hell are you doing out here?"

Rubbing his shoulder, the old man didn't look at Jason when he finally answered.

"Norton's missing," he said.

20

I don't think I much like you, Unca Carl," Jason said on their continued journey into Pahrump. He still held Swofford's pistol. Swofford had put his second gun away inside his windbreaker.

Swofford said, driving one-handed, "What's with the long hair and earrings?" He wiggled one hand in a *mezzo-mezzo* gesture. "You not so sure which way you go?"

"Ah," Jason said. "I see I'm in the company of the old fool there's no fool like. What an honor this is. When I meet the chicken that wasn't counted before it hatched, my joy will be complete."

Swofford humphed.

"Hey," Jason said. "What did you do to my car, anyway?"

"Pulled out the distributor rotor."

"I see," Jason said.

———

IN PAHRUMP, SWOFFORD pulled into an ugly pre-fab gas station. Jason got out, walked to the back of the minivan, and kicked the passenger-side taillight in.

"What the hell is your problem?" Swofford demanded.

Jason held out one hand.

"My distributor rotor," he said.

"Under your front passenger seat. You really are a god-damn kick in the pants, aren't you?"

"Don't touch my car, Carl. I don't like it."

"Your car's a piece of junk," Swofford said.

"You got three more taillights I can see," Jason said. "Piss me off some more."

WHEN THEY WERE back in the gassed-up minivan, Swofford said, "When did you last see Norton?" He turned the engine on and started the air conditioner.

"I don't know you're even really Carl Swofford," Jason said. "And even if you are, I don't know you. You got anyone can vouch for you?"

"Plenty, but you don't know them. So now what, young wise guy?"

"Now I guess you'd better figure out a way to convince me, old cranky guy."

Swofford looked impatient. "And you're not going to tell me anything until you're convinced."

Jason gave him a look that was intended to convey *Duh*.

"I'll make some calls," Swofford said. "If we find someone suitable, you can talk to them."

Jason said, "In person,"

"Norton could be in danger," Swofford said. "Don't you care about that?"

Jason raised his eyebrows idly.

Swofford looked away and shook his head. "You . . ."

He trailed off and muttered.

Jason said, "Imagine my discomfiture if I spill the beans to a bad guy."

"Okay, we'll do it your way. We'll go waste a ton of time making you happy when we should be using it to find out what happened to Norton." Swofford pulled a tiny cell phone from his shirt pocket, dialed, and waited. "It's me," he said after a minute. "We're inbound." He listened for a moment and then closed the phone.

"We're going into town," Swofford said. "You got an objection?"

"Oh, probably," Jason said.

21

L as Vegas!"
   Jason made the requisite cocking
sound when his thumb dropped, and he shot at Swofford
with his forefinger. The Strip was still several miles away, a
bizarre, jumbled line of rectangles, spires, and distant
obelisks that broke the desert like the wreckage of a gargantuan Martian city.

"Welcome to Mars Port," Jason said. "Chief import:
rich tourists. Chief export: poor tourists."

Swofford turned on the radio. Somebody drawled over
steel guitar about all the women in all the towns in a way
that was utterly indistinguishable from the other drawlers
who'd been through the same women and towns previously. Then a drawling deejay came on and talked about
what an individualist the singer was.

"I'd heard they liked country music here on Pluto, but I
didn't believe them," Jason said.

Swofford ignored him and exited the highway. A few minutes later, they walked through two sets of glass doors into the Stardust and were abruptly immersed in cold cigarette smoke and a vast noisescape of random electronic beeps. Jason listened while he followed Swofford across the floor. The hundreds of brief blips from computer soundchips were all in the same perfectly tuned "do-re-mi" diatonic mode, but they were overlaid with clinking beverage glasses and a recording of "On the Road Again" that was jarringly out of tune with the perfectly intonated chaos. It sounded like a herd of Philip Glass clones playing Pong in a western bar.

They threaded through rows of determined old women grimly playing nickel slots and went into a coffee shop, where the din of the games was muffled but relentless. Swofford scanned the room and headed toward the back with Jason following him.

Leslie Bookman was sitting in a back booth with half a glass of something fizzy, looking vaguely attentive to the room but mostly tired. She lifted her eyebrows at Swofford and then looked past him and smiled at Jason. He smiled back. She was fortyish and good-looking: dark hair with some gray, blue eyes, and crow's-feet that deepened with the smile. He'd met her around the same time he'd met Platt.

He took off his denim jacket and bundled it on his lap as he sat down. The gun he'd taken from Swofford was in its large inside pocket.

"Hi, Jason," she said when they sat down.

"Hi, Leslie," he said. "You're my proof of Grampa Cheerful's true identity?"

"He's not so bad," she said. "We've had a bad week."

"Can we get on with this?" Swofford groused.

Jason said, "He says he's Carl Swofford."

She nodded.

"And he's looking for Norton Platt because he disappeared."

"Yes. If you're satisfied that things are as they should be, I'd like you to go over all the contact you've had with Norton recently, and try not to leave anything out."

"I'll do anything I can to help," Jason said. "Hear that, Carl-my-boy? A little politeness and I wheel open the floodgates."

"Go fuck a pony."

Leslie Bookman looked back and forth between the two of them. "A little personality conflict here?" she said.

"Yes," Jason said. "I have one. Hence the conflict."

She glanced at each of them. "Maybe I should spend some time with Jason myself."

"Welcome to him," Swofford said, pushing out of the booth. "I'll go check in with John."

Jason said, "Carl, you want your gun back, maybe?"

"In a public coffee shop? What kind of stupid is that?"

"Daaaaaah," Jason said. "Run that by me again, George." He presented his bundled jacket to Swofford. "It's in there," he said. "You're welcome. I want the jacket back. It won't fit you anyway."

Swofford seemed about to say something uncivil, but instead he turned and walked out of the coffee shop. Jason put the bundled jacket on the booth seat. Leslie Bookman said, "You two don't seem to like each other very much."

"I hurt his arm."

Her look was assessing. "You might think about laying off a little."

"Okay."

"At any rate, it's nice to see you again."

Jason smiled. "Same here." He liked Leslie Bookman. "I assume you two have been in Platt's house?"

"Yes, we have."

"How about his minivan?"

She looked at him for a full ten seconds. "Carl didn't tell you anything, I take it."

"We were pretty busy disliking each other."

"Norton's minivan was bombed to slag in a Denny's parking lot in Glendale."

He remembered the flare he'd seen in his rearview mirror. He said, "Oh." She watched him. "Um," he said, "that's where I last met him."

She nodded.

"Was he in it?"

"We don't think so. Carl and I want to know everything you know."

Something chirped. She unhooked a cell phone from her hip and said, "Yes," listened for a few seconds, and said, "Okay, hold on."

She looked at Jason. "We're moving. I'd like you to stick close with us for a while."

"I need to get my music stuff and my car from Amargosa."

She looked doubtful. "You're driving that same car, aren't you?"

"Yes."

"I suppose the music equipment shouldn't be left sitting out there unsecured." Into the phone, she said, "What? No, he needs to . . . look, hold on."

She held up one forefinger to Jason and went over near the rest-room entrances to continue her conversation. Jason watched the other diners. They all seemed very happy to be sitting in Las Vegas. When Jason was seven, he'd had a hamster name Buster that had seemed ecstatically happy to sit in its little covered food trough until moisture condensed on the inside of the cover and Buster conked out from oxygen depletion. Jason's mother had eventually removed the cover so Buster wouldn't smother himself to death.

He looked up and verified that no one's mother was removing the casino roof.

Leslie Bookman came back and said, "We're moving out and heading back to L.A., with a stop in Amargosa to get your things. You can use the driving time to get your thoughts in order, and then when we get there, you can tell me everything. Let's go."

The Plymouth was where he'd left it, parked snug against the colonnade, impotent with its missing distributor rotor. Leslie Bookman waited in the burgundy minivan. Jason unlocked his room door and went in as Swofford raised the Plymouth's hood and began to reinstall the rotor.

Everything was where he'd left it. When he had packed all the music equipment into the Plymouth, he picked his laptop computer up off the bed and went into the hotel corridor through the room's interior door.

The bored desk clerk in khakis wasn't on duty. A nice woman in a salt-and-pepper ponytail checked him out of his room.

When she was done, Jason said, "Would you mind if I used your phone? I have a very important private call to make. It's not local, but I'll only take a few minutes, and I'll be happy to leave a couple of twenties to cover it."

Jason pulled three twenties from his pocket and put them on the counter. "It'll take me about five minutes."

"Is it local?"

"No. I just need to check my e-mail."

"I suppose that would be all right," she said. She drew a desk phone up from under the counter and turned it so it faced him.

She looked at the twenties. "You won't be too long?"

"Five minutes."

She took only one of the bills. "We have your address. I'll send you the change when we get the bill."

When she left him alone, he plugged the phone cable into the back of his laptop and hit the keys that were supposed to connect the computer to the phone line. Nothing happened.

He double-clicked to reveal the contents of his hard drive.

His chest clutched as an empty window appeared on-screen. There weren't any contents. The drive was completely empty.

His communication programs, his word processing program, all his e-mail, everything gone. Also gone, he realized with a second clutch of the chest, was his new music, all of it. He hadn't backed it up during his stay.

Someone had wiped his disk while he'd been away with—distracted by?—Swofford and Bookman. The vague feeling of paranoia he'd left in Glendale came back, less vague.

SWOFFORD WAS BACK in the burgundy minivan, and the Plymouth was running.

Jason followed the minivan west for a few hours on the 15 and 10 freeways, worrying. In early evening, as the minivan passed the interchange to the 210, he braked and cut across three lanes, almost hit the crash barrier at the very fork of the interchange and then the guardrail on the far side of his new lane, straightened out, and accelerated onto the 210 freeway transition. Leslie Bookman's puzzled face in the passenger window of the minivan receded on its westward journey from him on the 10. Fear and paranoia tailgated him along the transition road as below and away, on surface streets, the streetlamps switched on.

22

Swofford had said he'd tapped the Manor phone. For all Jason knew, there was a radio link or something from the phone tap to the minivan's cell phone, but he called the Manor anyway from a gas station pay phone, hoping Paul wouldn't answer.

Robert's voice growled, "Ahoy, matey!"

"Robert—"

"Ahaaaaargh!"

"Don't let on that it's me. Is Paul nearby?"

"Avast, yon scurrrrrrvy pus-baaaag!"

"Has he been asking about where I am?"

"Arrrrrrrh!"

"Has anyone told him?"

"Bloof!"

"Does 'bloof!' mean 'no'?"

"Heh heh heh heh!"

"Good. Don't tell him. Is Martin around?"

"Bleef!"

"Does 'bleef!' also mean 'no'?"

"Aharrrr!"

"Get out of the Manor *now* and don't return today. You know your clock?"

"Um . . . Ahaaaarrgggh!"

"The other way around."

"Arrrrr!"

"Bleeps and bloops."

"Aye, matey!"

"Knife boy at the tree. Your clock?"

"Ahaaarrrrarrrghaarrarrgghaharrrrrrrr!"

"Not the other way around."

Robert's only clock was on his VCR, and it always showed 12:00 noon. If he and Robert were on the same wavelength, "the other way around" meant midnight, and "not the other way around" meant noon. Jason hung up, hoping he'd been cryptic enough to have baffled eavesdroppers but not so cryptic that he'd baffled Robert.

A FEW MINUTES before midnight, he was sitting in the Plymouth behind a nightclub in Bay City, a few buildings down from the 10 freeway. The driver's side door was open, and his left leg was stretched out onto the pavement, but the engine was running in case something made him want to leave fast. *Bleeps and Bloops* was Jason's nickname for a weekly "new music" event he attended at the nightclub maybe three times a year. Every so often, there were performances of astonishing creativity and incandescence, but they were intermixed with a lot of random noise and artsy posturing. The ratio was approximately the same as pork to beans.

Robert had gone with him once. On their drive back to the Manor afterward, he stated to Jason that he was now going to try to "get behind" what the last act had been attempting when they slowly poured a paper bag of ball bearings onto the strings of a prostrate electric bass from an altitude of five and a half feet. Jason posited that the artist's intention was not worth getting behind. Robert countered that Jason was sadly tethered by the bonds of conformity, a slave to convention, and a cheesehead, and he passionately defended the pouring of the ball bearings. Jason thought it telling, however, that Robert had not been available for subsequent concerts.

It was dark behind the nightclub.

The carcass of a huge mid-1970s Pontiac with a lot of rust and a $39.95 paint job the color of pistachio sherbet but lumpier labored up the driveway on soft, balding blackwall tires and exerted itself toward the Plymouth. One dim headlight feebly illuminated the parking lot. The beast halted, hunkering and shuddering like an aircraft carrier with a bad hairball, and the engine dieseled and ratcheted after it had been shut off. Robert got out and ambled toward Jason. The hulking metal corpse behind him continued to shake violently, as though so intent on suppressing the disintegration of its overall structure that it was incapable of letting the engine die.

"Hey," Robert said in greeting.

"Whose car?"

"Mine."

"Really? When did you buy it?"

"About three hours ago, right after you called. I thought we might need it."

Robert grinned in pleasure at Jason's surprise and held his hands out toward the piles of stuff in Jason's back seat.

"Thanks," Jason said. It hadn't occurred to him that a change of cars would be a good idea.

"You're welcome."

The Pontiac issued a stupendous, stinking rattle and relaxed into temporary death.

They transferred everything from the Plymouth into the cavernous interior of the Pontiac. Jason parked the Plymouth on a residential street a block away while Robert got the Pontiac engine going again.

"Where to," Robert asked when they were headed for the driveway, seated in the twin depressions of the Pontiac's once-white front seats. When he braked before entering traffic, a horrendous squeal issued from the front wheels.

"It only does that always," Robert said.

Jason slid the Plymouth's iron jack-handle down between the passenger seat and the door. "There's people after me and I don't know why. Drive around aimlessly and we'll talk."

"Driving around aimlessly is itself an aim," Robert pointed out. "As is wanting to talk." He'd been signaling a left turn out of the driveway, but that apparently didn't strike him as aimless enough, so he flicked the turn signal switch and made a right. Nearing the next intersection, he looked uncertain.

"Try going north," Jason suggested.

"Okay," Robert agreed. He turned east. "I think this is north."

"What?" he asked when Jason was looking at him.

"I now understand why your ancestors wandered for forty years in the wilderness."

"Map, schmap," Robert said, holding up a hand. "Trust me."

23

"Have you ever been to Yosemite?"

Robert was lying on his back on the floor of an ugly motel room with two stunted double beds in it, his magnetic chess set in mid-game next to him, his forearms folded behind his head, staring at the ceiling. Jason had told Robert what there was to tell: Platt, Swofford, Bookman, wiped hard drive.

The laptop computer was open on the nightstand, and Jason was running a utility program from floppy disks, trying to recover his lost data.

"—what?" he said distractedly.

"Have you ever been to Yosemite?"

"—um."

A window came up that said the data recovery had not worked, and prompted him to try a different method.

"Grr," he said, and hit Enter. The utility program started its new attempt.

"Did you see *Sex, Lies, and Videotape*?" Robert asked.

"Hmm?"

"Did you see *Sex, Lies and Videotape*?"

Jason watched the disk scan.

"Uh . . ." he said, and forgot that Robert had asked him anything.

"Why would wolves have pointy ears?"

"What?"

"Why wouldn't they just have round ears?"

Jason glanced up momentarily. "Why wouldn't who just have round ears?"

"Wolves."

Jason didn't know why they were talking about wolves, but a good number of his conversations with Robert went like this.

"I don't know," he said.

"Me neither," Robert conceded.

Jason went back to watching the scan of his hard disk. It was halfway done and had not yet found anything.

Robert said, "Did you read 'Hills Like White Elephants'?"

"I know what mental jump you made to get to that," Jason said. "You went from wolves to elephants."

"Ah," Robert began meaningfully. "No." He rolled over to face Jason. "I was thinking about wolf ears being pointy. Then I thought that they'd be especially good at hearing pointy things. I tried to think of the pointy things they'd hear well: I thought of pencils, pine trees, pins, and plectrums, and then I realized that wolves aren't good at hearing pointy things; they're good at hearing things that start with *P*. So then I tried to think of what they wouldn't be good at hearing. *P* is the sixteenth of twenty-six letters in the alphabet. If you add thirteen to get the reciprocal letter, wrapping around to *A* when you reach *Z*, you end up with the letter *C*. Therefore, wolves are not good at hearing celery, calabashes, concubines, capybaras, concrete, civilians, cummerbunds, or citadels. Citadels are white and are located in the hills, and elephants"—he paused dramatically and flourished one forefinger—"wear cummerbunds."

"Ah," Jason acknowledged. "Cogently reasoned. But you forget: Do not rhinoceroses also wear cummerbunds?"

"Ah," Robert countered, "but *you* forget: Hills are not even the slightest bit like white rhinoceroses."

The utility program beeped.

"Hey, it found something!" To rejoice, Jason stood up and did The Wave, but since there was only one person doing it, it was more like The Guy Standing Up. He sat down and watched the scan continue.

"I think my favorite Muppet was Zoot," Robert reflected.

The utility program displayed a screen that said that the few files it had found were damaged beyond recoverability. It suggested that Jason purchase a more powerful utility program manufactured by the same company.

". . . um," Jason said, ". . . what did you say?"

"I think my favorite Muppet was Rolf."

Jason shut down the computer and closed its screen.

Robert said, "Without Platt, you have no useful allies."

"I've got you."

"As I said, no useful allies."

"And Martin."

"As I said."

Jason took off his shoes and lay on the thin bedspread of one of the double beds the wrong way around, with his head at the foot. As headlights passed outside, diffuse slivers of light swept like clock hands across the ceiling.

"This pisses me off," Jason said. "I do not like being nervous and at a loss."

"Okay," Robert said. "So let's think of something."

"What do you have in mind?"

"I don't know."

"It's a conundrum."

"From the Latin *con-*, against," Robert orated, "and the nonsense *-undrum*, nonpercussive musical instrument."

After ten minutes of silence, Robert snapped his fingers and said, "Hey! I don't have an idea!"

"I don't. Not. Do. I don't not," Jason said. He turned the right way around and untucked all the bedclothes with his feet so there'd be room in the bed. "Here is my plan. I'm going to go to sleep. If that doesn't work, maybe Martin will think of something tomorrow."

In a sudden attack of panic, he sat up and twisted around to look down at Robert. Robert's thumbs were up under his nostrils, and his forefingers were pulling the skin under his eyes down to make a pig face.

"Oink," Robert offered.

"You did reach him, didn't you?"

"The tree at noon."

Jason lay back down and started to doze, but another panic attack hit him and he sat up and looked down again. Robert the Pig gazed benignly up at him.

"Did you call him from the Manor, or from a pay phone?"

"Oink," Robert confirmed vigorously.

"Okay," Jason said. "Sorry. I'm going to get some sleep."

"I'll wake you if anyone breaks in and kills us."

"Just put the No Killing tag on the doorknob so the maid knows." Jason lay down and turned onto his stomach. The pretty rock in his shirt pocket jabbed his chest. If he took it out and put it on the side table, he might have to explain it to Robert. He turned onto his side and pulled the covers around him. "Good night."

"*Oink*-oink."

He faded out to the click of plastic chess pieces.

24

As it turned out, Martin did indeed have an idea. He explained it to Jason. The primary thesis of Martin's idea was that Jason was insane. A corollary to this thesis was that Robert was insane too. Martin explained this as they stood under a tree in a park where he and Jason had hung out when they were in high school. The park was pretty much the same, except that now the high school kids had ugly tattoos, pierced each other's eyebrows, and thought Alanis Morrisette was hot.

"What do you think of Alanis Morrisette?" Jason asked Martin.

Martin stopped in mid-rant and said, "What?"

"I didn't like how the conversation was going, so I redirected it."

Robert edged by in the Pontiac and turned the corner, brakes squealing hideously.

Martin said, "To get back to what I was saying—"

"Martin."

"—you're not listening—"

"Martin."

"—I don't want to hear what you have to say—"

"Martín."

"Damn! What!"

"This situation is not something I jumped into. As a matter of fact, it's something I jumped out of, but I don't seem to be able to get clear of it."

"Man—" Martin said. He shook his head as though discovering himself incapable of summoning appropriately colorful invective.

"I got people after me, Martin, and they're just going to keep coming. What do you want me to do, go home and wait for them?"

When Martin was done shaking his head, he shook it again with greater feeling.

"Man—" he repeated.

"I need your help," Jason said before Martin's anger and concern could congeal into irreversible obstinance. "Not like last time; not just because I'm depressed and guilty and galloping off on some stupid mission and I need to be baby-sat so I don't hurt myself. This is different."

"Read my lips: Let Someone Else Deal With It."

"Who?"

"I don't know who! Someone who does this kind of stuff and knows what the heck he's doing!"

"Who, Martin? Who?"

"Okay, fine, how about cops?"

"And tell them what? That I was hired by a freelance G-man to spy on my ex-friend who hid a 35-millimeter film container in my car and then tried to take it back after it melted, but I was too clever for them and gave it to the freelance G-man instead, but his minivan blew up and now other mysterious spook types are after me? Oh yeah, cops'll galvanize right into action over that. 'Yessir, Mr. Keltner, sir, we'll get L.A.'s finest right on this very serious dongle problem, sir.' "

Martin wasn't budging. "I still think you ought to let someone else handle it."

"*Who,* Martin? You tell me who, and I will go dump this on them. I do not want to be thinking about where Platt is, nor what the damn gadget is, nor whether people are good guys or bad guys, nor who those people were in the Taurus, nor how deeply into this Paul must be. I want to be off someplace writing music, not watching over my shoulder for people who *I don't even know why they're after me.*"

Robert rattled past again in the Pontiac.

Martin looked straight at him, stonefaced, for half a minute. Jason felt like saying more, but there was nothing more to say, so he stood and watched Martin's tension increase.

Martin pulled a cigarette pack out of his shirt pocket, tapped one out, lit it, and took a couple of nicotine hits, drawing out the process and looking at Jason. Jason just looked back at him.

Presently, Martin's tension seemed to reach a corner and disappear around it. He sighed. Reluctantly, he clapped Jason's shoulder.

"I got your back, bro."

Jason said, "Thanks."

Martin pointed at him warningly. "But don't you even start to think that you convinced me of anything. I got your back because I got your back, not because you made any sort of good sense."

"I'll take it."

Martin acknowledged this with a little dip of the head.

They turned and strolled slowly on the grass toward the sidewalk.

"If we don't figure out what is going on, it's going to figure us out first and come get us. Stupid Jeffrey with the monster gun won't be easy twice. You know?"

"Yeah."

"And then there's Platt. I want to know if he's alive."

"Jason—whatever. You sold me. I'm there."

"Thanks."

At the sidewalk, Martin said, "Just one thing. Don't get me killed. I'm really liking this life thing."

"Deal. How'd you get here?"

"I took the bus. Robert told me not to drive my car 'cause it was recognizable and he was going to buy a new one, so I left it at Direct Mailbox Systems."

The Pontiac pulled to an ugly green stop at the curb in front of them.

Martin said, "And look, here's the new car now. Isn't it just lovely."

Robert looked around furtively and waved them in.

Martin said, "Robert's about as inconspicuous as a really big actor in a butt-ugly green Pontiac. Can we get something to eat before we go talk to Paul? I'm starving."

"Before we go talk to Paul?"

Martin dropped his cigarette and crushed it with his shoe. "We were going to talk to him, right? It's not like we have anywhere else to start."

"Oh. Right. True."

Jason got into the Pontiac's back seat with all his music stuff, and Martin sat shotgun. Robert steered carefully away from the curb.

"I was right," Jason said. "Martin thought of something."

25

They were sitting in the Pontiac in the parking structure of the Glendale Galleria, eating corn dogs on sticks and drinking lemonade with the windows open. A disinterested breeze stumbled through occasionally. Me'Shell Ndegéocello was singing on the radio, with crackly interference from the metal parking structure. Robert and Jason were in front with the chess set on the seat between them.

"These corn dogs suck," Martin said in the back seat, looking for someplace to put his. "We should have gone to Roscoe's for chicken and waffles."

"You ever notice," Jason said, "how even flawlessly produced funky soul music sounds best in some crappy twenty-year-old car with only one speaker working?"

Robert moved a white pawn. Without looking up, he said, "You ever notice how my crappy twenty-year-old car with a radio is a crappy twenty-year-old car, whereas your crappy twenty-year-old car without a radio is a classic?"

"It is sad," Jason said. Robert moved a black rook and captured his pawn.

Still looking for a way to dispose of his sucky corn dog, Martin said, "How we going to find Paul?"

Robert looked up and said, "Oh! I probably know how to find Paul."

Martin said, "And?"

"I took a liberty. I thought maybe we'd want to pick up Paul's track again."

Jason said, "What did you do?"

"Well, I figured he was weasel enough to go through our rooms after I was gone, so I kind of left him a clue."

Jason said, "What, uh, what kind of clue?"

"A blank notepad."

Robert glanced uncomfortably at both of them as though waiting to be chastised. Jason looked at Martin to see if he thought a blank notepad was a non-clue too. Martin looked equally perplexed.

"Okay," Jason said. "It was blank, you say."

"Yes."

"To me, blank means nothing written on it."

"Right."

"Okay."

"Well," Robert amended, "I mean, no, not when I left it. But before that, I pressed hard with a sharp pencil, and then I tore the top sheet off."

Martin pointed at Robert with his corn dog. "Paul rubs it with the side of a pencil to bring the imprint out—"

"—and believes himself extraordinarily clever," Jason finished. "What did it say?"

Robert pulled a flattened squish of paper from his back pocket, unrumpled it, and gave it to Jason. It said:

4:00 P.M.•SUICIDE BRIDGE•PARK ON PAS SIDE.

Under that was a doodle of a house and a stick person, and the words

PAUL = MAJOR WEENIE.

"The little house drawing lends it a nice touch of phone-message verisimilitude," Jason said, handing it back to Robert.

"Lemme see," Martin said. "Here, take this." He took the paper and gave Robert the corn dog. "Nice stick house, there, Robert. Paul equals major weenie, huh?"

"Or major weenie equals Paul," Robert said. "Equations are symmetrical."

"The Suicide Bridge is a lousy place to meet him," Jason said.

"Uh huh," Robert agreed distractedly, his attention on his chessboard, "but it's a good place to watch him."

"He probably thinks the same thing about us," Jason said. "I wouldn't be surprised if we bump into him looking for us at some choice vantage spot."

Martin said, "So we find a choice vantage spot for watching the choice vantage spots."

"Okay, maybe," Jason said. "But I want to reiterate that the bearded guy with the Corvair, whoever he is, seems like someone totally out of Paul's league, and therefore also totally out of ours. He might be in on whatever Paul's doing. In fact, he might likely even be in charge. How are we going to deal with him?"

Robert moved a white bishop but kept his finger on it.

"Robert, you here with us?"

Robert returned the bishop to its square of origin and

said, "What if we don't? What if we separate Paul from him?"

"How?"

Silence in the Pontiac.

"Threaten him," Martin said.

"With what?"

Silence.

"Bribe him," Robert said, and appended, "With what?" before someone else could.

Silence.

Intent on the chess set, Robert took a large bite of Martin's half a corn dog.

After a few moments, Robert said, "Let's think from Paul's point of view. You've been tricked by your old friend, and you've ended up with a cigarette lighter when you wanted a dongle. What do you want next?"

"The dongle," Jason said.

"To kick the shit out of the old friend," Martin added.

Robert said, "Well, we obviously can't give him the dongle . . ."

"I think," Jason said, "that we should be very worried about the bearded guy."

"There are two obvious advantages to knowing where Paul's probably going to be at four o'clock," Robert said. "One is that we can be there. The other is that we can *not* be there."

"Not being there sounds good," Martin said. "I like that. Not being there. Good plan."

Robert tossed the bare corn dog stick behind his seat. "Does Paul's car have a cassette player? I always wanted to do this . . ."

26

Paul Reno brooded.

He was a man of action, but he never moved until it was time. Most people let their emotions cloud their judgment, but Paul was a different breed. People thought he was cold. They were right. He was. He was cold like a shark, he thought, gliding voracious and logical and emotionless through the crystal black sea. The image had recently become his favorite. Other people let the current push them, or flicked thoughtlessly in schools, but Paul was precise and deadly. People never knew until he really let them see. And then it was too late.

It was already too late. He was a shark, like it or not. No way to deny it anymore.

The dead weeds under the Colorado Boulevard Bridge were uncomfortable, and the stickers got through his socks. And it was hot. Jason wasn't due for another fifteen

..nutes, yet Paul had already been waiting, stalking, still-hunting for hours. Paul was a predator. That's why he'd thought of showing up early.

He could see the grassy little park-like area slightly above his position behind a concrete support pillar. Dirt and weeds sloped off below him. A few thousand feet down was a parking lot for some sort of large installation, behind a chain-link fence.

Jason was troubling. Friendship wasn't an issue; Paul had realized long ago that it would be necessary to sacrifice that particular friendship. A shark didn't allow the razor edge of its fine killer instinct to be dulled by loyalties.

Jason still trusted him, though, and that might prove useful, so he bided his time, gliding through the inky depths, conversing, moving naturally, waiting for the time to spin and attack. Why not, when he'd already crossed the line?

But there was still irritation. Jason had tricked him. It was an adolescent piece of trickery and Paul's own fault for allowing it, and it had been a fluke, but he would be more careful now.

For instance, he'd arrived hours early to watch.

Although he still had it in his pocket, he hadn't glanced at the white notepaper since his first reading of it. He didn't like the note at the bottom. PAUL = MAJOR WEENIE was not true, and he resented it. Robert was another irritation; the big guy just didn't grow up, and he wasn't as smart as he thought he was. Not smart enough for Paul.

Paul allowed the corner of his mouth to curve into predatory amusement. Robert wasn't even smart enough to hide his notepad messages.

Don't fuck with the shark.

John Tennant, now that was another story. The man was smooth. He knew what he was doing, and Paul approved of him. The older predator, battle-scarred and deadly dangerous. And he'd chosen Paul as his protégé. Not in so many words, but he'd heard of Paul, sought him out, and dealt with him in a way Paul understood, as two members of the same species. They were working together now, he and Tennant, to retrieve the little computer gizmo from Jason. If Jason got hurt, it was clearly his own fault. Shouldn't swim in shark-infested waters if you weren't ready for it. No one but yourself to blame if you got yanked under and mauled. Paul couldn't do anything about that. And there was no going back now. This shark was a great white, a man-killer.

Tennant had been cool about the cigarette lighter mix-up. He'd said that Paul had better get the real item back, and left it at that. Paul respected that. It showed class. And so he'd set out to do what he'd been asked. It didn't occur to him to wonder what might happen if he failed.

He shifted in the dead weeds and looked at his watch. It was 4:00.

At 4:10, he pulled the piece of paper from his pocket and looked at it again to verify the time.

At 4:20, he started thinking about leaving.

At 4:30, he looked around carefully one last time and gave up. Maybe they'd seen him when he'd found the notepad at the Manor. But no—he'd been careful. There hadn't been anyone home.

It was puzzling.

He hiked back up to the grass area and then walked a couple of blocks to where he'd parked his beige hatchback. He got in and started it up. Someone behind him boomed:

"Good afternoon, Mr. Phelps."

He jumped in his seat and swung around, but he'd

already recognized it as a recording. He punched savagely at the eject button on the tape player and yanked out the cassette. The hand-lettered label said "Cryptic Message of Mysterious Origin for Paul." The word *Mysterious* was written bigger than the rest, in wavery Halloween letters. He shoved the cassette back into the player.

It was Robert's voice.

"Your mission, should you choose to accept it, is to discuss a deal. Get out of your car and keep your eyes down. As usual, the secretary will disavow any knowledge of your actions. Good luck."

Then there was only tape hiss. Paul fast-forwarded it to the end, listening for the squeal that would indicate that there was something additional recorded. There wasn't. He turned it over and repeated the process. A long way into side two, there was a short *squibblip!* of noise. He re-wound briefly and let the tape play.

"There's nothing on this side!" Robert's voice yelled, and then the tape ended.

Paul's eyes narrowed. Okay. They wanted cute. Cute was fine. He'd play along for a while. Then, when the time was right . . .

Do not, Paul thought icily, *fuck with the shark.*

He got out. *Keep your eyes down. What the fuck does that mean?*

He kept his eyes down. That's why he didn't miss the purple arrow spray-painted on the sidewalk, pointing east.

ACROSS THE STREET from the grassy area, in the parking lot of the Benevolent and Protective Order of Elks, John Tennant watched Paul walking. He picked a cell phone up off the car seat and dialed it.

"I'm moving," he said.

"Keep us informed," said Leslie Bookman's voice.

He put the Corvair in gear. Just before Paul reached the bridge entrance, an old red Ford van roared through the intersection and accelerated toward Paul, who was approaching a second purple spray-painted arrow. At a bus bench fifty yards away and out of Tennant's line of sight, Robert, unshaven, unaware of Tennant, and dismissably homeless in an orange curly wig, cowboy hat, and western fringed skirt, stopped rooting through a wire trash can and got concerned.

27

At four-thirty, Jason and Martin were going through Paul's things. It was impolite to go through other people's things, and Jason was uncomfortable doing it.

"Wow," Martin said. He was standing over a stack of boxes, the topmost one open.

Jason turned to see what he was holding. Martin showed him a thick comic book in a tightly fitted plasticine bag.

Martin's tone was impressed. "Paul has a first-edition *Watchmen*."

"Yeah, he collects comic books."

"This is a graphic novel."

"You've never quite been able to explain to me the difference so that I understood it."

"Comic books are more . . . you know . . . comic booky."

"So . . . graphic novels are more graphic novely."

"Exactly."

"And in that moment," Jason said, "he was enlightened."

Paul's mattress was on the floor, with no bedframe. Jason tipped it up and looked under it. Bare floor. He opened a closed cardboard box. Unfolded clothing.

Martin said, "Hey, is this something?" He handed a white slip of paper to Jason. It said "L.A. Arts" and bore the date and time of the party.

"That's the party we went to, where Benton keeled over and died." He thought about whether the paper was a clue. "I don't see why he wouldn't have written it down."

Martin set it back on the table. "I wish I knew what we were looking for."

"If you find a bloodstained map pinned to an ammunition crate with an antique dagger, that would be a good thing to point out."

Martin opened another box. "Nope. Porno magazines." He leafed through one.

Jason said, "That slip of paper with the party info bugs me."

His phone rang downstairs.

"Uh oh," Martin said. They closed Paul's door behind them and ran down the stairs.

On the phone, Robert spoke eleven numbers and then hung up. To confuse eavesdroppers, the first two and last two numbers were nonsense. The remaining seven were the number of the pay phone Robert was at, with 1 added to each digit.

They left the Manor to go to a pay phone to call Robert back. Northbound on Marengo in the Pontiac, with Jason driving, Martin said, "How come the party info bugs you?"

"I don't know. There's no reason he shouldn't have written it down. I do that all the time, write things on little pieces of paper so I don't forget."

"Even if they're the same day?"

"Sure, so I don't forget the address or whatever."

"Ask Robert."

"Good idea."

They pulled into a gas station with a pay phone. Robert answered on the first ring. "I put the tape in Paul's car," he said. "He was walking the way he was supposed to go. An old red Ford van pulled up, and he got in. I don't think he wanted to get in."

"You got the license number?"

"It didn't have license plates."

"Who was in the van?"

"I couldn't tell. I think two people in the front, and I couldn't see into the back."

"Okay. . . . Hey, what's wrong with this picture: Paul had a slip of paper in his room with the date and time of the L.A. Arts party on it."

"Didn't you invite him to that?"

"Yeah."

"When?"

"That afternoon."

"Why would he write the date down for a same-day event?"

"That's it. That's what been bugging me. Is it safe to pick you up?"

"As far as I can tell."

"We'll be there in a few minutes."

Back at the Pontiac, Martin said, "I got it. The date. That's what's wrong with Paul's note."

"Yeah, Robert said the same thing. Paul got into an old red Ford van while he was following our wild-goose arrows. Robert didn't think he wanted to get in."

"Uh oh. What do we do now?"

"Pick up Robert and regroup. Let's talk about Paul's note on the way there. Apparently, he must have written it before the day of the party."

"Okay, so I guess that means he wanted to go to the party before you asked him. I wonder why. You think it was coincidental?"

"Could be, but I think it's probably most useful to assume that nothing is coincidental. Let's say he intended to do exactly what he did: meet Huey Benton and get the dongle from him."

"Okay."

"When I invited him, he was forced to accept. He was already going. He knew if he said no, I'd see him there and wonder what was up."

"You think he poisoned Benton or something?"

"No."

"Why not?"

"I don't know."

"Uh huh."

"All right," Jason said. "Point taken."

Robert was waiting for them in front of a Hughes market. They reshuffled so Martin was in the back, Jason in the front, and Robert driving.

"Where to?" Robert asked when they were on the road.

Jason said, "I wonder about Benton's computer stuff. Does anybody have a reason why we shouldn't enter L.A. Arts under false pretenses and try to get into his computer, assuming it's still there?"

Martin said, "Yes. The reason is what are you, fucking nuts?"

Robert said, "As long as our pretenses are going to be of the false variety, what's my character?"

Jason looked critically at Robert's six-five frame. "Someone who wouldn't be out of place in a computer research department, but who wouldn't need to know anything about computers."

Martin snickered. "Hey, how about a computer salesman?"

Jason and Robert both laughed. Then they looked at each other.

"No," Martin said, seeing the look.

Jason and Robert kept looking at each other.

Robert said, "Can I have a briefcase?"

"No," Martin said. "No. Time out. Stupid. Bad idea. Stupid idea. I'm a stupid, stupid person. I have stupid ideas and a great big stupid mouth that just flaps and flaps and flaps."

Jason said, "Let's go to the nearest computer store and then swing by that place we did the printing that other time."

28

At eleven the next morning, Ed Saunders the very tall computer sales guy and his unshaven, mustachioed, ponytailed assistant Joe marched into the L.A. Arts computer center towing a wheeled hand truck piled high with brand new computer boxes.

Saunders beamed myopically through his thick glasses at the student working the front desk, plopped his natty gray briefcase onto the pile of boxes, flipped open its latches, and said, "Good morning! Ed Saunders, Tiger Network Solutions." He held out a professional-looking two-color card from the briefcase. The card said

ED SAUNDERS • SENIOR ASSOCIATE
TIGER NETWORK SOLUTIONS
A SUBSIDIARY OF SPT INDUSTRIES

It had a phone number and e-mail address on it. The Tiger Network Solutions logo was a smug-looking cartoon tiger sitting at a computer.

The student smiled wanly at him without looking at the card. Saunders was keeping her from a pressing game of computer solitaire.

"I've got an eleven o'clock with Huey, Huey Benton," Saunders boomed cheerfully, continuing to hold out the card. "He'll be glad to know his eighty-four-fifty sixty-four/three gig with sixteen-x CD-ROM and V-net finally came in. Would you let him know I'm here, please?"

The student's wan look floundered. A salesman's appointment with a dead co-worker was out of her depth. She took the card and said, "Um, hold on, okay?"

"No rush," Saunders replied heartily. "We'll wait." He nodded happily at Joe, who looked bored. The student rose lissomely with Saunders' business card and floated out the door through which Saunders and Joe had entered.

"So far, so good," Jason whispered.

"Sure, easy for you," Robert said, *sotto voce,* "you've got no lines. I forgot my name and almost called myself Freg Saumblberd."

"Let's just hope no one recognizes me from the party."

"Don't worry. The fake mustache changes your whole face."

In a minute, the student wafted sylphishly back, trailing a man in his late forties in slacks and a pink shirt. As the man came forward, the student slipped lithely around and sat in her chair, watching.

"Mr. Saunders?"

"Call me Eg—Ed," Saunders beamed, offering his hand.

The man shook it. "I'm Corwin Lee. What can I do for you?"

"Did Huey forget our appointment? Today's the day we pick up his old computer and set up his new eighty-four-fifty sixty-four/three gig with sixteen-x CD-ROM."

"And V-Net," Saunders' assistant said.

"Well, yes of course V-Net," Saunders said impatiently. "You can't get them without V-Net anymore." To Lee, he said, "Did Huey forget? I sure hope so; that's one less client lunch on the old expense report this month, ha ha."

Lee gave him the obligatory smile and said, "Yes . . . I'm sorry, I . . . we've suffered something of a tragedy here recently. Huey Benton is no longer . . . he died only recently. I'm sure no one had any idea you had an appointment with him, or we would certainly have called and let you know not to come."

"He died?" Saunders said.

"I'm afraid so. It was very sudden."

Saunders was shocked. "How did he . . . do you mind my asking? How did he—?"

Lee nodded. "It was very sudden, as I said. He collapsed during a student/faculty event and hit his head."

Saunders was aghast. "That's horrible. God, that's awful. Did you know him well? Was he married?"

"No, we never spoke. I don't think he was married."

"That's horrible," Saunders said again, clearly overwhelmed.

He let the silence hang until Lee filled it:

"At any rate, what can I do for you now?"

"Oh, nothing complicated. I'm here to pick up his old computer and set up the new one."

"I see. Well. Let me see. Do you have some sort of paperwork I can look at? I'm just here from the performing arts department, filling in temporarily."

"I surely do," Saunders said. He put his briefcase up on

the pile of boxes again, opened it, and handed Lee some pink, white, and canary papers. His assistant rested his head on his arms next to the briefcase and looked unenthusiastic.

Lee riffled through the papers.

"So," he said. "You're just going to take the one and drop off the other?"

"That's the idea."

Lee studied the papers some more.

"Well," he said, handing them back. "I suppose this is probably all right. I just didn't have anything that said you were coming."

"That's all right," Saunders said. "I understand it's a difficult time. I wish I could just come back when everything's sorted out, but Huey put me off the last three times I called him, and the deal on this baby requires that I get the old computer back now."

"I see," Lee said uncertainly.

"If I don't bring it back today, we'll have to go through a whole new purchase requisition, and I won't be able to credit the core return. Because of the depreciation timetable. Now, that's not a problem on my side, but your purchasing department is . . . well . . ."

The mention of L.A. Arts' purchasing department seemed to cause sudden concern for Lee.

"No, no, let's not go through purchasing," he said. "They'll never get it done in time. This is time-sensitive, right?"

"That's absolutely right," Saunders assured him.

"That would help me justify bypassing purchasing. And there's no other way to get the credit?"

"Not until the next rebate offer."

"When will that be?"

"Your guess is as good as mine. Before this one that's

now ending, it was almost a year and a half. Oh, and it's only certain models. We don't know that Huey's will qualify again."

"I see. I see." Lee seemed torn. Saunders waited understandingly. Presently, Lee said, "I will get a copy of that paperwork?"

"Absolutely. That's standard. The canary copy is yours. And if you want, I'll get you a buff duplicate of the original pink signed PO referenced to the green blanket order."

"That would be great, " Lee said. "Thanks."

"Terrific," Saunders said. "Let me just get your signature here. We'll have your new computer set up and the old one out of your way in just a few minutes."

29

"This can't be," Jason said.

Benton's computer was set up on a table in their groundfloor motel room. Jason was in a chair near the computer, typing on the keyboard and trying to get used to the brick-sized trackball that Huey Benton used instead of a standard mouse. Martin was lying on one double bed, practicing with his butterfly knife. Robert sat on the other, near the door, watching the knife intently. His magnetic chess set was set up on the bed next to him, in mid-game.

"This can't be," Jason said again.

Martin said, "You've been saying that for the last ten minutes."

"And I've been meaning it for the last ten minutes."

Still intent on Martin's glittering knife, Robert said, "So?"

"This thing's got no hard drive. It shouldn't even be

starting up. There's no floppy it could be booting from, no CD-ROM, no nothing. But here it is, up and running. This cannot be."

Robert said to Martin, "Lemme try something."

Martin shrugged. "Okay." He closed the knife and offered it to Robert.

Robert refused. "No, put it on the bed, and then go for it as though you're going to attack me."

Martin sat up, facing Robert, and put the knife on the bed next to him.

"Okay?" he said.

Robert nodded seriously. Martin grabbed the knife. As he began, deftly, to swing the jointed, clicking knife into an offensive position, Robert reached across with one big hand and swatted it across the room. It shot bladefirst into the wall and stuck with its hinged parts dangling, three feet from Jason.

"Dang!" Martin got up to unstick the knife from the wall.

"That's what I thought," Robert said, nodding.

"You guys want to watch that?" Jason complained.

Robert said, "Sorry."

"Oh, by the way: Did I tell you that Paul said you two were a couple of stereotypes because Martin's always practicing with a knife and Robert reads a lot and carries a chess set around?"

Martin blew drywall dust off the knife blade and inspected it closely. "Did you tell him *why* Robert carries a chess set around?"

"Nope."

Robert squinted at Martin and said, "I will beat you next game."

"You just keep practicing there, chief." Martin's eyes

glinted, and in a few seconds, he broke down in a display of gleeful cackling.

"Have I told you 'shut up' today?" Robert inquired. "Jason, so, I take it you didn't tell him what got Martin interested in knife-fighting, either."

Jason glanced at Martin, who stopped cackling and began to study the ceiling.

"Not because he thought it would be useful on the mean streets of L.A.?"

Robert smiled indulgently. "No, because I got him with a leg sweep six times in a row. Now suddenly he's into weaponry."

"It's not fair," Martin said. "Your legs are like eight feet long."

"I am almost good enough now," Robert said. "I predict that next time we play, I will beat you in fewer than twenty moves."

"You just predict as much as you like, there, Bobby Fischer," Martin soothed. Then he busted up again. Robert attempted hauteur but did not achieve it.

"I hate trackballs," Jason said. "Trackballs. Hey. Hey, wait a minute here." He reached for the trackball.

A shuddering *thump*, and the door flew open, splintering the doorframe. Two male figures stood poised in the doorway.

Robert kicked the door closed.

Everyone looked at each other.

A very ridiculous moment passed.

"Shit!" Martin said.

As Robert lunged shoulderfirst toward the door, scrabbling for its security hasp, someone on the other side gave it a solid kick. Robert threw his weight against it, but it was already stopped by a boot toe. A hand got in around the door edge from outside.

Martin darted to the door and sliced his blade down over the knuckles of the invading fingers as Robert stomped on the boot toe. There was a cry from outside and the fingers and boot pulled back quickly. The door still wouldn't close; someone on the other side was braced against it.

Jason took a few running steps and launched himself at Robert, striking him shoulder-to-shoulder and slamming him against the door. The door crashed shut and Martin flicked the eye-level security hasp closed with the knife. Another kick bowed the bottom of the door and made the whole wall shudder, but the hasp held.

Jason grabbed the room phone and dialed zero.

A woman's voice said, "Front desk."

"We're in room twenty-six and someone's trying to break in."

"Again?" the woman said in a peeved tone, and hung up.

Jason looked at the telephone.

Martin looked at him questioningly. Jason indicated mystification and hung up.

"We called the cops!" he yelled at the door. "They'll be here any minute!"

The battering stopped and a brief, indistinct dialogue took place on the other side of the door. Then another kick landed, more an expression of anger than an attempt to get in. Footsteps moved away.

Robert shifted the corner of the curtain and peered out.

"They've got their backs to us."

Jason joined Robert and looked out. The Pontiac was parked head-in to the motel room door. The two men were past it, walking rapidly toward a white Taurus wagon with body damage to the rear right quarter panel.

"That looks like the car that was tailing Paul," Jason said. "It got away from me. I hit it with the Plymouth."

"Want to follow it?"

Martin said, "If they followed us here, they already know what the Pontiac looks like. If we follow them, they'll recognize us right off."

"It looks like they're going toward that white car," Robert said urgently. "If we're going to follow them, we have to go now."

Jason hesitated. "How much gas did you put in after we left L.A. Arts?"

"A full tank."

The men got into the Taurus.

Jason looked from Robert to Martin. "Are we really up for this?"

Martin said, "I already said I was."

When Jason turned a questioning glance at Robert, Robert looked startled. He said, "Yeah!" in a surprised tone.

"Okay," Jason said. "I guess that leaves me."

He didn't know what to do.

"You're the man," Martin reminded him.

He felt no click of resolve or moment of truth. Martin and Robert were both waiting expectantly. The bad guys were getting farther away. He waited for the click or moment. It didn't come.

This was exactly how he felt when he reached an impasse during composing. It was the point where he would abandon a piece because it just wasn't working.

Maybe things only worked when you did them even when they weren't working.

He said, "Urgh."

Then he said, "Robert."

Robert displayed attentiveness.

"Start up the Pontiac. Try not to let them see you. Martin, I need help getting the computer into the car."

Robert nodded once, pulled the security hasp open, and went out the door in a lumbering crouch. Jason disconnected the computer, handed the keyboard and cables to Martin, and carried the computer itself outside.

Robert had the Pontiac going, and the white Taurus was trying to get out of the driveway into dense traffic. The passenger turned to watch them as Martin dove into the back seat and yelled, "Ow!" The seats were only slightly less than blistering hot.

Jason handed the computer in and jumped into the front, trying to minimize his contact with the seat. "Follow that car."

Robert said, "Sure thing, boss," in a movie cabbie voice. The Pontiac lurched into reverse. When Robert braked, something clunked instead of squealing.

"Hey, mine does that same clunk." Jason reached for the seat belt and dropped it as it burned his fingertips. "How big is the gas tank on this thing?"

The Taurus headed out of the driveway ahead of them.

Robert said, "Vaster even than my ego. It took forty-five dollars."

Martin cranked the rear windows down in short, non-skin-scorching spurts as the Pontiac nosed into the right-hand lane. The Taurus was two cars ahead of them.

Martin leaned forward. "What are we going to do when we catch them?"

"We're not going to catch them. We're just going to follow them and see what happens when they run out of gas."

There was a long silence.

"That's your great plan?" Martin yelled. " 'See what happens when they run out of mother-lovin' *gas*'?"

"Hey, it was spur-of-the-moment," Jason protested. "I didn't have twenty minutes to plan something clever."

"Oh," Martin said reasonably. "You didn't have twenty minutes. Well, that's different. Didn't have twenty minutes. I can see that. Hey, I guess that would explain"—he leaned forward and yelled—"why this plan *sucks!*"

The Taurus swerved one lane to the left, and Robert swerved to follow. A battered little yellow pickup cut out around them without slowing and beeped at them.

"If you need to get over fast," Jason said, "remember the First Rule of Driving a Beater: Aim for the expensive cars."

The Taurus cut over another lane.

"Benz behind on your left," Martin reported.

Robert wrenched the wheel.

"Hey, that works," Martin said, peering back at the newly stopped Mercedes and its cursing driver.

"A joy of joys to drive is the car that looks like it's not going to stop," Robert said.

"And in fact doesn't" Jason said. "Second Rule of Driving a Beater: You always have right-of-way."

The Taurus hung a sharp left and entered a freeway on-ramp, onto the northbound 101. The Pontiac followed it up the ramp, relative wind gusting through the open windows as it reached freeway speed.

"Well," Robert said, "this car chase stuff must be old hat to you."

Jason said, "Except this time the good guys have a V-8 engine, so the bad guys can't outrun us. I hope."

Robert said, "They must have followed us from Benton's office."

"That's what I figure, too."

"Maybe we're not very good at this."

Martin said, "No, you think?"

The Taurus accelerated and ducked into the next left lane.

"Cadillac, behind on the left," Martin called.

Robert wrenched the wheel over.

30

They closed on the Taurus, Martin calling out expensive car positions, Robert concentrating and steering, and Jason looking out for the highway patrol. The driver of the Taurus tried everything. He sped up; he slowed down; he slowed down and then sped up. He went left; he went right; he feinted and deked and swerved and played little fakeout games on the transition roads. But at freeway speeds, the Pontiac had raw, immediate power, and Robert used it well. They stuck directly behind the Taurus.

The 101 veered from its collision course with the ocean and became the Pacific Coast Highway. Churning, white-foamed turquoise stretched past the horizon on the left and gray-brown rockslide cliffs loomed on the right. Tall stilt-houses perched half-over the cliffs like tense, expectant wooden spiders. The salty beach wind that blasted through the open windows was twenty degrees cooler than the air inland.

In Oxnard, the Taurus settled down in the leftmost lane, doing the speed limit.

"What's going on?" Jason pondered after it had been there for a while.

Robert shook his head and shrugged.

Martin said, "It's like they're trying to keep with us."

Jason frowned. "You're right."

The cliffs ended and they approached Santa Teresa. Greenery obscured the view of whatever was on both sides of the freeway. The Taurus was still solidly at the speed limit in the leftmost lane.

Jason stopped frowning. "Cell phone."

"Cell phone?" Robert asked, and then nodded. "Cell phone. You think they're calling for reinforcements."

"Yeah, or arranging a reception at the final destination. Either way, they're reeling us in."

"Are we going to let them keep reeling?"

Jason said, "Anybody got a better idea?"

"Yes," Martin declared from the back. "I think banging myself real hard in the head with a hammer would be a better idea. I think drinking sulfuric acid would be a better idea. I think applying a white-hot poker to my tongue would be a better idea. I got lots of better ideas. Thank you so much for this opportunity to share them."

"Those are very good better ideas, Martin," Jason said. "They will be considered with care and gravity."

Martin flopped onto the back seat. "Yeah, you say they're great ideas, but I don't see us getting off the freeway."

Robert said, "Where do you think we're being reeled to?"

"I dunno." Jason looked in the glove box. The only things in it were Robert's magnetic chess set and a hard, sugarless lemon-flavored candy in a twisted paper wrapper. "You got a California map?"

"Yes."

"Here?"

"No."

"What's up this way, up north here?"

"Um. Mexico?"

Martin said, "Santa Teresa, Santa Maria, San Luis Obispo, um, Paso Robles, King City, Salinas. And there's tons of other little towns called, like, San Blahblahblah or Santa Blahblah all in between, too."

"Then what?"

"Silicon Valley, San José, Bellamy Park, San Francisco, Oregon, Washington State, British Columbia, Yukon Territory. I can keep going. Alaska, the North Pole, the moon . . ."

Robert said, "This has all revolved around computer things. If I was a bettin' man, I'd bet that if we're still on the road in an hour, we're going to the Silicon Valley."

"Sounds as likely as anything," Jason said. "How far is the Silicon Valley from here?"

Martin looked up and his eyes moved as he figured. "Um . . . Maybe two hundred and fifty miles?"

"Okay. That means that if reinforcements are coming from there, we'll probably meet them halfway, which is about a hundred and twenty-five miles. Two hours from now, maybe less. How's the gas situation?"

Robert glanced down. "Three-quarters of a tank. I'm being very smooth with the thing, the what is it, the pedal thingy."

They went through San Luis Obispo, Paso Robles, and a string of smaller towns with Mexican names. Afternoon became evening. Nobody talked for a while.

After about an hour without conversation, the Pontiac decelerated abruptly and lurched toward the center divider. Martin said, "Watch it, watchitwatch*watchit!*" Jason lunged for the steering wheel and overcorrected the course into the next lane and Robert snapped awake and insisted, "Queen to—oh, no!" He stomped convulsively on the brake pedal and something metallic in the front part of the car immediately responded by making a horrific grinding noise and not slowing down much.

Jason and Robert did contradictory things to the steering wheel, but the car eventually came back into true behind the Taurus.

After a long stretch of scenery, Jason said, "When's the last time you slept?"

"Last night."

"How long?"

Robert looked sheepish. "About an hour."

"You were playing chess all night."

"Not all night. I slept for an hour."

"Great," Martin said. "The driver's falling asleep and we can't stop to switch."

"I'm fine," Robert said overly brightly.

"Okay, " Jason said, "how do we keep Robert awake?"

"I'm fine."

"You're not fine. You just fell asleep in the fast lane. What should we do to keep you awake?"

"Play chess?"

There was a long pause. Hopefulness radiated from the driver's seat.

Jason said, "Robert, is that one of your better ideas?"

Robert looked offended and said, "Sure it is. Chess exists in the mind, not on the board."

"Yeah, that's what we need, you drifting off in deep thought."

"I won't drift off."

"Ixnay," Martin said, terminating the debate, "on the goddamn esschay."

"All right," Robert said. "In that case, keep me talking."

Jason said, "Okay. Tell us a story."

"About what?"

"Um . . . Let's see. Since you'd drift off into deep thought if we asked you to make something up, let's go with true stories. How about . . . Someone you know who did something unusual."

Robert considered the topic. "I know this guy who caught the killer of a performance artist."

"Someone not in this car."

"Okay, let me think. I get to embellish . . ."

31

My great-grandfather Harry Goldstein came here in the late nineteenth century. Fourteen years old, and he'd already made enough money rolling cigars to have already sent his family ahead of him, one by one.

"My knowledge of my family history is kind of spotty, but I imagine that Harry probably does odd jobs when he gets here, shines shoes, or does whatever immigrant children of that period wind up doing. But that's before the beginning of the story I'm going to tell you. The back story is that Harry gets married, has kids, and owns a few businesses. The business that this story is about is a rug store."

Martin said, "Rugs like toupees, or rugs like rugs, like rug rugs?"

"Like rug rugs. Harry's got some savings or something—people from the Old Country were big on savings—so he puts it all into this rug store, every penny. It's in St. Paul, next door to the DeCri Coffee Shop. I know that because my grandfather always makes a point of it when he tells me this story.

"Harry's made some sort of import-export connection, and he's got Indian rugs in piles, and living room rugs stacked in rolls on shelves. Did they have bathroom rugs in those days? I keep having to unimagine them because they might be anachronistic, but I don't know for sure."

Martin and Jason both indicated ignorance of bathroom rug arcana.

"It doesn't matter. Anyway, there's a bell on the door and a lot of dust from how the rugs are shipped, so when a customer comes in, the bell rings and the sun glances off the door glass and brightens the dust motes. My whole image of it is, what do you call it, like an old picture, not black and white—"

Martin said, "Sepia."

"Right, right, sepia. Like an insurance commercial. Harry wears a white shirt and black vest and yarmulke with a fedora over it and I'm guessing a vest and pocket watch, although I don't know that for sure because I only knew him as an elderly man in baggy suits. Considering his experiences in pogrom-avoiding and cigar-rolling and old-country-fleeing and store-opening, I don't imagine indecision in his body language.

"Oh, I forgot: There had to be bars on the store windows and doors. My grandfather never mentions them when he tells me this story, but they had to be there, or the middle part of the story doesn't make sense.

"So Harry takes his wife out to celebrate their new life in the merchant caste and opens his store up for business.

"He sells some rugs or he doesn't the first day, I don't

know. It doesn't matter. But the next day, Harry's leaning against his counter next to his empty cash register when the bell on the door tinkles and a couple of guys in hats with wide bands walk in.

"One of the guys says, 'We want to talk to the owner.'

"Harry says, 'So talk.'

"The guy says, 'You the owner?'

"Harry says, 'I'm not Milton Berle.' "

Interrupting, Jason said, "Milton Berle was like fifty years later."

"It doesn't matter who he said he wasn't. Sid Caesar. Whoever. Ernie Kovacs. Harry says, 'I'm not Ernie Kovacs,' is that better?"

"No."

"Okay, George Burns. Harry says he's not George Burns. So the guy says, 'Hey, settle down, nobody accused you of being George Burns. We're here about your insurance.'

"Harry hasn't caught on yet. He says, 'What are you talking about?'

" 'Fifty dollars a month,' the guy says. 'Insurance.'

" 'Do I look like I have fifty dollars a month? If I had fifty dollars a month, what would I need with a rug store?'

"The guy shrugs and says, 'You're new here and nobody told you. We understand that. We're reasonable people. You take this week, on us, no charge. We'll come back next week. But don't make us wait too long. It would be a shame if anything happened to such a very nice place of business.'

" 'Insurance like this,' Harry says, 'I don't need.'

"Okay, I made up the stuff about the gangsters. But it could have been that way, because late one night my grandfather, who is six years old, sees his father shaving to go out.

" 'What's wrong, Papa?'

" 'They cleaned me out,' Harry tells him. 'Not a rug left in the store.'

" 'Where are you going, Papa?'

" 'To see the mayor.'

"Someone had broken into the DeCri Coffee Shop, come through the wall into Harry's place, and stolen every rug he owned. That's why there had to have been bars on Harry's windows, because why else would they have broken in that way?

"Now, Harry was some kind of big deal in Jewish small business. He knew the mayor well enough that the mayor had given him an honorary police badge, which my grandfather says could be used back then instead of bribe money if a cop pulled you over for speeding."

Martin said, "Okay, so this story takes place before Milton Berle, but after cars."

"I guess so," Robert said, "and also obviously after graft. Anyway, Harry goes to see the mayor. He tells him, 'I got cleaned out today, and I wasn't insured. It's ruined me. I want to know who's responsible.'

" 'Yes, we know who that was.' So the mayor tells Harry which gang it was that cleaned him out. It's a Chicago gang. Next thing you know, Harry's cleaned out his bank account and bought a train ticket to Chicago."

As Robert paused to launch into the next part of the story, the Taurus suddenly changed lanes to the right, near King City.

32

Robert changed lanes to follow the Taurus.

"I'm betting on a rendezvous," Jason said. "If they're changing lanes, they're either going to exit or they're preparing to receive incoming help. Or they're just screwing with us. We ought to keep an eye out for any cars that seem to be maneuvering for position or whatever."

Robert asked, "What do we do then?"

"Well . . ."

After a long silence, Martin's voice from the back seat said, "I just want to tell you what an awesomely splendiferous goddamn plan this is turning out to be."

"I'm doing my best, Martin."

Martin said, "White Tauruses behind us. Two on the right and one on the left."

Jason said, "You're kidding." He swiveled around and looked past the piles of gear out the back window. Three more new white Taurus station wagons hung back in the two adjacent lanes. "Not exactly hard to spot, are they? These guys are obviously unclear *viz* the object of your garden-variety 'being inconspicuous' notion. But to our delight, they are also obviously unclear *viz* the unorthodox methodology with which we choose between and subsequently adopt viable lane-change options."

The trailing Tauruses eased closer to the Pontiac. All three drivers had their left hands to their heads. They looked as though they were probably holding telephones.

"Might I suggest," Robert observed, "that this conclusion leads logically to certain actions which, if engaged without a certain subtlety of execution, might serve to, as the saying goes, tip the blackguards off?"

"Dash it, you're right. I throw myself unhesitatingly into your capable hands."

"Very good, sir." Robert wrenched the wheel left and hit the brakes.

The Pontiac shuddered and the Taurus to the left screeled and nose-dived into the emergency lane.

"The gentlemen in question," Robert explained as the Pontiac straightened out in its new lane in front of the car it had just cut off, "were in the process of acquiring what I have heard referred to as a 'pincer action' by the more sordid denizens of the underworld, wherein two or more of the enemy bracket the victim, thus allowing no avenue of escape."

"Brilliant!" Jason cried. "But however did you manage to outwit the scoundrels?"

"I ascertained that the left hand of the driver was occupied at a distance from its steering wheel. It was only a matter of selecting the ideal moment to apply the manoeuver." Robert bowed in his seat.

Martin said, "What the *hell* are you two talking about?"

"You really should read more," Robert said.

The rearmost of the three new Tauri accelerated past them and then cut quickly between the Pontiac and the car originally being pursued. That car peeled off all the way to the right, into the exit lane, while the Taurus that had been behind and to their right pulled up nearly even with them, hemming the Pontiac in and preventing it from following the original car, which was now exiting.

Martin said, "Well, you wanted to see what would happen when they ran out of gas."

"This isn't fair. They weren't supposed to have friends. Whatever happened to no line cuts and no keepies?"

All three new Tauri kept their positions, one behind, one to the right, and the original one ahead. The center divider was to their left. Jason was a little concerned about being caught in the formation, but not horribly so; in the eventuality of an intersection between old Pontiac and new Taurus, he was pretty certain of what outcome he'd bet on.

A few miles later, Martin said, "What does *viz* mean?"

It was nearly a hundred miles before anyone said anything, which was just before something else happened.

33

Evening gloom deepened into darkness. Robert switched the Pontiac's flickering headlight on. It turned the back of the leading white Taurus dim yellow. At the Santa Clara city limit, Robert said, "Although I am not completely certain in my statement that *viz* is like *e.g.*, I can state with an excess of cheerful confidence that we are about to run out of gas."

Jason leaned toward Robert so he could see the dimly lighted gas gauge. Its needle was at the orange line that marked the unhappier end of the Empty/Full continuum.

The Taurus to their right pulled suddenly alongside, and the gray-haired driver pointed off the freeway.

Jason said, "I think he wants us to get off at the next exit."

The driver pointed again.

Martin leaned up over the front seat. "You think we should?"

"I don't know," Jason said, "but isn't going with these people the whole reason we're here? I vote we exit."

"I vote we should do that, too," Robert said.

Martin said, "I vote we apologize for butting in and go have some steaks."

"Democracy is a beautiful thing," Jason said. He gave the gray-haired man a thumbs-up.

Martin plopped back onto the back seat. "Another miscarriage of justice for the African-American," he said.

"Hey," Jason said, "at least we let you eat with us."

"Who lets who, now?"

The Pontiac shuddered and its engine cut out briefly.

"What was that," Martin demanded.

The engine cut out again, more joltingly.

Martin said, "I asked you what that was."

"I hate to be the Bear of Bad News," Robert said, "but . . ." He pointed at the gas gauge and roared like a bear.

"Out of gas," Jason translated for Martin.

The Pontiac shuddered, belched, died, and began to decelerate. The Tauri kept pace.

Robert wrestled the powerless Pontiac into the emergency lane, bumping over a rusted muffler, a woman's tennis shoe, and some empty plastic transmission fluid bottles. The brakes scraped noisily. The Tauri pulled over with them, one ahead and two behind.

"What's our plan?" Robert asked.

"It depends on theirs."

Martin smacked the back of Jason's head.

"Ow!" Jason turned around in surprise. "What was that for?"

"I *hate* it when you sound smart like that but you're really only just treading water."

Still turned around, Jason saw the doors of the Taurus behind them open. Two men unbuckled in the yellow of the Taurus' dome light and got out. One was blond and young-faced, the man Jason had seen in the Taurus that had been after Paul. The other seemed the same age, but older in the face. Jason fished the jack-handle out from between the seat and the door and jammed it into his front pocket so it ripped the pocket's fabric. It dangled inside his pant leg with its angle inside the pocket so it wouldn't fall in completely. He watched for a break in traffic and got out.

The driver's door of the Taurus a few yards in front of the Pontiac opened until it hit the stout concrete highway divider. The gray-haired man slid out and stood in the angle of the door.

The jack-handle was cold against Jason's leg. The two drivers approached, backlit by their own headlights. When they were close, the blond looked at the Pontiac and laughed.

Jason shouted, "Either of you guys got Auto Club?" The highway traffic was thin, but its noise was contained by greenways and concrete baffles. An indistinct clangor resulted, over which normal speaking voices didn't carry.

"Funny guy," the older-looking driver said loudly. "Let's have that computer, funny guy."

"No," Jason shouted.

The driver said, "Yes," and pulled his coat back. A gun glinted in the overhead lighting.

Jason turned toward the Pontiac. "Martin, hand me the computer."

Martin looked surprised.

Jason waggled two fingers in a let's-have-it gesture. "Come on."

Robert persuaded the passenger's seat forward to make room, and Martin awkwardly handed the computer out the door.

Jason took it from him and gave it to the Taurus driver. None of the passing headlights slowed down so someone could ask why he was doing that.

"There you go," he said.

"You're not as dumb as you look, funny guy," the blond driver said.

Jason glanced suddenly behind both men. He nodded toward the oncoming traffic. "CHP."

The men both turned quickly to look. Jason hooked a thumb and forefinger into his front pocket and got hold of the jack-handle. There was no highway patrol car. The men turned back.

"Hey, look at that," Jason said. "You're as dumb as I look."

The blond took a step toward him. Behind Jason, the gray-haired man called, "Let's go, Barry."

Barry stopped his approach and glared at Jason. Jason withdrew the jack-handle, let it tap against his leg, and looked interested.

"Barry," the gray-haired man said, "leave the guy alone and let's go before the CHP really does come by."

Barry gave Jason a dangerous look that was intended to make him wake up in cold sweats for the rest of his life.

"Bye bye, Barry," Jason said.

Barry pointed at him with one forefinger, meaningfully. A momentary primal male thing happened in Jason's abdomen and biceps, and he pointed the jack-handle back at Barry. Barry gave him a soundless little laugh and turned to attend to the computer.

The computer and the older-looking driver went into

the Taurus. Barry stood next to it. The gray-haired man, still standing in the angle of his open door a few yards in front of the Pontiac, said, "Don't you know how to plan ahead?"

"Right," Jason said, "we were supposed to plan on driving all the way out to Where God Lost His Shoes."

The gray-haired man folded himself back through his half-opened door. Barry pointed at Jason again and got into his car. Jason figured it would be redundant to point the jack-handle at him again, so he didn't. All three Tauri waited for a long break in traffic and then pulled into the fast lane as Jason stood by the Pontiac and watched.

Barry's Taurus passed a little too close to Jason. He expected it and had time to get the jack-handle ready, swing it solidly at the side mirror, and then drop it in a whirling clatter because it hurt considerably to whang a car going twenty miles per hour with a tire iron going seventy.

The formation of Tauri accelerated away into traffic, one of them with a newly modified side mirror. Jason flapped his still-vibrating hand vigorously at the wrist and, at a break in traffic, darted into the fast lane and grabbed the jack-handle.

"What the hell was that macho bullshit with the tire iron," Martin exploded as Jason poked his head through the window.

He dropped the jack-handle on the front floorboard. "That's exactly what it was. Trunk key, please?"

Martin glared at him as Robert handed him the key. He opened the trunk of the Pontiac and took out the tightly capped gas can he'd filled in Death Valley.

The tank soon had five gallons of gas in it and the engine was running again. Jason sat in the passenger's seat, rubbing the hand that had been holding the tire iron.

Robert put it in gear.

"No," Jason said. "Wait."

Robert explained, "Getting away. They are. As we speak."

"That's okay. They're already too far ahead."

Robert squinted at him. "I sense it. Your fiendish, cunning plan. It is fiendish, cunning, and fiendish, and a plan. Like a lurking lurker, lurkishly it lurks in the deeply deepest sockety sockets of those deep deep eye socket—"

Jason said, "See if I'm missing something important here. The original Taurus we were chasing couldn't've had time to get a tank of gas and pass this location yet, right?"

"Right," Robert said tentatively, waiting for Jason's conclusion.

In conclusion, Jason looked happy and said nothing more.

"Oh!" Robert said as he got it, and grinned widely.

Jason turned and beamed at Martin.

"Okay," Martin said. "I admit that's moderately clever. Wait for the car again, follow the car again, yeah, okay. But don't get too proud of yourself. They got the computer."

"I'm going to be cocky about that, too, but I'm going to do it later. Right now, I need to take the gas can and start walking for gas so when the original Taurus comes by, we look like we're down for the count, dead in the water, long in the face, uh, out like a light."

"Big like a moose," Robert helped.

"You guys open the hood and look like you're fixing stuff. If the Taurus goes by, give it a minute and then come get me. If a CalTrans tow truck stops to help you, tell them you thought it was out of gas, but it was just a clogged fuel filter and you blew it out and now it's fixed. Got it?"

"No." Robert nodded.

Jason paused to compose a clearer set of instructions, and Martin said, "I got it, don't worry. Start walking."

Jason got out with the gas can and walked north in the emergency lane. In a few minutes, a honking car approached behind him, and the white Taurus with body damage swished by on his right. The men in it were the two from the motel. Jason caught a brief flash of waves and victorious grins as it passed him.

A few seconds later, the Pontiac came up behind him in the emergency lane. The Taurus was far enough ahead to be nearly indistinguishable from traffic.

"The scab-licking cloacas jeered insensitively at us," Robert said as Jason got in.

"At me, too," Jason said. "I'm thinking maybe—"

Robert stomped on the accelerator, smoking the rear tires and surging wildly into the fast lane. In the line of sight between two foreshortened lanes of traffic, Jason caught an impression of the white Taurus about half a mile ahead.

"I'm thinking," Jason repeated, "that I kind of like arrogance in an adversary. Overconfidence is a good ally. As long as we're not spotted, finding their secret headquarters will be cake."

Robert said, "Cake?"

"Successful avoidance of visual surveillance will result in significant reduction of difficulty in goal acquisition, and facilitate the surmounting of task obstacles."

"Oh!" Robert smacked his forehead. "*Now* I understand!"

"Twit."

"I thought cake was better," Martin said from the back seat. "And I'm looking up *cloaca* when we get home."

34

The white Taurus went fifty miles before it exited. Either they hadn't been spotted, or the men in the Taurus wanted to be followed. There were no evasive maneuvers, no sneaky moves at all. Even if they'd been spotted, that was probably okay with Jason; if they were following the Taurus into some sort of trap, it would at least bring them closer to whatever it was they'd be closer to.

The gas gauge was riding the "E" mark again as they followed the Taurus in a right turn off the offramp.

Martin said, "Welcome to Silicon Valley."

"It's not what I expected," Jason remarked as he looked out at a well-lighted, flat town of widely spaced industrial parks, greenbelts, and corner mini-malls.

Robert let another car get between the Pontiac and the Taurus. "What did you expect?"

"I guess geodesic domes and Jetson cars."

"It is," Martin said. "This is all just camouflage."

They went straight for almost ten minutes, staying a block behind an apparently unconcerned white Taurus until it entered the driveway of a small industrial park on the left. Two rows of beige pre-fab buildings faced each other efficiently across a narrow parking lot. A lighted sign at the driveway entrance said that they were at 121 North CD-ROM Drive, and went on to name the high-tech-sounding companies that were located in the pre-fabs. None of the names meant anything, but they all sounded really zippy.

A yellow sign against the pre-fab building on the left said "Parking for Synervision/Chronitex Only." Across the parking lot from Synervision/Chronitex was another building with a blue sign that said "CyberCalc Technologies, Inc." and a white one that said "MicroVue/Codec Inc." Some people were hanging around, smoking.

The tail of the white Taurus disappeared behind Synervision/Chronitex as the Pontiac approached the driveway. White Tauri were briefly visible parked behind it until the Pontiac passed the driveway and the other building blocked the view.

"That name sounds really familiar," Jason said.

"Which way?" Robert asked.

"Somewhere else where we can try to figure this all out."

"Motel," Martin said, pointing to the right.

"The car would be too obvious in the parking lot. Where else is there?"

"I don't see anywhere else. We got the motel, we got the liquor store, we got the industrial park. We got nowhere else."

Robert said, "What if we disguise it?"

Jason said, "Disguise what?"

"The car."

"As what?"

"We could paint it."

"What color, exactly, do you think would make it hard to recognize?"

Moments passed as they all envisioned the Pontiac in various hues.

"Okay, that's out," Jason said. "So, what do we—"

Martin said, "Why don't we just park around the block?"

THEY ENDED UP in a second-floor motel room with a non-functional baseboard radiator and a painting of a duck. Someone had painted the radiator white, evidencing less skill but more inspiration than the duck artist.

The room overlooked the parking lot. Past the parking lot was the street, and on the other side of the street and a few hundred feet west were the computer companies. Jason still hadn't figured out what was so familiar about "Synervision/Chronitex."

He restored his online software from a backup copy on floppy disk and connected his laptop to the Net via the room phone line. He and Martin sat on one of the beds, waiting for the laptop to access an Internet search engine. Robert sat in a chair next to the bed, peering through the barely open drapes. His chessboard was in Martin's pocket, so he was actually paying attention to the industrial park.

When the search page appeared, Jason typed "Huey Benton" and hit enter.

The search engine went through its records of the Internet. In a few moments, another page appeared:

• SEARCH FOR "HUEY BENTON" RESULTED IN 46,968 MATCHES.

"Technology makes life easier," Jason said. He clicked on a button labeled Search Again and typed "Huey Benton AND dongle."

• SEARCH FOR "HUEY BENTON, DONGLE" RESULTED IN 0 MATCHES.

"Try 'computer,' " Martin suggested.

• SEARCH FOR "HUEY BENTON, COMPUTER" RESULTED IN 307,996 MATCHES.
• SEARCH FOR "HUEY BENTON, GENIUS" RESULTED IN 64,966 MATCHES.
• SEARCH FOR "HUEY BENTON, WUNDERKIND OF ALL COMPUTER THINGS, GOD OF HERRING" RESULTED IN 0 MATCHES.
• SEARCH FOR "(HUEY BENTON) AND (COMPUTER OR GENIUS OR DONGLE)" RESULTED IN 3 MATCHES.

"There," Jason said. "That one's useful." He clicked. A listing of the three matches appeared:

• 1. LISTING OF THE FACULTY AND STAFF OF L.A. ARTS
• 2. LISTING OF THE L.A. ARTS COMPUTER DEPARTMENT
• 3. THE GENIUS THAT IS ME

"The genius," Martin read, "that is me."
Jason clicked on it:

> **!!!!ThE GeNiUs ThAt Is Me PaGe!!!!**
> **THE FUTURE IS HERE!!!!**
> Click here to enter it . . .

Jason looked at Martin. "Five bucks says it's a manifesto."

"No bet."

Jason clicked. The Genius That Is Me Page disappeared and was replaced by another:

THE FUTURE IS HERE!!
The set top box. . . . .
The multimedia revolution. . . . .
The bourgois home computer
stranglehold. . . . .
FORGET them ALL!!!
As usual, a fat, lazy, grasping middle
class appropriates a true revelution,
turning the beautiful free exchange of
information into a **stinking corporate
qagmire** of mindless games and disgusting
sex products! With power comes RESPONSABILITY
but where is the responsability for these
vile applications of innocent data? Where
is the **other side** of the **bottom line**?!!
Click here to find out . . .

Jason clicked. A new page:

IT IS RIGHT HERE!!!!
The only way to balance the greed of the
corporate-financial system, is to strike
where it DOES NOT EVEN KNOW IT IS VUNLERABLE!!!!!
But it is vulnerable and I am the one who
knows how TO STRIKE!!!
If something happens to me **the world must
know** and perhaps there is some small chance
justice will prevail in this time of a soft,

```
lazy people inured to the harsh injustices
   perpetratd by the corporate-financial
  system!!! If you have the right stuff,
              click here . . .
```

Jason clicked. Presently, another page appeared:

```
Sorry, you do NOT have the right stuff.
```

"I beg your pardon." Jason tried again.

```
Sorry, you do NOT have the right stuff.
```

Jason shook his head. "Programmers. Talk about misguided machismo."

Robert said from the window, "I read that programmers are the rock stars of the nineties."

"Let me guess," Jason said. "You read that in a programmers' magazine."

"Yes. I believe it was *Big Hard Throbbing Disk Digest.*"

Martin said, "One of the artists I work with named Dawn, she uses a program that models human figures in three-D. She says if programmers were the rock stars of the nineties, they'd get breasts right."

Robert looked one-eyed at Martin as though he wished he had a good response.

Jason disconnected the laptop from the phone line. "We'll mess with that web page later. I don't feel like playing guess-my-clever-game with a coy computer geek. Instead," he announced, "I will explain why I said I was going to be cocky, back there on the freeway. I don't think having Benton's computer is going to do them any good."

"Why not?"

"Remember it didn't have a hard disk, and I said it shouldn't be able to run, because there was no system software?"

"Yeah."

"It's not just that it shouldn't be able to run without any system software; it's that it's impossible."

"But it did."

"Yes. Exactly. It did. That means it had system software. I have a hunch where it was hidden. Anybody want to guess?"

Martin looked tired. "Don't make us guess, Miss Marple; just tell us."

"Most trackballs attach via the serial port. This one uses the SCSI port. I wondered why. I think it's because there's a chip in the trackball with an operating system on it. If I'm right, it probably has other things on it, not just system software. After all, why go to the trouble of turning a trackball into a start-up device unless you want to use it on a variety of computers? And why be able to use it on a variety of computers unless it has some function besides just starting up?"

He connected the trackball to his laptop, changed some settings, and restarted.

In a minute, the words DEVICE#2NOTFOUND appeared on the screen. A little timer appeared and began to count down from sixty.

"Device number two," Robert said. "Do you think that's—?"

"Yeah." Jason nodded thoughtfully. "I bet it's the dongle. Ten bucks says you need both the trackball and the dongle in order to access whatever else is on the chip."

"You know what this means for us," Martin said.

Jason and Robert both looked at him.

"It means leverage," Martin said. "We have half the system."

"It also means," Robert said, "that if they figure out that we have it, we will be what I believe is termed *quarry*."

The counter reached zero, and a message came up: DVLS/A6 NOT MOUNTED.

"What the hell does that mean," Jason murmured. "DVLS . . . Dedicated Velocity Level System. Dynamic Version Logic Simulator."

Robert said, "Dungbeetles Very Likely Stink."

"You guys are funny," Martin said. "I just thought it said *devils*."

Robert said, "Deluded, Vanessa Likes Sam. Dastardly Villians Lack Sophistication. Double Value Lurking Sackcloth."

Something was nagging at Jason, but he couldn't figure out what.

He looked at the screen again: DVLS/A6 NOT MOUNTED.

Startled, he said, "Oh!"

"What," Martin asked.

Jason stared and pointed at the screen. "Martin's right. It's *devils*."

"It could be anything," Martin said. "How do you know it's *devils*?"

"The CD-ROM game Platt was working on at Light Wizards was *Devils of Alpha-Six*."

Everyone looked at the laptop.

DVLS/A6 NOT MOUNTED.

"Oh, man!" Jason smacked the top of the nightstand in sudden realization. "I am such an idiot. No wonder Synervision sounded familiar. That's the company that contracted Light Wizards."

Everyone looked at the laptop again and was baffled.

35

I don't get it at all," Jason said. "How does the CD-ROM game Platt was working on fit into any of this?"

They talked about it until it was time to eat, which was soon. Martin went downstairs to the motel coffee shop and brought back fried, breaded cheese sticks; fried, breaded shrimp; fried, breaded chicken strips; and three root beer floats, which, although neither fried nor breaded, seemed not inconsistent with the underlying theme.

Jason logged back onto the Net and went through Huey Benton's series of web pages again.

```
        If you have the right stuff,
            click here . . .
```

For the hell of it, he clicked again, and a different page came up:

You have the **right stuff**. Please wait . . .

"Hey, it's working this time!"

Martin looked over his shoulder. "What did you do differently?"

"Nothing."

"You must have done something differently."

"No, nothing. Maybe he's got some sort of random thing that sometimes shows you the page and sometimes doesn't."

"Why?"

"Because he can? I dunno. Oh, wait. I get it."

Martin ate half a cheese stick and looked quizzical.

Jason shook his head. "The right stuff. Ha ha." Jason tapped the trackball with a forefinger. "This right stuff. If the trackball's not attached, you don't have the right *stuff* to access the page. Cute."

The page was replaced by a new one.

Hello, Partner! :-)
If you are reading this, I am **long gone** and
you are accessing my web site. You are
probably logging on from my computer at L.A.
Arts. If not, then congradulations on
figuring out my little hardware trick. This
page had just been generated by an autonomic
applicatoin and posted automaticly on the
web. This process does no occur if it has
been less then 2 days since my last security
reset. In other words, if you are reading
this, I am either more than 2 days dead or
beginning my life of luxury somewhere
without extredition.
Next page . . .

There were some pictures along with the text on the next page. As he waited for them to load, Jason skimmed the text aloud for Robert and Martin:

"Looks like newspaper articles. Um, let's see . . . Data/Media Group retained by Silicon Valley start-up Synervision to provide assets for CD-ROM games . . . there's a picture, but we can't see it yet because it's still loading. Um . . . Synervision announces delays of scheduled game releases . . . L.A. Arts computer wiz on cutting edge of video . . . L.A. Arts computer guru Huey Benton . . . blah blah blah . . . cutting edge . . . take us into the twenty-first century, yadda yadda . . . He was working on data compression for Synervision."

Martin said, "What's data compression?"

"Making information smaller so more of it can go through a cable in less time." He skimmed the rest of the story. "Data/Media was working on compressing video signals for use in computer games."

From his post at the window, Robert asked, "Would that be very lucrative?"

"Sure. A bloodthirsty ten-year-old boy decapitates a monster; if it spurts more gruesomely than the competitor's monster without requiring more system resources, you're rich." He skimmed over the rest of the text on the screen. "And thus is the multimedia industry forged. That seems to be all the content in the articles. The pictures are coming up . . . here's one of Huey Benton shaking hands with the president of Synervision. Anybody recognize this guy?"

The man was nondescript, confident-looking, white, middle-aged, and even-toothed. He wore blue-lensed sunglasses and had thin lips.

"Nope," Martin said. "I don't know anybody with money."

Robert came over from the window and looked and shook his head.

A picture with the caption "Data/Media founders" began to appear. Robert and Martin crowded a little closer to watch.

"Well," Jason said when both founders were clearly recognizable, "that's a twist."

One of them was Huey Benton. The other was Ian Hibbit.

"Hmm," Robert said.

Martin said, "Oho . . ."

They sat and stared at the picture of Huey Benton and Ian Hibbit.

"Okay," Jason said when, despite still not knowing anything, he felt less confused. "Martin, could these pictures be fakes?"

Martin said, "Yeah, they could be, but they don't look like it."

Pause.

Jason said, "Ian Hibbit seems to have been Huey Benton's partner."

Robert said, "Hibbit could have killed Benton for control of the company."

Pause.

Martin said, "If Hibbit knew Benton was going to die at that party, and someone hired Paul to steal the dongle from Benton, then . . ."

Jason said, ". . . then it stands to reason . . ."

Robert picked up the thread and said, ". . . that it was Hibbit who hired Paul."

"Platt said Benton's death was clearly accidental. He called the coroner's report 'unambiguous.' "

Martin nodded. "If Hibbit and that big guy Jeffrey with the gun and the other guy, what was his name—"

Robert said, "Hibbit's driver? Lowell."

"—came after Paul at the Manor—"

Jason and Robert said simultaneously, "Paul double-crossed Hibbit."

Robert said, "Selling to a higher bidder?"

"The bearded guy in the Corvair," Jason said. "That could have been Paul's buyer."

Martin said, "Hibbit hires Paul to steal the dongle. Paul steals the dongle, but instead of giving it to Hibbit, he arranges to sell it to the bearded guy."

Jason said, "Unfortunately, it's Paul we're talking about, so instead of hiding it someplace intelligent, he sticks it in my engine where I find it, so he can't deliver it to either of his two buyers."

Martin said, "So the bearded guy and Paul come after you at the Pantry and make off with your cigarette lighter."

"Which, by the way, I want back."

Martin whistled softly. "If we're right, I'd say that Paul is in some real deep shit."

Robert said, "I wonder if he knows he is."

Jason said, "When I gave the dongle to Platt, Platt was working for Light Wizards, which was contracted by the company that hired Benton. Then Platt disappeared. What's that about?"

Long silence.

Robert said, "I hesitate to say it, but if this dongle is so valuable, maybe Platt sold it and left the country with a lot of cash."

Jason said, "I'd say that didn't happen."

"Me too, but I thought I should say it."

Martin said, "What did the Synervision guys in the Taurus want with Benton's computer?"

Jason said, "Maybe they just want the data compression research results. After all, they paid for it. It might even be legally theirs."

Robert said, "And without Benton's dongle and trackball, they can't access it."

"Right, but they might not know about the trackball."

Robert said, "We have a lot of loose ends here. I'll name the ones I can think of right off. Loose end the first: If Platt isn't dead, he's disappeared. Why?"

"Because it's been seven years and he has to get back to Vulcan for the Pon Farr."

"Loose end the second: Who is the bearded guy?"

"The evil fallen elf whom Santa Claus cast out of the Workshop."

Robert sighed. "Are you even listening to my questions, or are you expending all your energy thinking of funny answers?"

"Thinking of funny answers. Let's see what's on the next page."

He clicked.

100,000:1? GET REAL!!!!!!!

Maybe in a hundrd years but not now and not
for your **vile garbage.**

I HAVE STRUCK A BLOW FOR THE REAL TECHNO-
INTELLIGENSIA!!!! EXPLOIT THE OPPRESSOR!!!!!!

Oh yes and FUCK YOU!

This page has just been posted permanently
on the web.

Martin said, "What does that mean?"

"One hundred thousand to one sounds like a ratio," Robert said.

Jason nodded. "I bet it's a data compression ratio. It seems awfully high, though."

"I don't get it," Martin said. "A hundred thousand what?"

"A hundred thousand to one," Jason said. "That means that the data comprising a hundred thousand video frames could be compressed to the usual size of one normal frame."

"Is that possible?" Robert asked.

"Not as far as I know," Jason said. "And more importantly, not as far as Huey Benton knew. Know what I think?"

"What?"

"I think there was never any data compression. It was all a hoax, and this is Benton's egotistical way of confessing."

Robert said, "Dostoevsky believed that guilty people yearn to confess."

Martin said, "Are we the only ones who know about this?"

Robert said, "No, it's been well discussed by literary analysts."

"About this web page, you dweeb," Martin said. "Not about Dostoevsky."

"We may very well be," Jason said. "At least, until someone else happens upon it. And judging from this, Hibbit doesn't know it's a hoax either."

"Right . . ." Robert nodded. "I wonder what Paul's up to."

36

Paul Reno was slowly realizing he wasn't in charge.

There wasn't really room for Jeffrey on a van bench seat, and the squeeze did nothing to make him more attractive. Paul especially disliked the way his forehead squinched up before he landed a blow.

Paul was on the rear bench seat, which faced Jeffrey's. His shoulders were down low on the seatback, his arms pulled back and down to disappear into the split between the seat and back. Ropes bound his hands to the welded base of the bench seat, and his knees were on the carpeting, his feet under the seat and bound near his hands. Ian Hibbit squatted with his back to the sliding door, facing them. Lowell was driving.

Still flinching from Jeffrey's last blow upon Paul, Hibbit said, "Is that really necessary?"

Jeffrey gazed slackly at Hibbit. "You said hit him."

"I think that's enough for now."

Jeffrey fell into simian inanimacy, a brooding, overlarge ceramic monkey.

"Mr. Reno," Hibbit said. "I think you have been lying to me."

"No," Paul said, "I—"

"I think," Hibbit repeated, "and Jeffrey thinks, that you are lying to me."

Paul glanced at Jeffrey, who gave no indication of thinking anything of the sort or indeed anything at all.

"What's this going to accomplish?" he asked, but not too defiantly.

Hibbit said, "It's really only a vague notion. Threaten you physically and you'll come through with the dongle. You were paid half in advance in good faith, as per your requirements. You did not deliver."

"Look, I did what I said I did."

"Huey is dead, it's true, but I don't see how you can possibly take credit for an accidental death."

"I already told you—"

"And I already showed you what happens when you lie to me. Jeffrey?"

Jeffrey shifted his weight.

"No—"

Jeffrey hit Paul in the stomach.

When Paul was done gasping and retching, he croaked, "Is it my fault Jason found the dongle?"

"Mr. Reno." Hibbit leaned toward him. "Despite my agreement to hide your involvement by doing the dirty work of going to his apartment to get the item myself, and despite the fact that my attempt failed, yes, it is entirely your fault."

Jeffrey said, "And I want my gun back, asswipe."

Paul's glance darted toward Jeffrey again. Jeffrey's eyes were evil peas beneath the deep jut of his brow.

"Look," Paul said. "I just need a little time."

"You've had a little time."

"Just a little more."

"Where is it?"

"Jason's got it."

"Where is he?"

"I . . . I don't know."

"Then what good are you to me? Why should I not have Jeffrey kill you now?"

"Because Jason will be a major pain in the ass to you. He's always a pain in the ass. You saw."

"We'll be better prepared next time."

"So will he."

"Do you have a suggestion?"

"He trusts me. You help me find him, I'll get your dongle. We can . . ." Paul's glance flickered toward Jeffrey. ". . . we can work out a discount on my fee." He tried to smile.

Hibbit's eyebrows flew up. "A discount? A discount? I think not! I think when you deliver the dongle to me, I will tell Jeffrey not to kill you. I think that will be sufficient payment, don't you?"

"I'll get it for you, whatever it takes."

"And if Mr. Keltner does not want to give it to you?"

"No one forced him in on this, so if he gets hurt—"

"And if you find yourself in the position of being the one who has to hurt him?"

"Then I'll hurt him. Like *that*."

Paul's hands were tied. "Like *that*" was less effective without a punctuating fingersnap.

Hibbit smiled back. "Mr. Reno, Jason Keltner does not have the dongle."

Paul's smile stayed on his face but went dead.

Hibbit said to Jeffrey, "Watch him."

"Why not kill him?"

"We may. For now, just watch him." Hibbit climbed around to the front seat.

Paul looked at Jeffrey. Jeffrey didn't get to kill him yet. He didn't seem happy or sad or much of anything about it. Lowell gunned the red van up Interstate 5, taking the ugly inland route toward Santa Clarita. Nothing to look at but cows for a few hundred miles, and Jeffrey.

37

When Robert got tired, Martin took a watch. It was hard to tell what was going on at Synervision. Barry the blond guy and his partner could still be in there, or they could have left already and gone home for fish sticks.

Jason started to sketch out a surveillance chart on hotel notepad paper. Robert set up his chess set and beat himself in six moves.

"Robert," Martin said presently. "What kind of vehicle picked up Paul at the Suicide Bridge, again?"

"An old red Ford van."

"Like this one?"

Jason and Robert went to the window and looked through the drapes. The red van was signaling a right turn into the motel driveway. When there was a break in traffic, it made its turn and parked.

"That sure could be it," Robert said.

The driver's side door of the van opened, and Lowell got out, stretched, and went into the motel office. The oxidized roof of the van hid any other occupants.

In a couple of minutes, Lowell came out of the office. He went to the passenger's side and spoke to whoever was there, pointing in the vicinity of where Jason, Robert, and Martin sat. They all pulled back from the window. Lowell went around to the driver's side and got in.

Despite the fact that Hibbit was through a wall and two hundred feet away, Jason whispered, "Did they find us, or is this just a coincidence?"

Robert said softly, "They're not taking any pains to stay out of sight. I don't think they know we're here."

Martin murmured, "This is the only motel around. Like I said before, there's this motel, there's the liquor store, and there's the industrial park. If Hibbit deals with Synervision, he probably always stays here."

The van pulled out of its parking space and parked nose in to the motel, almost directly below their room. The second-floor walkway blocked the view, so there was no telling who might be getting out of the van. In a minute, more than one non-petite person thudded up the stairs and walked toward their room. Jason found his hand gripping the top of one of the two motel room chairs. It was the only weapon within reach.

The footsteps paused, and then the door to the room directly to their left was opened. The people went inside and the door was closed.

"No way," Martin breathed.

Jason whispered, "I wonder if Paul is with them."

They crouched at the shared wall, listening intently, but there were no telling sounds from the other room. After an hour, Jason and Martin went back to the window and Robert

kept listening to the other room. Jason tried to explain his surveillance chart to Martin, but discovered himself too exhausted
to assemble cogent sentences. Martin made him lie down for a
nap and promised to wake him for his turn at watch.

ALL HE REMEMBERED about the dream as it was obliterated by
consciousness was that it was in black-and-white and there
was an important and mysterious thing that everyone
wanted. It was all very complicated, but in the dream, he'd
cleverly intuited through a web of double crosses and secret
agendas. There was a beautiful, deceptive woman in there
somewhere, too, with veiled eyes and her sights set on Jason. Some people's dreams were cryptically prophetic or
strangely enlightening. Jason's were old detective movies.

When he opened his eyes, Martin was looking at him
innocently and Robert was at the barely parted window
curtain. Robert's little chess set was in Martin's hand.

He whispered, "Why didn't you wake me for my turn
at the window?"

"He's awake," Martin said softly. "Hey, uh, Jase?"

"What?"

"Who's Bonnie?" Martin grinned. "Look there. I believe he's embarrassed."

Robert said in a stage whisper from the window, "It's
not fair ambushing him when he wakes up."

Martin said, "Forget that, I want details. Who's the
dream girl?"

Jason stretched. "Standard-issue dream girl. Anything
interesting happening?"

Robert said, "You're not going to get anything out of
him."

Martin said, "He's a guy. We brag about this stuff. It's
how we're built."

Robert said, "Maybe guys could learn to be a little more like women once in a while."

Jason rubbed his eyes. "You ever hear a bunch of women away from home talking about men? It's horrible."

"Eye color," Martin pressed.

"What? Why?"

"Just fishing for details. What color eyes?"

"Maroon."

"Hair."

"Bald with pink tufts."

"Tall or short?"

"Who cares?"

"Straight or curvy?"

"Amoebalike, with horrifying pseudopods that reshape at will. Instead of all the physical stuff, you ever thought about maybe asking 'smart or dumb'?"

"Why bother? It's you. She's smart."

The pretty rock lay against his chest in his shirt pocket.

Robert said, "You're not going to get anything else out of him."

Martin's hands went up in surrender. "Okay, okay. I'll lay off for now, but I am going to get the details out of you at some point. I'm patient."

Robert snorted. "What new and strange definition of 'patient' is this?"

Martin said, "Aw, just tell us, Jase!"

"So," Jason said, "how's the surveillance going?" The rock bumped lightly as he got up.

AFTER A DAY of not leaving the room, they were very hungry and the surveillance chart contained data of no apparent significance.

At Synervision, no more cars had arrived or departed.

The employees of the other companies in the industrial park mingled and smoked outside when the lunch truck arrived. Employees of Synervision did not come out. Synervision had received no UPS or Federal Express deliveries.

In the next room, people moved around. Attempts to eavesdrop with a water glass had revealed nothing. Twice, someone left the room and came back fifteen minutes later. These were assumed to be food runs.

"This," Jason said, dropping the surveillance chart on the motel room table, "tells us nothing."

Robert said, "There's one good thing about sitting here for a whole day. Since no one's come after us, we can reasonably assume that neither Synervision nor Ian Hibbit knows where we are."

"That's true. I wish we had *The Art of War* here so we could see what Sun Tzu had to say about the advantage of surprise."

"He said it was an advantage."

"You are, as ever, very helpful. Do we have any other advantages?"

"We have the trackball," Martin said.

Robert said, "We have a good view of Synervision and extreme proximity to Hibbit and maybe Paul. The guns I took away from Lowell and Hibbit are in the car."

Jason said, "It seems to me we should be able to do something with those things."

Robert's gaze disconnected, and he looked thoughtfully at the corner of the room and rocked a little. Jason stared at his hands and tried to think, but nothing formulated.

After a few minutes, Martin cleared his throat softly and whispered, "Anybody thought of anything?"

"No," Jason said. Robert shook his head.

"Because I was thinking," Martin continued, "that

maybe the reason we can't think of anything is that we're the only ones without our own goals."

"We don't have an agenda," Robert rephrased.

Jason said, "I thought our agenda was we want to find out who's after us and make sure they don't get us."

Robert said, "Yes, but that's a reactive agenda. Before we can pursue it, we have to wait for someone else to act. I believe what Martin's suggesting is that we consider formulating a more productive agenda."

"The problem with that—" Martin began.

Robert said, "—is that we don't know enough to formulate an agenda that makes sense."

Martin indicated with one gracious hand that Robert had accurately spoken his thoughts.

"When no clear course of action suggests itself," Jason said, "pick something at random."

THEY LEFT THEIR room quietly and went downstairs. While Martin slit the sidewalls of the red van's tires, Jason and Robert went into the coffee shop. Jason called the motel front desk from the pay phone there and asked for Hibbit's room.

When Hibbit answered, Jason said, "Listen and don't talk. The police are about to surround your room. Go into the room immediately east of you, just you and Paul Reno. Leave Jeffrey and Lowell where they are and don't tell them what's going on. If I see all four of you leave, I'll tell the cops where you went. All your tires are slashed, and the police will be here any moment. If you try to steal a car and get away, I will ram you with mine, and if you flee on foot, the police will get you. When it's all over, go to the motel coffee shop, show me your hands are empty, and keep them where I can see them."

He hung up, called the police, and reported gunfire in Hibbit's room.

38

Sitting in the motel coffee shop seemed safer than being in the room next to Hibbit's when the cops showed up. The wing that contained the coffee shop was at a right angle to the wing that contained the rooms, so it was a clear view across the parking lot. The first police car showed up three minutes after Jason's call, and three more arrived within another minute. Two officers went into the motel office and spoke to the desk clerk, who immediately looked worried and began making phone calls. Presently, doors on both floors began to open, and tenants hurried into the motel office. Since the office adjoined the coffee shop, Jason could see the tenants asking questions of the desk clerk, who professed ignorance and shooed everyone into the coffee shop. The coffee shop filled up quickly with people and nervous tension, and everyone got a free cup of coffee and watched the police work. Jason had a stack of pancakes in front of him, half-eaten, and Robert and Martin had been fed too.

Two of the police officers went past the stairway and around to the back, one stayed at a point near both the driveway and the motel office door, and five approached the door with guns drawn and a small battering ram. Electric excitement replaced the usual coffee shop chatter and clatter as people pointed and speculated.

Robert said, "This was an efficient use of our energy."

Martin raised his coffee cup. "Noooo shit."

The police officers could not be heard in the coffee shop, but after a tense pause during which Jason presumed them to have identified themselves, the battering ram was used on the door and the five officers streamed into the room with guns aimed. Cheers went up in the coffee shop.

"There you go, baby!" a large man in the booth next to theirs boomed.

Jeffrey came out, escorted by three officers, his hands cuffed behind him.

"All right, all right!" the man next to them yelled, bouncing in his seat. The officers brought Jeffrey down the stairs and put him into the back of a police car. Lowell came out in front of another two officers. Similar whoops went up for him.

"Two down," Jason said, looking at Jeffrey and Lowell cuffed in the police cars.

It took a while for the police to leave, and then it was a good hour before people got tired of talking about the disturbance and started returning to their rooms. After a while, the door to the room Jason had rented opened and Hibbit came out.

"I still don't see why you had to warn him," Martin said.

"I told you," Jason said. "I don't want Paul arrested, and

there was no way to get him out without Hibbit going with him."

"You already know this," Robert said, "so pardon my saying it, but maybe Paul deserves to be arrested."

Hibbit went down the stairs, paused to inspect the tires of the van, and walked across the parking lot toward the coffee shop. Robert and Martin got up. Martin went to a pay phone near the rest rooms, behind Jason, and Robert strolled over to the motel office and flirted with the desk clerk.

Hibbit entered the motel office and then the coffee shop. He displayed empty hands and approached, taking in Martin at the pay phone before he slid into the booth. Robert went out the office door to get Paul.

As arranged, Hibbit's hands stayed in view. "Show me a gun," he said.

"I don't have a gun."

"Well then," Hibbit said. He began to draw his hands back toward himself.

Jason picked up his fork. "But I can tine you right through the eye."

Hibbit looked hesitant.

"I'm very keyed up," Jason said allowing his tension into his voice. He saw the corners of Hibbit's eyes twitch. "And fast with a fork. Just ask my pancakes."

Hibbit stared at Jason and then flicked his eyes briefly down to look at the pancakes.

"He is! He is!" Jason said in a pancake voice, making them talk-wiggle with the fingertips of his left hand. "And if the pancakes flatly lie—" He angled his head to indicate Martin, behind him.

Hibbit looked. Robert had briefly coached Martin for maximum menace when flashing Hibbit's own gun at him. They'd found information on the Internet that told them how to unload the gun. It had no ammunition in it. Jason didn't tell Hibbit that.

"Hands on the table," he said instead.

Hibbit complied. "What do you want?"

"A meeting with your client."

Hibbit stared at him and then burst out laughing. "Why on earth would I give you that?"

"Because I have the second device."

"What second device?"

"The second device without which the dongle doesn't work."

Hibbit stopped laughing but didn't look convinced.

Jason said, "Didn't know that, did you?"

"Where is this supposed device?"

"Central Park."

"Pardon?"

"Galactic cluster NGC-2055."

"Pardon?"

"They're nonsense answers, you idiot. I'm not going to tell you where it is."

"How much do you want for it?"

"I'm not selling to you."

"Then what—"

"I think you thought if you killed Benton and took the dongle, then you'd be able to keep all the Synervision money yourself."

"I? Kill Huey?"

"Right, you didn't do it, fine. If the dongle ever shows up again, Synervision will discover it doesn't work without the second device. I have the second device. Without it, the data compression doesn't work and you don't get any money."

Hibbit paused. One of his hands moved about a six-teenth of an inch.

He's got a gun. Jason's leg muscles tensed for a cross-table lunge.

Hibbit didn't go for a gun. He said, "It seems you're in, then. How will I contact you?"

"Keep a room here, under your name. I'll check in regularly."

Hibbit rose. "You'll not gain the advantage of me again, Mr. Keltner."

Jason said, "I'm gaining advantage of you again right now, Mr. Hibbit. I'm leaving. You're not. My friend with the gun will stay and watch you for a while."

"And if not, he will do what? Shoot me here in public?"

"If not, I will not deal with Synervision. Now, sit."

Hibbit's jaw muscle clenched and he sat.

Jason stood. "Good head for business."

Outside the coffee shop, the Pontiac came around the corner and stopped at the curb so he could get in. As Robert pulled into traffic, Jason turned to look in the back. Paul's arms were tied behind him, and a knotted rope held a gag in his mouth.

"He was already tied up," Robert said. "It suggests both rampant egotism and questionableness of my moral fiber that I left the gag on him for no other reason than that I would then continue to be the loudest person in the car."

Paul glared at him. Jason picked Martin's knife up off the floorboard and leaned over the seat to cut the rope that held the gag. Paul spit out the rag and said, "What the fuck do you think you're doing?"

"You want us to give you back?"

"Well, whatever. You think you can just—"

"Paul?"

"What."

"I'm tired of you talking to me like that."

"I think this is—"

"Paul, if you talk to me like that again, I will hit you twice in the nose while your hands are tied."

Paul said, "Yeah, right. Like you'd—"

Jason dropped the knife on the front seat. He swiveled slightly on his knees to get a better angle, and punched Paul in the nose. Paul's head snapped back and bounced against the seat back, and Jason punched him a second time on the rebound.

"You—you—" Paul's eyes were wide and his tone was disbelieving, almost a whine. Blood ran from one nostril onto his upper lip and part of his cheek. Jason's knuckles were wet with it.

"I made the condition and the consequence clear. You fulfilled the condition; I provided the consequence. Now sit up, and don't kick or bite, or I'll take the knife to you."

Paul looked offended. "What kind of —"

"I said sit up."

Paul sat up. Jason slid back around to face forward in the passenger's seat and turned the rearview mirror so he could see Paul. He wiped his knuckles off on the front of the passenger seat where it wouldn't show. Robert was whitefaced and he was blinking rapidly. Paul snuffled in the backseat.

They swung by the coffee shop again and Jason got into the back with Paul. Hibbit was still sitting where he was supposed to sit. Martin saw them, came out, and got into the front.

"Paul looks like shit," he said. "Hi, Paul. You look like shit."

Paul didn't respond.

"Petrol, James," Jason said. "And then home."

39

In a dim, dirty motel room twenty miles from Synervision, Jason said, "Spill it."

Paul said, "Why should I? You don't know shit."

Jason said, "Behold shit: You were hired by Hibbit to steal the dongle from Huey Benton at the L.A. Arts party. That's why you said you were going to have money coming, back when I took you to my jam session at Fifth Street Dick's. When I invited you to go to the L.A. Arts party, you looked a little taken aback. That's because you were already planning on going."

Paul looked as nonchalant as he could, tied up with rope.

"So," Jason continued, "you robbed the dead guy. Then—I don't know why, maybe you were afraid of keeping it on you—you hid the dongle in my engine, which was a really stupid place, since it started to melt."

Paul looked startled and said, "I wrapped it in wet paper towels."

"That's probably why it wasn't completely melted, but it was still a total bonehead move on your part. You made a deal with the bearded guy and left it in my car until the deal could go down. Hibbit visited you, but he thought I was you. I figure this means you'd only dealt in e-mail or on the phone. You told Hibbit I had the dongle, so he came downstairs and accosted me, but Robert and Martin got the drop on him in the parking lot. After you disappeared with Jeffrey's gun, I bluffed Hibbit into thinking that I was in a position to deal for the dongle.

"You knew I was going to be playing in Bay City, so you knew my car would be at the nightclub. You tried to get the dongle from my engine, but I interrupted you. The first of many white Tauruses appeared, trying to get the dongle from you. I helped you get away, but I had to stop chasing the Taurus when my carburetor linkage fell apart. Guess what I found when I popped the hood to fix it!"

He waited for Paul to guess. Paul didn't.

"Anyone?"

"Julie Newmar," Robert guessed.

"The dongle! Good thing I found it, or you and the bearded guy—who now had Jeffrey's gun, I wonder how that happened—would have gotten it when you ambushed me in the Pantry parking lot. Lo," he concluded. "I know shit. So, here we are. Who's the bearded guy?"

"What are you going to do if I don't talk, hit me again?"

Martin said, "I might even if you do talk."

Jason thought in silence that became uncomfortable as it stretched out. Martin picked up a plastic-wrapped drink glass from the side table and went into the bathroom and ran the tap. The pipes shuddered loudly.

When he was back, sipping, Jason said, "Water hammer."

Paul said, "Huh?"

"That pipe noise is called water hammer. You promised the dongle to two independently dangerous people and then lost the merchandise. Here's the only deal I'm willing to offer. I'm now a player in this game. The better you talk, the better your cut."

"I want fifty percent."

Jason didn't care. He said, "Twenty," to keep up appearances.

"Forty-five."

"Thirty."

"Forty or no deal."

"Fine. Who's the bearded guy?"

"I don't like these ropes."

Jason looked at Martin. Martin came over reluctantly and cut Paul's ropes with his knife.

Paul rubbed his wrists. "His name's Tennant." He looked smug. "Totally out of your league."

"I don't doubt it," Jason said. "Who is he and how'd you meet him?"

"I don't know who he is. He contacted me. He knew I was getting the dongle for Ian Hibbit and he said he'd pay better."

"So you said yes."

"Sure. You know me; I'm no fool. I took the better offer."

"How much was the better offer?"

"Thirty grand, half up front."

"How much was your original deal with Hibbit?"

"Twenty, half up front."

"What were you going to tell Hibbit when you'd given the dongle to Tennant?"

"Tennant said he'd deal with it."

"And you took that to mean—"

"That he'd deal with it."

"Who wiped my hard disk?"

A smile teased at the corners of Paul's mouth. "I'll hold that information for later."

"All right," Jason said, "where's Norton Platt?"

Paul looked confused. "Huh?"

"Okay—So, what do we do with you now?"

"Don't I have any say in any of this?"

"Go ahead."

"I need to make sure I get my cut."

"I guess that means you're staying with us."

"Like glue."

"Glue doesn't stay with; it sticks with."

Paul looked as though neither glue nor literacy was important and said, "Whatever."

Jason said, "I think we should head south. I don't like being in their territory. I'd rather operate closer to home."

Robert said, "Maybe some of us should stay here and watch Synervision."

"That makes sense," Jason said. "Paul and I go back home and you two stay here?"

"I don't think we need two people here," Robert said. He picked his chess set off the bed, withdrew two pawns, and put them behind his back.

"White pawn stays," he said to Martin.

"Left."

Robert showed the white pawn in his left hand.

JASON GAVE MARTIN five hundred dollars and they dropped him off around the block from the motel across from Synervision. Then they hit the road back home.

40

Some primal beacon seemed to be drawing every motor home in the world back to its ancestral lair in Southern California. It wasn't a fast trip home in the Pontiac.

On a stretch of two-lane highway where Robert was unable to pass a very slow herd of five, he said, "I think you're doing an excellent job in many respects. I am concerned about the increasing ease with which you do violence."

In the front passenger's seat next to Robert, Paul snorted.

Jason was in back. He said, "You think hitting Paul was uncalled for?"

"Yes," Paul interjected.

"Not entirely, but I'm concerned with the change in you, not with the warrantedness of the act."

Jason considered that.

"You think both punches were uncalled for?" he said.

"Yes."

"Not just the second one."

"No."

"What do you think I should have done instead?"

"I don't know," Robert said, "but considering how creative you've been in other facets of this affair, I think you could have thought of something."

Jason mulled that. "Is violence inherently bad?"

Robert didn't answer while he popped the Pontiac over to the left to see whether there was room for him to pass the pilgrimage of motor homes, and then returned to his lane.

He said, "I don't know that I can answer that, but I judge the question to be a red herring. The issue that I believe merits inspection and introspection is whether doing violence is bad for you personally. My opinion is that unless you truly want to embark on a life of violence—which you don't, last we discussed it; you want to be a musician—then it is."

"We become what we do?"

"That strikes me as what means to you what what I said means to me."

"Huh? Never mind, don't repeat it. I think I got it."

"I sure didn't," Paul cut in. "You guys intellectualize too much. Jason didn't like what I said, so he hit me. It's only natural. Sometime, someone else won't like what he says, and they'll hit him. What comes around goes around. Somebody fucks, somebody gets fucked. It's the way of the world."

"A valid viewpoint," Robert acknowledged, "for those with six legs and a neural ganglion the size of a pinpoint."

"Hey, I just tell it like it is. Tell me you don't see it all around you every day."

Robert said, "I don't see it all around me every day."

Paul shrugged. "Then you're blind."

Robert edged the Pontiac left for a view past the motor homes and then moved back into his lane.

"Or," he said, "you are."

"Robert," Jason said, "I'm not sure this is an escalation of violence. I have hit Paul before."

"Once, during a time of extreme anguish and personal crisis for you," Robert said. "And you had just discovered his reprehensible act against you personally. Neither of those circumstances exists now, but your action was the same. I interpret identical reactions to decreasing stimuli as relative escalation."

"If I adopt your view, does it mean I have to apologize to Paul?"

"It doesn't have to do with Paul," Robert said. "It has to do with you."

"You guys," Paul said, "have no idea what you're dealing with."

"And that," Robert said, "is why violence might turn out to be necessary after all."

Jason said, "Both of you shut up or I'll kill you."

ROBERT AND PAUL fell asleep soon after Jason took a turn at the wheel. Driving with the Pontiac radio turned down low, he wondered about Platt and considered alternatives to violence. He concluded that he could have avoided hitting Paul, but that it had been unavoidable with Swofford. He was unable to think of a way to make on-the-spot differentiations. He also thought about Paul's statement at the L.A. Arts party, that Jason's comment about dancing white people had been racist. He decided it might have been, but it didn't matter.

Paul was sleeping against the passenger-side window. Jason hoped that Huey Benton really had died from falling over drunk and hitting his head.

41

"We have the dongle," Hibbit's voice said. "The client insists on a demonstration of the fully functional system."

Jason had been leaning against the pay phone next to a urinal in the blue-tiled men's room at a roadside Denny's. He straightened and said, "You have the dongle? Already?"

"By strange coincidence, it came into our possession today."

Jason wondered if that meant the worst for Platt. "I don't like negotiating money. If the demonstration works, the price is twenty-five thousand dollars."

"That is—"

"Twenty-five, no negotiation. Your dongle is worthless without what I have. You yourself are worthless to Synervision."

A few seconds passed.

"I will advise the client of your request."

"I assume the meeting place will need an AC outlet for the demonstration machines."

"Electricity and space adequate for two computers and peripheral equipment. And privacy. That is all you need worry about."

"I'll call you with the meeting place details."

"Mr. Keltner, my people at Synervision grow impatient. When will your call come?"

"Your people's impatience troubles me not. You'll hear from me as soon as I think of a good place."

He hung up and called Martin at the motel.

"All quiet here, chief," Martin told him. "Nothing to report except one short brown dude going a little ape shit. Lots of time to practice with the knife, though. You ought to see me, man. I'm a regular Kung Fu Graham Kerr. No cucumber is safe."

"Why don't you look into rental cars," Jason told him. "I don't know when we'll be able to come get you. Did I leave you enough money?"

"Yeah, plenty. Will do. Okay, talk to you later."

"Kung Fu Graham Kerr?"

"Damn. Thought I got that one by you."

"You did," Jason said. "I still don't get it."

Robert and Paul were sitting in a half-booth in the back, eating barbecued chicken wings with ranch dressing and celery. As he approached, he heard Paul say, "No, the celery is supposed to be eaten separately."

Robert said, "The experienced chicken wing eater knows otherwise."

Paul said, "Look, they give you ranch dressing so you can eat the wing and then dip the celery in the dressing." He demonstrated by dipping a piece of celery in the dressing and eating it.

Robert presented a wing for Paul's consideration and said, "Observe." He dipped the wing in the dressing, ate the meat off the bone, crunched into a piece of celery, and chewed.

Paul looked at the resulting spot of barbecue sauce in the ranch dressing and said, "That's disgusting."

Jason sat, facing them across the table. "They say they have the dongle. We need to think of a good place for the meeting. It needs privacy and an AC power source. All other factors are up for discussion."

Robert nodded and said, "Let's discuss what could go wrong for us at such a meeting."

"Being overpowered," Jason said. He reached for a wing. Robert and Paul both watched closely.

"Right," Robert said.

Jason picked up a piece of celery, stuck the wing onto it like a Popsicle, and nibbled on the chicken.

"What else," he asked.

Robert said, "Being ambushed."

"Right, being ambushed. What else?"

Paul said, "They could take what they want and not pay."

Jason ate a large spoonful of ranch dressing. Paul looked eager to disavow his association with the proceedings.

"Experts agree," Robert said. "That is not how to eat chicken wings."

"I'm not eating chicken wings," Jason said. "I'm eating ranch dressing and enjoying a chicken-and-celery palate cleanser."

"Oh, yes," Robert verified. "In that case, your etiquette would be correct." He looked sidelong at Paul. "It is also well known that if you were eating celery, no chicken, and ranch dressing on the side, you would do it like this." He set the ranch dressing bowl on his head, wiggled a chicken wing like a cigar, and threw all the remaining celery sticks into the air.

"I'll go wait in the car," Paul said, rising.

Jason said, "I'd rather you didn't."

They looked at each other for a long moment, and then Paul sat back down. Robert took the salad dressing bowl off his head.

"Thank you," Jason said to Paul. "My biggest concern at this point is that if the compression algorithm is a fake, which Benton's web page does seem to indicate, then we have to go on faith that the demonstration will work. Benton must have had a way to make it seem like it was working all along, or Synervision wouldn't still want it. The question is, does Hibbit know how to do it? Robert, you have ranch dressing in your hair."

Robert looked concerned and said, "You *were* done with the celery."

"I wasn't," Paul said.

"No, no," Robert clarified. "I meant"—he nodded as though prompting—"you *were* done with the celery."

Paul just looked at him.

Jason said, "Yes. You are accurate. Unbeknownst to us, we were done with the celery."

Robert got up. "Are we finished eating?"

IN THE PONTIAC again, Jason in the driver's seat, they entered the freeway.

Motor homes dotted the vista ahead like chrysalises. Jason imagined the complete life cycle: The slow growth of subcompact car larva to motor home chrysalis, and the deliberate, agonized emergence of a Boeing 737 unfolding itself damp and unsteady from within the now-useless Winnebago husk.

The Pontiac caught up to the nearest of the damned things and was unable to pass.

In the back seat, Robert repeated, "What else?"

"Oh, so now you're focused," Jason said. "Okay. Ambush, overpower, not pay, demonstration might not work because compression algorithm is fraudulent. I don't see that there's anything we can do about ensuring success at the demonstration. Hibbit was Benton's partner, so he's the only one who'll know how to make the demo look like it's working. We hope."

Robert said, "On the other hand, Benton's web page seemed to indicate that Hibbit was unaware of the fraud."

"Right. So, either Hibbit was in on it and therefore knows how to make it look good, or he wasn't in on it, in which case he might know how to do it or he might not. Which leaves us nowhere and no recourse. I think we have to go on faith that the demo will work. Let's talk about the things we can control."

Robert said, "Paul, do you have any thoughts? Ambush, overpower, not pay."

"Oh," Paul said. "Am I included in this conversation?"

Jason said, "Do you have something to contribute?"

"Well, I don't know. My thoughts on the issue didn't seem welcome."

"They're welcome," Jason said. "What are you thinking?"

"I think you're out of your league."

"Certainly," Jason said, "some of your other thoughts must be even more welcome than that one."

Robert said, "Let's just go with that. Let's assume he's right. How could we compensate for being out of our league?"

"Let's see," Jason said. "What advantages are mentioned in Sun Tzu. . . . I remember there's the advantage of terrain, the advantage of numbers, and the advantage of generalship. Then there's a bunch of stuff about deception. Is that all? We don't have the advantage of numbers and we don't know anything about the other side's generalship. Deception is a given. That leaves terrain."

Robert said, "It's also translated as 'conditions,' which would include both terrain and weather."

"If we're meeting indoors, how does either of those help us?"

"Do we have to meet indoors?"

Paul humphed. "Jeez, where else would you meet, in the park?"

"Not the park," Jason said. "We need working electricity and some privacy, not to mention that it would be bad if it rained. But the thing I like about your idea, Paul, is that it would let us see people coming, unlike in a room or building, which could be surrounded without our knowledge. Even if we tried to compensate by posting sentries, the sentries could be found and overpowered."

Still stuck behind the same Winnebago, Jason pulled slightly left to see ahead and then slipped back behind the motor home as opposing traffic sped by.

"A remote mountaintop," Robert said.

"That would let us see them coming," Jason said, "but unless we want to roll boulders up the mountain so we can then roll boulders down the mountain, I really don't see much of a tactical advantage. And we'd have to carry a generator up for electricity, too, and there's still the question of rain. And we'd have to worry about being shot and left for dead and not being found until a scout troop happened upon our bodies in a ravine while orienteering."

Robert asked, "Is there a merit badge for that?"

"For being shot and left for dead, or for happening upon dead bodies of the stupid?"

"For rolling boulders up and down mountains."

"Hey, you know what we could really use for this? A castle with a moat."

"Right . . ." Robert said. "Or a stone fortress with anti-siege implements."

Paul shook his head. "Oh, brother."

"We are aware, Paul, that the ideas are outlandish," Jason said. "We're getting big and ridiculous so that we can then bring it down in scope and end up with something unexpected and usable."

Paul said, "I dare you to show me how saying, 'We should have a castle with a moat,' could possibly do any good."

Silence hung in the ugly Pontiac like a Christmas-tree-shaped air freshener. Robert's chin was on one fist. He was staring blindly out the window and rocking a little.

Jason eased over in his lane to try to pass again and couldn't. He struck the steering wheel in frustration. "*Damn* these motor homes!"

"Motor homes," Robert sang absently as he rocked and thought. "Mote- mote- motor homes."

Robert suddenly turned away from the window and looked at Jason in the rearview mirror, wide-eyed and startled. Jason knew they were suddenly thinking the same thing.

A wide grin blossomed on Robert's lips. Jason smiled back at him in the rearview mirror.

"Heh, heh, heh," Robert cackled, grinning. "Moat-moat-moat-moat—"

42

The actual rental of the motor home was costly, and neither Jason nor Robert had a credit card. The steep cash deposit depleted most of Jason's remaining funds. The motor home was a clean twenty-two-foot model with a side door, a bed over the cab, a kitchenette, a dinette, and a bathroomette, and it got eight miles to the gallon. An externally mounted gasoline compressor fed by the main gas tank provided alternating current to interior outlets.

Jason specifically requested insurance.

On the freeway, the pavement under and around their meeting room would be moving at a relative velocity of sixty-five miles per hour, isolating them as would a moat around a castle, and discouraging marauding Visigoths. In order to avoid giving the Visigoths time to assemble helicopter and jet-skateboard assault teams, Jason would provide Hibbit only with an initial meeting point. Their subsequent departure from that point in an RV would surprise everyone but the good guys.

Martin was still in Silicon Valley, probably practicing with his butterfly knife and watching out the window.

Two white Tauri pulled into the Manor parking lot and parked without regard for the painted spaces. Four people got out. There was Hibbit, carrying two laptop computers; blond Barry; the gray-haired man from the freeway incident; and another, who looked important and wore blue reflective sunglasses like a skier, but did not carry skies. He was the man pictured at Huey Benton's web site, the CEO of Synervision. He wore a light gray summer suit and was the only one in the group with no sweat rings under the arms.

Jason was squatting next to some dead grass, scratching Waldo the cat behind the ears. He stood as the men approached.

Ian Hibbit said, "This is Mr. Green." Hibbit's gaze flicked around a lot, not settling on anything.

The blue-lensed man nodded slightly and didn't offer his hand. The lenses revealed no evidence of eyeballs.

Jason said, "I am Mr. Keltner."

The eyeless blue reflected back at him and the man said nothing. The rest of the group waited for a cue. The man had a thin face and a good tan and used an expensive-smelling aftershave.

Jason indicated Waldo and said, "This is Mr. Waldo. Mr. Waldo will be acting as cat today."

The head turned slightly so the blue lenses could take in the cat. The lips didn't move and the blind, blue gaze came back to regard Jason.

Ian Hibbit looked from Green to Jason and back. "Is there any reason for further delay?"

Jason shrugged *nope*. As he started around the group of

men, Barry, his blond arch-enemy from the freeway, grabbed his elbow. Barry's hand was warm and moist. His damp, squinting face pushed closer to Jason. "Where do you think you're going?"

Jason said to the blue lenses, "Malibu Ken has my arm."

Barry said, "Why not just shoot him and take the goddamn thing?"

Green regarded Jason.

Jason said to him, "Because the goddamn thing isn't here to take."

Hibbit blinked. "What? Why not? Where is it?"

"Cynical type that I am, I thought you might be tempted to take it before we'd done the demonstration."

"How," Hibbit said, "are we supposed to do a demonstration without the very piece being demonstrated?" He turned to Green. "How?"

Jason said to Green, "Are we doing this or not?"

"Get on with it," Green said.

Jason said, "Malibu Ken has Super Arm Grip Action."

Green flicked a finger and Barry released Jason's arm.

The motor home was idling a block away, with Paul behind the wheel.

"There's room for four in back," Jason said. "Me, Hibbit, Mr. Green, and I assume the guy with the briefcase."

"What is this?" Mr. Green said.

"Privacy and an AC power supply," Jason said. "In full compliance with your specifications."

Green turned to Hibbit.

Hibbit said hurriedly, "Er, this is not acceptable."

"It is to me," Jason said.

Hibbit looked at Green. Nothing was said.

"The device is here?" Hibbit verified.

Jason said, "No."

"Then—"

Jason said, "I'm not screwing you. Why would I, when I can just perform as agreed and get money?" He opened the side door and swept one arm grandly toward it. "After you."

At a tilt of the head from Green, Barry and his partner went in and came back out. "It looks okay," the partner said.

"After you," Jason said. Hibbit, Green, and the briefcase carrier went in. Jason followed.

The motor home's two air conditioners were going, and the coolness was icy to exposed skin. Hibbit sat at the table and nervously began plugging in and configuring the two laptop computers. Jason's eyes met Paul's and they both looked at the laptops. It would be bad if the demonstrations didn't work.

As Jason reached to close the side door, he saw Green give Barry what might have been a meaningful look, so he expected to see a white Taurus behind the motor home at some point.

He closed the door and sat on the twin bed. Paul pulled into traffic.

"The second device," Hibbit said, holding one hand out.

"Are the computers all ready for it?"

"Indeed they are, damn you. The second device."

Hibbit's upper lip was moist. Jason said, "We have a while before the demo starts."

"Give me," Hibbit said tensely, "the device."

"You'll have," Jason said reasonably, "to wait."

Paul glanced meaningfully back at Jason again. Jason raised his eyebrows in subtle agreement. It would be bad if Hibbit didn't know how to fake the compression demonstration.

Barry and his partner followed them in the white Taurus. Jason watched them out the motor home's back window. Out on the 210, heading away from the city and into open spaces, Jason opened the side door and Robert's Pontiac pulled alongside and matched speed at about fifty-five miles per hour. Robert's window was down.

"You're leaking something," Robert yelled. "Under the engine. It's dripping."

Jason shrugged helplessly. There was nothing he could do about it now. He gestured toward himself, and Robert extended out the window an old billiards cue scavenged from the storage under the Manor stairs. The trackball was duct-taped securely to its tip. Jason pulled the cue and trackball into the motor home and shut the door.

He carefully unwrapped the trackball, saving the tape, and handed the device to Hibbit, who attached it to one of the laptop computers. He looked at Green. Green reached into his inside coat pocket and withdrew the dongle.

Jason watched the dongle as Green handed it to Hibbit, and worried about Platt. Hibbit attached it to the other computer and restarted everything.

If the leak were something important and the engine cut off, the advantages of being in a moving motor home would disappear. If Green had someone following them, they'd be easily overpowered. Jason shot a glance at what dashboard gauges he could see from the rear area. Nothing was red. Not yet, anyway.

"Right," Hibbit said. "This will demonstrate the data compression. First, I will show you that there is nothing on the hard disk of computer two except the operating system and the decompression software."

He showed them.

"Now I will show you the uncompressed data which will be compressed during the course of our demonstration." He withdrew a CD-ROM from his coat pocket and displayed it. Its label was hand-lettered; "Devils of Alpha-Six." He inserted it into the first computer. Jason hoped again that he knew what he was doing, that he was aware of Benton's scam and knew how to make it look as though the compression were working.

Robert was not within sight, but Jason knew he was near. They had plans for several contingencies, but mechanical failure of the motor home wasn't one of them. There was no way to contact Robert now and arrange anything. If the engine died and they had to pull off to the side, everyone would just have to improvise. Everyone but the Synervision people—Jason had no doubt that Barry and his partner would know exactly what to do in such a situation.

Hibbit clicked on an icon on laptop number one, and a color movie filled the screen and began to play, with sound. In it, monsters trooped around on a space station and spaceships screamed around planets. A row of white numbers along the bottom counted off minutes and seconds.

Hibbit said, "This is ninety-three minutes of footage." To prove it, he fast-forwarded for a while, and then skipped ahead randomly. Then he clicked, and the movie stopped. He dragged the movie icon onto another icon labeled Compress&send.

Almost instantly, the same footage was playing on laptop number two. Its visual quality was very slightly degraded.

"The compression does create artifacts," Hibbit said. "But it is well within agreed tolerances." His voice was eager and strained. Jason shot another glance at the dashboard. The temperature gauge looked a little high. Then again, they were traveling up a slight incline with the air conditioner going.

Green said, "How do I know it's not playing the footage from the first laptop, just using the second screen?"

"Ah," Hibbit said. "Yes, indeed." He disconnected the cable between the two computers. The movie continued to play on the second screen. Hibbit fast-forwarded to demonstrate that the monsters and spaceships were there in their ninety-three-minute entirety.

Green said, "Maybe I'll just take it and save myself"— he almost smiled—"twenty-five grand."

Jason said, "Or maybe we'll just drive to the police station. Got a full tank here, and a motor home in perfect working order. No reason we couldn't just head right for the LAPD."

The corner of Green's mouth quirked, and he pointed his chin at Briefcase Carrier, who handed the briefcase to Jason. Jason unlatched it, saw a lot of money that he didn't count, closed it, and said, "We're done."

Hibbit shut everything down and disconnected the laptop computers. Jason duct-taped the briefcase to the billiards cue and opened the side door. Robert was alongside in the Pontiac.

"It's still dripping," Robert yelled over the relative wind noise.

Jason gestured helplessness with one hand and extended the billiards cue across the few feet between them, struggling against stiff air resistance. When the briefcase was finally in the Pontiac, Robert waved and peeled off toward an offramp. Barry and his partner didn't follow. Jason leaned forward slightly in the doorway and looked for fluid loss from the front of the motor home, but he couldn't see anything.

Nothing broke as Paul drove the motor home back to the Manor, and the temperature gauge never reached the red. While it idled in the Manor parking lot, Jason looked at the front. A steady drip from the engine compartment fell to the hot asphalt. When everyone was out, Paul backed it out of the parking lot and left Jason and Robert with the Synervision people.

Standing in the parking lot next to a white Taurus, Green considered Jason. "Twenty-five grand," he said. He shook his head and laughed. "Twenty-five measly fucking grand."

Green turned to Barry. "I'm done with him," he said. "I don't care what you do." Green and Briefcase Carrier got into their car.

When they were gone, Barry smiled. "We got unfinished business," he said to Jason, "you and I."

Barry's partner leaned against the Taurus.

"You win," Jason said.

Barry cracked his knuckles and walked toward him. "You don't get out of it that easy."

"I'd really prefer that I do."

"What's the matter," Barry said. "You chicken?"

"Yeah."

"You chicken?"

"Yup."

"You a little baby chicken?"

"Fluffy yellow. I apologize for starting up with you. I don't want to fight you."

Barry's partner didn't seem interested. Right up in front of Jason, Barry said, "Really, why not?"

"My friend Robert says I'm tending to be too violent."

"Aw," Barry said. "Isn't that nice."

"I'm leaving now," Jason said. He turned away.

Barry kidneypunched him and he went down to his knees, shocked at the pain. He tried to move away, toward the corner of the Manor. A boot crashed into his rib cage and he fell on his side. Through a glaze of tears, he saw huge, cheap athletic shoes run around from the corner of the Manor. He squinted up and focused. As Barry went down from the leg sweep, yelling and going for his gun, Robert got hold of his arm and audibly dislocated his shoulder. Barry yelled louder, and the gun clunked onto the asphalt. Barry's partner leaned against the trunk and scratched his side.

Robert said to Jason, "When I said I was concerned, I didn't mean—"

"Gun," Jason gasped. Barry went for it. Robert kicked him in the jaw and picked up the gun.

Jason groaned and held his side.

Robert hoisted Barry up and turned him to face Jason. Barry winced and glared resentfully down at him. The partner belched.

Jason got up slowly. He didn't straighten up all the way. As he walked unsteadily toward Barry, he removed one of his earrings.

He stopped in front of Barry. Barry was red and breathing hard.

"You beat me," Jason said. He slipped the earring into Barry's shirt pocket. "You can show them the evidence." He looked at what Robert had done to Barry's face. "I got a few real good punches in, caught you off guard, but you really beat the shit out of me, and then when I was down, you ripped my earring out of my ear." He glanced at Barry's partner, who shrugged as though that was okay with him. "Do you really see any reason to come back here?"

Barry shook his head.

"Good," Jason said. "Because you really do win. If you did come back here, you'd hurt me bad. I understand that. You're tougher than I am, and I just don't want to get beat up again."

Barry nodded, his fire confused out of him.

"Thank you for understanding," Jason said.

Robert put both hands around Barry's shoulder. Before Barry realized what was happening, Robert had snapped the shoulder back in place, and then he caught Barry as his knees buckled. Then he let him go. Barry and his partner got into their car and went away.

43

Robert brought the Pontiac to the curb outside the motor home rental place. Paul climbed into the back.

"I wonder what that leak was," Robert said.

Paul said, "That drip that Jason was looking at? That's just condensed water from the air conditioner. They all do that." He handed Jason a check. "Here's your deposit back. They don't give it back in cash. Not that I don't trust you or anything, but I'll take my cut now."

"It was?" Robert said. "They do? The air conditioner?"

"Hello?" Paul said. "We've got money to talk about here."

Jason slid the check into his pocket. The briefcase was on the passenger-side floorboard. Trying not to hurt his side, he tossed it one-armed back toward Paul without looking.

"Ouch!" Paul yelped. "Hey, what's the—"

"Twenty-five thousand dollars," Jason said. "A one-hundred-percent cut. You can return the fifteen grand you got from John Tennant and the ten grand you got from Ian Hibbit. If you're lucky, which you are, and a slick talker, which you are, you can be free and clear with everybody but me."

Paul looked suspicious.

"Or you can think you're smarter than everyone else, which you do, and keep it, which you probably will. Either way, it's yours. I just gave you back the full value of my interference in your business. We're even."

Paul still looked suspicious. "Robert, you heard him, right? You're my witness. I get all of it."

"Oh, sorry, what was that?" Robert said after a moment. "I didn't hear you—I was musing on the nature of greed."

Paul opened the briefcase and counted the bills. When he was done, he closed it and put it on the seat next to him.

"Hey, Paul?" Jason said.

"What?"

"How'd Huey Benton really die?"

"Like I know? Hey, like you said, I was just there to get the dongle from him. You think I killed him?"

Jason turned around in his seat to look at Paul. Paul's face was expressionless.

Jason tapped the seatback idly. "I assume you will be moving out of the Manor."

Paul said, "Why would—"

"I assume," Jason said, "you will be moving out of the Manor."

Slowly, Paul said, "I might do that."

"Good. You satisfied I've paid you what you're owed?"

"Yeah."

Jason nodded. He got out of the car and stood on the sidewalk, holding the door.

Paul glanced at Robert and then at Jason. "What the fuck is wrong with you?"

"Paul," Robert said, "please get out of my car."

"Man, what's eating you? This is between Jason and me."

"Paul," Robert said, "please, I'd really appreciate it."

"Well," Paul said shortly, "since you asked nicely." He squeezed out of the back with his briefcase and stood facing Jason.

Jason looked back at him.

Paul stood there for a few seconds and then gave a humorless little "huh," and turned and started walking. Jason watched him go. When Paul was half a block away, Jason got back in the car.

"So now what?" Robert said, pulling into traffic.

"Now Paul might throw a tantrum and damage some of my things back at the Manor, but I don't care. You know what I really want?"

"What."

"Half a fried chicken with onions and gravy, a stack of waffles with butter and maple syrup, some iced tea with lemonade in it, sweet potato pie, and a cup of coffee."

" 'Scoe's it is."

"First I have to call Martin and tell him to come on back down as soon as he sees the Synervision cars return. He should have a rental car. Then after we eat I want to get my own car back from where we parked it. Ow." His bruised side twinged. "After that we're done, aren't we."

"Almost. As soon as Martin's back."

"I'm not worried about Martin." Jason's fingers explored his side. "I'm worried about Platt."

PAUL'S CAR WASN'T there when they got back to the Manor two hours later. Jason went in and checked his e-mail.

```
You have 1 new mail message.


From: METAMUSIC
To: NOTE ON
Subj: . . . that ends well


All is well. Verify that you can debrief
tomorrow 1400 hrs at your place.


N
_*_
```

Jason replied with one word: VERIFIED. He went upstairs and told Robert.

Full and exhausted in his own dark apartment, with his own car parked outside and everything wrapped up, Jason eased himself down onto his futon and fell deeply asleep.

44

He wasn't sure why or how long he'd been talking on the phone.

"Wait," he repeated, "what?"

Martin's voice said, "Jason!"

"What."

"Jason!"

"What."

"Jason, stand up and walk around. You're asleep."

"Get up, stand up," he sang.

"Are you standing?"

"Da-*dump*-dump-da-*dump*. Great bassline."

"Jason!"

Careless of his hurt left side, Jason sat up against the wall and hurt himself. His clock radio said 3:36 A.M.

"It's three-thirty-six A.M.," he said, massaging his side.

"You don't say!"

"What do you want?"

"Are you awake, or do I have to piss you off some more?" Loud pushbutton tones issued from the earpiece as Martin pressed random buttons. Jason yanked it away from his ear.

"I'm awake," he insisted. Pushbutton tones reverberated weakly in the bedroom.

The tones stopped. Jason put the phone back against his ear.

Martin said, "You awake now?"

"I'm awake, I'm awake. I'm awake. What do you want?"

"You need to get out of there."

"Why?"

"The dongle doesn't work."

"Yes, it does. You weren't there. You're falling behind the times."

"Jason, listen to me carefully. You listening?"

"Yeah."

"Okay, listen, then: It. Does. Not. Work."

"What do you mean?"

"I got it on my scanner radio. I overheard a conversation between Hibbit and some other dude named Green. You are in some deep shit."

Jason let his head fall onto his knees.

"What was the conversation?"

"All the Tauruses came back. Then a little while later I heard this conversation between Green and Hibbit. Green said the Synervision programmers said the dongle was a fake, and Hibbit was totally shocked. First he said Green must be mistaken, and then when that didn't fly, he said you and Paul must have switched it for the real one. The white Tauruses all piled back out of the driveway pretty soon after. That was maybe two hours ago. I'm behind them in the rental car, but I pulled off to call you from this pay phone. I gotta get back to it before I lose them for good."

"Aw, man . . ." Jason closed his eyes and let the back of his head thump against the wall. His brain swam in fatigue toxins. "Where's Hibbit?"

"I don't have the slightest idea, but I figure he wasn't at Synervision or they wouldn't have had this conversation on the phone."

Jason opened his eyes. "Okay, I'll roust Robert."

"You retaining all this? I gotta go."

"I'm retaining. How should we stay in contact if I'm not here and you're using pay phones?"

"I dunno, chief, but I gotta jam."

"Bye."

Jason hung up and let his head fall onto his knees. Sleep was a gorgeous word. He slipped momentarily back into it. As he slumped, his bruised side caught and made him gasp, and he got up.

HE DIDN'T KNOW what else to do, so he and Robert got into their two cars and ended up at a Denny's a few minutes from the Bay City fishing pier. Jason figured the Synervision people wouldn't know to look there.

They sat where they could see their cars and waited for their food. Jason bought a newspaper from a vending machine outside. They stared at it glassily over coffee and didn't eat their pancakes. Jason's left side throbbed.

Robert looked up from the sports section. "What is a field goal?" His eyes were half-lidded and pouchy. His chess set sat, closed, on the table.

Jason said, "When the goalie gets a rebound and takes the puck off the field."

Robert nodded dully. Jason put his head down on his arms and closed his eyes, but his eyes wouldn't stay still under their lids. It wasn't restful.

Robert said, "No it's not. Is it?"

"No what's not; is what?"

"A field goal."

With his head still down, Jason shrugged.

Robert crumpled the sports section, put it on the seat next to him, and said, "Hmm."

When he didn't elaborate, Jason said, "What."

"Hmm."

Jason peered up. "Stop saying 'hmm' and tell me what."

"Hmm. I was just thinking about the fact that the leak in the motor home was normal condensation from the air conditioner. Don't you think it illustrates our pathetic stations in life? We don't even have enough money to know how normal air conditioning behaves. Don't you find that depressing?"

"No. What I find depressing isn't that I'm giving up a station in life for art. It's that I'm giving up the station and then not getting the art done."

"We need to make more money," Robert decided. He rooted through the newspaper for the business section, and his forehead creased in concentration as he read the first thing that hit his retinas.

"What is Triple Net?" he asked.

"If you're a fish who travels a lot, you get Triple Net in case you break down."

Robert eyed him squarely and said, "I do not believe you."

"Look, I'm too tired. I'd like to improve my station in life too, but I don't know what Triple Net is."

"I'm too tired too." Robert's face drew into focus and

became thoughtful and almost awake. "How do we know the e-mail is really from Platt?"

"It said so."

"Is that totally reliable?"

"No."

"Is there any way to verify it?"

"Not one I know."

Robert sat pensively. Then he said, "What if the message is not from Platt, and it was a trap?"

"A trap for what? We don't have the dongle, we don't have the trackb—"

"Yes, but thanks to Hibbit, Synervision thinks we do."

This trickled like clear water through Jason's sleep deprivation several times before it finally snagged and made sense.

"Aw . . ." He let his head fall back onto the flat top of the booth.

"And if it wasn't from Platt, then who was it from?"

"Not Synervision, because it was sent before they had any reason to trap us."

"That leaves Hibbit and Tennant."

"Not Hibbit, because he knows we don't have anything he wants."

"That leaves Tennant."

Jason nodded.

"Could what was on your wiped hard drive have given Tennant enough information to fake an e-mail to you?"

Jason thought about it. He put his head down again. "Maybe."

"So," Robert said, "either Hibbit knew it was a fake and knew how to make the demo look right, or he didn't know it was a fake and he just parroted what he'd seen Benton do, and it worked at the demo."

Jason said, "He parroted."

Robert said, "I can't understand you when you talk into the table."

Jason raised his head. "He parroted. If he'd known it was a fake, he wouldn't have stuck around and had the phone conversation with Synervision. He wouldn't have waited for them to find out they'd been scammed; he'd have beat feet out of Sparta. Martin said he sounded shocked that it was a fake. I bet he genuinely was. Now that Synervision's discovered the scam, Hibbit's got himself off the hook by im—imp—impl—shoot, what is it, means 'make to look involved,' shares a root word with 'imply,' four syllables with the accent on the first syllable—"

"Implicating."

"Right, implicating us. By saying that we must have somehow switched the dongle for one that didn't work. What do you want to bet that Hibbit's on the way out of the country while Synervision comes after us?"

"Some," Robert said after brief reflection, "might not envy us."

"I thought we could just give everything back. Paul would have another chance at redemption without doing anything to earn it, and there'd be no reason for anyone to bother us." Jason put his head down and bumped his forehead softly and rhythmically on the table. Robert's chess set rattled a little. Jason turned his head sideways to look at it.

"We should have predicted this," he said. "It is incredibly stupid that I did not predict this."

"Check," Robert reminded him, "is not mate."

Jason glanced up at Robert. "Won even a single game yet?"

"That is totally not relevant."

"I don't like waiting." Jason stared at the brown, fake woodgrain an inch and a half in front of his face.

"Then let's not."

"But I don't have a plan."

"Okay," Robert said. He got up, put a ten-dollar bill on the table, and started walking away.

"Where are you going?"

"You tell me."

"Tell you what?"

"Where I'm going."

"I don't know."

"Then make something up."

"You are a very annoying person," Jason said.

"Better men than you have called me annoying."

Jason sighed. "The bad guys are southbound. They left two hours before Martin called me, and it's been another hour since then. They're at least two hours away. If we head north, we'll meet up with them in about an hour."

"Well," Robert said smarmily. "It looks like you had a plan after all."

45

They went north on the 101 in two cars, drinking lukewarm coffee in to-go cups. The plan was to intersect the path of the Synervision Tauruses. That was the whole plan. There was no more plan. That was it.

After a while, Jason got into the exit lane with Robert behind him in the Pontiac and exited the freeway. At the bottom of the offramp, he motioned for Robert to come alongside. A pleasantly warm breeze blew in when he rolled the window down.

He yelled to Robert, "The freeway divides. We won't be able to see oncoming traffic. Let's go find a turnoff or rest stop on the southbound side where we can see them coming."

Robert nodded. They got back on the freeway, heading south.

———

EARLY MORNING TRAFFIC was steady and fast past the mouth of the turnoff. The cars that had been driving the longest still had headlights on. Although it would have been more efficient to sit in their cars and be able to tear after the Tauri at the first sign of them, Jason and Robert were leaning against the Plymouth's hood. Jason was moving his torso around, trying to make his stiff left side more pliant. It hurt when he moved, but it also felt better.

"How do you feel?" Robert asked.

"Like I got punched and kicked."

Robert nodded. "You won," he said.

"So," Jason said, without looking away from traffic. "Last we left your great-grandfather, he had used all his money to buy a train ticket to Chicago."

"Oh, right," Robert said. "Uh . . . okay." He stared at the ground for a few seconds to get back into the story. "Right. So: rug store, Harry got cleaned out, found out who did it. So:

"HARRY TAKES THE train to Chicago, and when he gets there, he gets directions to the address the mayor gave him and he walks to the headquarters of this gang, because he spent most of his money on the train and he can't afford to take a cab and still have a hotel room for the night.

"I don't know if he talked his way past a beautiful but hard-bitten receptionist, or maybe he blustered through a bunch of pug-uglies in fedoras and striped suits picking their fingernails with knives. The details in the family story here are nonexistent. But I doubt that he just walked in and the kingpin's sitting there behind a sign that says, 'The Kingpin Is In.'

"Whatever it was, he got in. So there he is in a room

with the mob boss and probably a few of his goons. Maybe they're shooting a little pool with their jackets off.

" 'Who the hell are you,' the mob boss says.

" 'I'm Harry Goldstein. You knocked over my rug store in St. Paul.'

" 'Rug store'? The mob boss looks at his goons for comic support, and they laugh with him. 'I don't know what you're talking about. I'm a businessman.' "

Jason said, "Your mob dialogue is a little stale."

"It's six in the morning. You can have a story with stale dialogue or you can wait until I feel like telling it better."

"Go ahead."

"Where was I?"

" 'I'm a businessman.' "

"Right. So Harry says, 'Well, I'm a businessman too, and you knocked over my business. It wasn't insured. I've got a wife and kids, and you've ruined me, and the police aren't going to do anything about it because you've got them greased.'

" 'So what do you want me to do about this?' says the mob boss. 'Even if I knew something about this, which I don't, what do you want from me?'

" 'I want you should give me my merchandise back.'

" 'That, I cannot do. Even if I did know anything about what you're talking about, the merchandise would be long gone by now. You came all this way for nothing.'

" 'You ruined me, you dirty so-and-so. I've got a wife and kids, and they're going to be out on the street in a week. Now, what are you going to do about it?'

"The boss's goons get attentive. The boss puts down his pool cue. 'You trying to push me around in my own place of business?'

"Harry says, 'Mr. Big Time Gangster comes into my place of business, steals my merchandise, ruining me, and gets his nose out of joint over a little push?'

"There's silence in the place, except for the clock over the pool cue rack. The goons have their eyes on the boss, the boss has his eyes on Harry.

"This frozen moment stretches and stretches. Then the boss reaches into his vest pocket. 'You want to know what I will do for you? This. This is what I will do for you.' There's a long pause, and then he pulls out a business card and hands it to Harry.

" 'When somebody comes into your place and gives you a card like this,' he says, 'you add a couple of zeroes onto the price until you make up the loss. Capiche?'

" 'I got it,' Harry says. He nods at the goons and turns to go.

" 'What,' the mob boss says, looking around the room. 'I get no thanks for this? You give me no thanks for this?'

"Harry turns around. 'For returning what you stole from me, I should thank you?'

" 'I didn't have to do this, Harry Goldstein,' the boss says.

"Harry looks at him for a minute. 'For giving back to me what you took, I won't thank you,' he says. 'But shake your hand, that I'll do.'

"So he shakes the boss's hand and the goons all relax mostly, and he catches the train back to St. Paul. All the next month, people come in with business cards and buy thousand-dollar rugs."

Robert stopped talking.

Jason let the silence hang until he was sure the story was over and then said, "What's the point of this story?"

"It didn't have a point. It's just a family story. You asked for a true story about someone I knew who had done something unusual. There it is. It was the truth. You want a story with a point, you have to give me time to make something up."

Jason nodded and let the story sink in. Traffic blew by.

"If they cleaned out all Harry's merchandise," he said, "where'd he get the rugs that the people bought for a thousand dollars?"

Robert's mouth opened to speak and then closed. He said, "I never thought of that."

"Oh." Jason watched traffic. "What do you think Paul's up to?"

Robert thought for a while. "I don't know. I don't think I see him fleeing the country, but I also can't imagine him returning the money to Hibbit and Tennant and trying to clear his karma."

"Yeah."

"What are we going to do when we see the Tauruses?"

"We can either make our presence known or try to follow them without being seen." Jason pulled a quarter from his pocket and flipped it, slapping it onto his arm. "Heads we're sneaky; tails we're us. Call it."

"Heads."

He uncovered it. "Tails."

They leaned against the Plymouth's hood and Jason thought about the Harry Goldstein story, trying to fit it with a moral. In half an hour, three white Tauruses sped by.

46

few miles from the rest stop, the Pontiac rear-ended the rearmost Taurus. They had planned to coordinate their efforts, but the Plymouth's old slant-six engine couldn't keep up with any of the other cars on an upgrade. Jason was a good quarter-mile back and losing ground with the accelerator floored.

Two more Tauruses passed him on both sides. Three-quarters of a mile ahead, the first group of three Tauruses converged on the Pontiac and began to force it to the right. The Pontiac swerved and banged against them, but the general movement was toward the shoulder.

"Brake!" Jason shouted at Robert. At the same instant, the rearmost Taurus jolted as its brake lights came on, and the Pontiac lunged left. But the bracket re-formed in only a few seconds and again forced the Pontiac to the right. The two other Tauruses caught up to the forward three, and all five eased the Pontiac onto the shoulder, white sheep herding an ugly green dog.

The whole caravan came to a stop. The doors of the Tauruses flew open, and men spilled out.

Three nondescript brown sedans with government "E" plates and two marked California Highway Patrol units sped past Jason and closed on the Tauruses. The Plymouth strained to maintain forty miles per hour on the upgrade as the sedans reached the cluster of cars and stopped sharply. Men in uniforms and three-piece suits flung open car doors and crouched behind them with weapons drawn. All the Synervision people's hands went up.

As Jason drew near, he saw Robert, out of the Pontiac with his hands on the roof.

Unsure whether to stop, he slowed. His gaze locked with someone who looked familiar, a man with brown hair. The man stared at him and started for one of the brown sedans.

He punched the gas, and the Plymouth accelerated slowly from thirty-two to thirty-four miles per hour. The brown sedan swung out into his lane and began to close, and he placed the face. Tennant, without the beard.

Without a plan, knowing he couldn't beat the sedan to the next exit, he steered the Plymouth off the freeway and halfway down an embankment planted with straw-colored dead grass, bringing it to a sliding, nose-down stop in neutral.

He yanked the emergency brake handle up and shoved the driver's door open. Tennant was coming down the embankment, out of his sedan, in a fast scuffle of dust and dead grass. There was nowhere to take cover. With self-preservation ruled out, Jason took a few running steps back toward Robert.

Tennant said, "Freeze," and Jason did. He looked back.

Tennant was behind the Plymouth, aiming Jeffrey's huge patchwork handgun at him.

"Hand it over," Tennant said. "Right now."

"I don't—" Jason said, and stopped to get his voice under control. "It isn't—"

"Shut up," Tennant said. "I want it now."

Jason looked helplessly at him, and the ugly green Pontiac caromed over the edge of the freeway and bounced down toward Tennant in a clanking halo of dirt and dead grass bits. Tennant froze. The Pontiac crashed to a stop only a couple of feet from him, throwing gritty dust over Tennant and Jason. The big engine revved loudly, and Robert's head came out the window and yelled, "Throw it down or I will run you over."

Tennant aimed the ugly handgun at Robert.

"Throw the gun down," Robert insisted. He revved the engine again.

"Get out," Tennant yelled.

The Pontiac engine revved again. Then it choked and died.

In the silence, Tennant aimed the pistol more decisively at Robert's head. "Get out now!"

Jason could hear Robert setting the Pontiac's emergency brake. Then the door opened and Robert got out.

"Over there with your friend," Tennant said. Robert started toward Jason. Tennant kept the gun on him.

"Hand it over," Tennant said to Jason.

"It doesn't work," Jason said. "Benton was scamming Synervision. Hibbit didn't know. Synervision has it. I don't have it." He was babbling. He shut up.

Tennant said, "Bullshit," and raised the gun.

At a loss, Jason said, "I want my cigarette lighter back."

Martin came over the edge of the embankment at a

dead run. Jason and Robert both looked up, and Tennant turned. Jason tensed and formed a vague plan that had something to do with running toward Tennant and attacking him.

Tennant aimed the gun at Martin and fired an instant after Martin leaped off the plane of the embankment feet-first and connected solidly with the back of the Pontiac.

Martin fell to the ground behind the Pontiac, and something went *ping!* very loudly as the Pontiac's emergency brake failed.

Its full weight fell against Tennant, pinning him against the bumperless back of the Plymouth.

"Martin!" Jason yelled. Tennant teetered and the gun whirled toward Jason.

"John!"

Jason looked up the embankment, where Norton Platt had appeared.

Tennant whirled back around to bring the gun to bear on Platt, but the Pontiac shuddered as a solid thump sounded from behind it. Martin was kicking the back of the Pontiac. Tennant grimaced and yelled, losing his balance as the two cars slid a few inches down on the dry dirt and dead grass. Martin's eyes peeked over the trunk of the Pontiac.

As Tennant regained his balance and aimed through the Pontiac windshield at Martin, and as Martin began to duck behind the Pontiac, and as Platt stepped off the pavement and onto the embankment, something groaned under the Plymouth and then went *ping!* and its emergency brake failed. It was a major third higher than the Pontiac brake failure, Jason noticed vaguely, do-mi. The Plymouth began to roll away from Tennant, and Tennant became the only thing holding up the Pontiac. He flailed for balance, the ugly gun fired, and Robert spun and went down. The Plymouth, Tennant, and the Pontiac crashed clumsily down the embankment to the ditch at its bottom.

Martin and Jason scrambled through the kicked-up dust toward Robert, and Platt took the embankment in a few plunging strides. At the bottom, he bent between the Pontiac and the Plymouth. He pulled handcuffs from a back pocket and then put them away again.

Swofford's face appeared at the edge of the freeway.

"Dispatch an ambulance," Platt yelled up at him.

Swofford nodded and pointed down the highway. He stepped off the pavement onto the crest of the embankment, looking only at the dusty wreck at the bottom.

Robert sat up and brushed himself off.

"Lie back," Martin told him angrily.

"I'm okay. He didn't hit me. I fell down dead so he wouldn't want to shoot again. Did the spin-around look real? I took stage combat last year."

Martin stared at him, livid.

"I'm glad you're not dead," Jason said.

"Thank you," Robert said. "So am I."

"I'm glad you're not dead," Jason called down to Platt.

Platt glanced up at him and then knelt and spoke to Tennant. He was too far for Jason to hear what he said, but Jason's impression was of comfort and bedside manner.

47

Martin drove Jason and Robert in a blue rental Escort. They were following a white Taurus again, but Platt was driving it.

Nobody talked in the Escort until Jason said, "So?"

Martin said, "Platt was in Santa Clara all along, at that same motel."

"You're kidding."

"No, man. It's the only place to stake out Synervision from."

"Why didn't you tell me?"

"Platt told me not to. He knew Swofford had your phone tapped, and Swofford trusted Tennant, so anything we said could get back to Tennant. We didn't want him to know where Platt was."

"Okay."

"He was also worried that Paul was with us. That's why he didn't show his face when we were there. First he was waiting until he knew what we were doing. Then after you two dropped me off to start watching Synervision, I went up to my room and he was sitting there. Nearly scared me to death. I told him what we were up to, and he figured that for anything to move toward a conclusion, he'd have to put the dongle back in action."

Jason said, "Do you know how the scam worked?"

"Platt showed me. After he cleaned up the melted glob on the circuit board, there was a little thing under there. He called it a storage device, kind of like a hard disk. It had the movie on it."

"So all the dongle did was contain the movie. It was stored in the dongle, ready to play on any system that also had the CD and the trackball attached."

"Yeah."

"You said Platt decided to put the dongle back in action. How'd he do that?"

"Actually," Martin said modestly, "that part was my idea. He called up Synervision, said he was from Light Wizards, and that Huey Benton had left a little device there last time he was in. He said he'd already messengered it up to them and wanted to let them know to expect it. We packaged up the dongle and I went in as the messenger when Hibbit wasn't around to recognize me."

"So then you heard the conversation on the scanner radio—"

"No, man, you know I don't have a scanner radio. I was hoping that would tip you off that there was more going on than I was saying, but you were too out of it to catch on. I couldn't tell you Platt was alive because Swofford had your line tapped. In the meantime, Platt had *their* line tapped. That's what he was doing at the motel, watching and listening. First he blew up his van so both sides would think the other got him, and then he settled in and just waited. I dunno about you, but I think that's pretty slick. When we saw the Tauruses piling out of the driveway to come and get you, he called the FBI guys he was working with and said everything was about to come to a head. Then we took off after them. Now here we are."

"Here we are," Jason said. "Robert, how'd you show up so suddenly? Last I saw you, you had your hands on top of the Pontiac surrounded by a lot of law enforcement types."

"I saw Tennant take off after you. I looked around and saw Platt. He saw what was up and told the law enforcement types to let me go, so I got right in my car and went after you."

"Thanks."

"You're welcome."

After a while, Robert said, "Martin, while you were at the hotel together, did Platt tell you who Tennant is?"

"No." Martin shook his head. "But I got a feeling they know each other. Maybe even tight."

THE HOSPITAL LOOKED and smelled like a hospital, and the waiting room was no better. They sat on orange-cushioned seats with Platt, Swofford, and Leslie Bookman, leafing half-heartedly through magazines. Jason thought about the Harry Goldstein story.

When the doctor came out and told them Tennant had died, Platt nodded and thanked her. Swofford touched his shoulder. Platt looked at Swofford, raised his eyebrows briefly, and left. Leslie Bookman went with him. Jason didn't have anything to say, so he didn't say anything.

Swofford looked at Jason for a long time. Jason

pretended not to notice, but when the gaze wore on, he looked up and said, "If you're not going to say anything, stare at someone else."

Swofford looked mostly tired. "Norton says you're a lot like me, but I don't see it." He looked at his hands. "I should explain."

"Yeah," Jason said.

"Platt, Bookman, Tennant, and I were working with the FBI CCS—"

"CCS," Martin interrupted.

"Computer Crime Squad."

Jason said, "You were after Hibbit and Benton for scamming Synervision."

"No. We were after Synervision. We didn't know there was anything going on with Hibbit and Benton when we first got involved."

"After Synervision? For what?"

"Are you familiar with public-key encryption?"

"Yes."

Robert and Martin shook their heads.

Swofford said, "Short version: It's what keeps your ATM cards and larger bank transactions secure. Synervision was working on cracking public-key encryption."

"Did they?"

"No."

Robert said, "So the computer games were fakes?"

"Synervision made games. They just never finished them or shipped them. The games were a front for their need for phenomenal data compression."

"Why'd they need that?"

"I just told you. For cracking DES. You want the techie stuff, here it is: They were attempting a brute-force approach using time-memory trade-off attacks and pre-calcing the key space."

"Right," Robert nodded sagely. "Sure, you could pre-key the timespace thingy."

Jason said, "So did it work?"

"Not without the data compression. Probably not with it."

"But the data compression—"

"—didn't exist. We didn't know that."

"And Platt worked at Light Wizards because—?"

"It was worth a stab. Bookman, Tennant, and I were doing more conventional surveillance. Norton thought he might have a shot at alternate infiltration through the company that provided the visuals for the games, because they had to work closely with the data compression people."

"He hired me to watch Paul because he found out Paul was involved with Hibbit."

"Yes. And then after we lost you, we picked up Paul's trail." Swofford shook his head almost imperceptibly. "I didn't know John had his own reasons for keeping after Paul."

"How come Platt had to disappear? How come he couldn't just tell you?"

Swofford didn't answer.

"Carl?"

"Maybe I wouldn't have believed him."

After a long silence, Robert said, "That's understandable."

Jason said, "How'd Huey Benton really die?"

"He got drunk, fell down, and received a fatal blow to the head."

"So Paul didn't kill him."

"No."

"And neither did Hibbit."

"No."

"Do you know if Hibbit's been found?"

"No."

"So nobody dunnit, and the mysterious item is worthless."

Swofford nodded.

"Some mystery. Who's Tennant?"

Swofford cleared his throat. Silence drew out. Finally, he said, "Norton turned out all right. I thought John did too."

Robert said, "He meant something to you."

Swofford sat, and nobody spoke for a while.

Jason said, "He wore a false beard in case his description ever got back to Platt."

Swofford nodded. Finally, he stood. "Norton turned out all right," he said. "There will be a post-game wrap-up soon. Norton will let you know when."

He left.

Jason said, "Why would Tennant go to the trouble of disguising himself with a false beard and then use a unique old car that could be so easily identified?"

Robert said, "Maybe he didn't expect to have to come to Paul's rescue on the spur of the moment, and that was the only car he had available."

"I think it was what Tolstoy said," Martin said.

"You mean everybody wants to confess?" Robert said. "That's Dostoevsky."

"Whoever," Martin said. He stood. "I don't know about you guys, but I really want to go home."

48

I t was late afternoon when they parked behind the Manor. They sat in Martin's blue rental Escort.

"Well," Jason said.

Martin said, "We should eat."

"Okay."

Warm light slanted through the trees along Marengo. They walked to Old Town without talking and got Mexican food and icy margaritas on the rocks. The evening walk back was dull and very pleasant.

At the Manor's front door, Martin said, "You want to come up for a while? I'll make Ibarra."

Jason said, "Sure."

They hung out in the Manor's main kitchen while Martin made an almond and a cinnamon flavored Mexican cocoa. Patrice from the attic apartment came down to check her mail and took a cup back up with her. Soon

Chuck from upstairs and Tony from the room next to Jason's came in and said they'd heard there was hot chocolate. Martin handed out mugs and made more.

They went upstairs. Martin and Robert lay on top of the covers on their beds. Jason sat on the floor against the wall with his legs under the wobbly card table. They sipped from their mugs and fell asleep.

49

The floor was uncomfortable and the pretty rock was jabbing his chest, but that hadn't been what woke him. He heard his door squeak closed downstairs.

Robert and Martin were asleep in their clothes on their beds. Jason touched Robert's shoulder.

Robert moved. Jason touched his shoulder again and said, "Hey. Robert."

Robert's eyes opened and he looked at Jason. "Yes," he said clearly.

"Wake up. Someone's down in my apartment."

"The blue one, did you have the golf hat, the hat?"

"There is no golf hat. You're dreaming."

"I am? Hold on. Hello." Robert shook his head. "Hello. Hello. All right, I don't think I'm dreaming anymore."

"Someone's in my apartment." Jason went over to

Martin's bed and shook him a little. Martin continued to breathe heavily.

"Martin," he whispered.

"That doesn't work," Robert said. He got up and turned the light on. Immediately, Martin snuffled and put the inside of his elbow up over his eyes.

"Martin," Robert said in a normal voice.

"What."

"We have a problem. We need you to wake up."

"No."

"Martin."

"What."

"We have a problem. We need you to wake up."

"No."

"Martin," Jason said.

"No."

"Someone's downstairs in my apartment."

Martin peered out from under his elbow. "Who?"

"I don't know. I just head them go in."

"Call the cops."

"Yeah, but we can't use the phone in my apartment. We have to walk to the gas station."

It was impossible to get downstairs quietly, so they just clomped outside as quickly as they could. No light issued from between Jason's miniblinds.

It was a five-minute walk to the gas station. The heat wave had finally broken. It was cool out. "Hey," Martin said as they approached the pay phone. He pointed.

A small beige Toyota hatchback was parked catercorner from the gas station.

"That's Paul's car," Robert said.

They looked at each other. Then they turned around

and walked back to the Manor. They stood on the porch and Jason knocked on his own front door.

"Paul?" he called softly.

There was motion in the front room.

"Paul?"

Paul's voice came through the window. "Yeah."

"What are you doing in there?"

"Waiting for you."

"Is it safe for me to come in?"

"Yeah." Then in a new tone, "Yeah. What do you think I'm gonna do, shoot you?"

Jason opened the door and went into his front room. The light was off. Paul was sitting on his couch.

"Hello," Jason said.

"Hello."

Robert and Martin came into the room behind Jason.

"So," Jason said. "What's up?"

Paul said, "I came back."

"I see that."

Robert said, "How come?"

Jason said, "How come you came back?"

"I don't know."

"Did you spend the money?"

Paul jerked his head to indicate the briefcase leaning against one end of the couch.

Jason moved into the room, and Robert and Martin came in behind him. "Why'd you come here?"

"I don't know."

"Is there something you want from me?"

"I don't know."

"Is there something you needed?"

"I don't know."

Robert said, "Is there something you want to tell us?"

Paul said nothing.

Jason said, "What is it you want to tell us?"

There was no answer. Jason sat down on the piano bench. Robert sat on the floor, and Martin leaned in the short book-shelved passageway that went to the pseudo-kitchen. They waited.

"I killed that dead guy," Paul said.

Martin said, "Which dead guy, Benton or Tennant?"

Paul looked up in shock. "Tennant's dead?"

Jason said, "Are you saying you killed Huey Benton?"

"Yeah. I killed him."

Jason glanced at Robert and Martin. They both looked confused.

"Paul," he said. "How did you kill Huey Benton?"

"You remember on the news a few years ago, how people died from drinking coolant?"

Robert said, "You're talking about the wineries that extended their wine by adding coolant to it?"

"Yeah."

Jason said, "That's how you killed Benton?"

"Yeah." Paul interlocked his fingers in his lap. They trembled slightly.

"You put coolant in his booze?"

"Yeah. He was drinking this green, sweet stuff. I thought it would hide the taste and the color."

"You used the coolant from my trunk."

"Yeah."

"You went out and got it while I was in the men's room when we first got to the party."

"Yeah. I poured it into a half-empty bottle from the party and hid it under my jacket."

Jason shuddered. "Just before he fell down, he said,

'Steal my fucking drink, would you.' That's because he couldn't find the bottle while you were out tampering with it."

Paul shrugged.

"Did you come back here to turn yourself in?"

"I don't know."

Everyone sat silently. The couch creaked.

"Who wiped the data off my laptop when I was in Death Valley?"

Paul said, "Eve Something. I don't know what name she told you."

"Who hired her?"

"Tennant. He knew you were out there somewhere—"

"—because Swofford knew, because he had the Manor phone tapped," Robert said.

"I don't know anyone named Swofford," Paul said. "I told Tennant a girl would probably work on you."

Jason said, "That's how Tennant had my e-mail address, to send me the fake message from Platt."

Paul said, "I don't know."

"I need to make a call," Jason said. The pretty rock bumped against his chest when he got up. He gave Robert and Martin a subtle head shake so they wouldn't tell Paul anything and went into his bedroom. He dropped the rock in the bathroom trash on his way.

Platt sounded exhausted on the phone.

"I'm sorry to call," Jason said. "Something's just happened that I don't understand."

"I know the feeling," Platt said. "What is it?"

Jason told him.

"I see."

"We haven't told him anything to contradict his account."

Platt sighed. "I'll be out."

"Thanks."

On his way through the bathroom, he picked the rock out of the trash and went outside to drop it in the orange Dumpster at the far end of the parking lot. Halfway across the lot, he got impatient and winged it viciously at the Dumpster. It banged the metal hard and he turned back toward the house as it was still skittering on the pavement.

PLATT SET UP a video camera and Paul confessed to killing Benton with coolant. Platt handcuffed him to the bathroom sink and came back out into the front room, where Paul couldn't hear them.

Jason said, "I thought Benton's death was definitely from the head trauma."

Platt said, "He's telling the truth as he knows it."

Robert said, "Was the coroner mistaken?"

"Not necessarily. Do you know what the treatment is for ethylene glycol poisoning?"

Martin said to Robert, "That's the stuff in coolant."

"Ah." Robert nodded.

Jason said, "No, what's the treatment?"

"Administration of hard alcohol."

"But I thought people died from it in wine."

"In wine," Platt said. "Not in booze. Booze is the countermeasure."

Robert said, "Ohhh—"

"So it's not murder," Jason said.

"It's still attempted murder," Robert said.

"But nobody died from it."

"But he did make the attempt."

"But it wasn't even poisonous under these circumstances."

"But he thought it was."

"But it wasn't."

Martin said, "If I think a foam-rubber knife is dangerous, and I stab you with it . . ."

Platt said, "He tried."

"I know he tried," Jason said, "but don't you think there's some gray area here, even if it's a very narrow gray area? No one was harmed. In fact, no one could have been harmed."

"Well," Robert said, "not quite. Benton's dead."

"Of unrelated causes. And there's no evidence. The coroner found only a head wound and a high blood alcohol level."

"The coroner could take a second look," Platt said.

"If someone asked them to," Jason said.

Martin looked puzzled. "Why are you defending him?"

Robert said, "Not to say that this is an excuse for anything, but he has shown remorse and come back voluntarily. On the other hand, he still tried to kill Benton."

Jason said, "Nobody's saying he didn't. He's messed up and he doesn't know the difference between right and wrong, but he figured out that he needed to come back and try to make right. He had to know he'd be setting himself up for a murder conviction. It just seems like such a waste to send him to prison."

"That's fine," Robert said, "but what does it have to do with the fact that he tried to kill Benton?"

"I just think Paul's . . . I dunno . . . kind of a stray . . . but worth saving."

Platt looked sharply at him.

Jason said, "If he goes to prison, it's just such a waste. I know that's lame, but it's the best I can put it. I guess I'm out of good arguments."

Platt was still looking at Jason.

"What," Jason said.

Platt shook his head. "Just a moment of déjà vu," he said. "The earth turning." He closed his eyes, breathed deeply once, and said tiredly, "Wait here."

He went through the short passageway and into the bathroom.

"Earth turning?" Martin said.

Jason shrugged.

Platt came back, behind Paul. Paul was shaky, and he didn't look at anyone directly. His hands were cuffed together.

"All right," Platt said. "Here's the situation. Paul has admitted to attempted murder in front of four witnesses and a videotape. The coroner's report didn't find ethylene glycol in Benton's body, but if they're given reason to look for it, they might. Jason thinks Paul is 'worth saving.' Robert and Martin aren't sure where they stand on the issue. Is that accurate?"

Everyone but Paul nodded.

"What Paul did was not just a crime against Huey Benton, and not just a crime against society, but a crime against the circle of people around him. When he poisoned Benton, he betrayed the trust and rights granted him by those closest to him. Agreed?"

There were a few moments of thought, and then the agreements trickled in.

Paul didn't agree. "It was just between me and Benton. These guys have nothing to do with it."

"I don't need concurrence from you," Platt said. "I'm going to make you an offer. If any of your friends here can't live with it, the offer's void. Got it?"

"Whatever."

"All right. Here's the deal." Platt drew in a deep breath, held it, and let it out. "Paul, you will apprentice yourself to me until I say you're done. If you cross me, the videotape you just made goes straight to the FBI."

Jason stared at Platt and then looked at Robert and Martin. Robert looked fascinated. Martin looked something else. Maybe angry.

Paul said, "You want me to be your apprentice."

"That's the first part of the equation. The second part is that, in addition to answering to me, you will answer to Jason, Robert, or Martin whenever they want."

"Why?"

"Because you have no morals and they do. Also, it puts some of the responsibility for your progress and well-being on the people that wanted a second chance for you."

"What do you get out of this?"

"None of your business. Right now, you don't get answers. You just get to accept or refuse the offer."

"How long do I have to decide?"

"Right now."

"This is slavery."

"I have no objection to that assessment. Would you prefer a murder conviction?"

"Well," Paul said, looking at Jason. "It looks like I have no choice."

"We're not done yet," Platt said. "Everyone has to agree. Jason, do you agree to this?"

"Yes. I do."

"Robert?"

Robert looked up at the corner of the room and rocked a little. In half a minute, he stopped rocking, looked at Platt, and said, "Yes."

"Martin?"

Martin had been studying Paul. "I don't like it," he said. He shook his head. "Not at all. Paul?"

Paul had been looking distractedly around the room. He looked at Martin.

"You're a liar," Martin said. "You tried to kill some-body. And you're just generally a snake in the G.D. grass. Even without those things, I don't like how you treat peo-ple, and I think you've got Jason snowed. You don't de-serve anything that's being offered to you."

Paul said nothing.

Martin said, "But I'll agree to it."

Platt said, "You should be certain."

"I'm certain I'm right about Paul," Martin said. "I'm also certain Jason's not seeing him clearly. But I'm also cer-tain Robert's very smart and has a good reason for deciding yes. And I'm almost certain that being a secret agent man and all, you can handle whatever tricks Paul has up his sleeve. And I gotta say, there was a time when I didn't de-serve what was being offered to me, so I can't begrudge it when it's offered to another man. So I'll vote yes." He stepped closer to Paul. "But believe you me: You fuck up the opportunity these good people are giving you," he said, "you spit in their faces, and I promise"—his forefin-ger went into Paul's chest—"I will take it very personally. You be crystal, crystal clear on that."

Paul said nothing. Martin stepped back, meeting Paul's glower with his own.

"Well, then," Platt said to Paul. He smiled. "You're mine."

Paul said, "I just want to go on the record as saying that this stinks. I come back and try to do the right thing, and you take advantage of me for your own ends and push me around. What are you going to do, have me paint your house?"

"Not painting," Platt said. "Moving furniture. You can start tomorrow." He took the cuffs off Paul. Paul rubbed his wrists.

Platt said, "Your wrists aren't sore. First lesson: Dramat-ics just annoy people. Cut it out."

Paul rubbed a little longer.

"Go wait in my car," Platt said. He pulled his keys from his pocket and gave them to Paul. "It's the Chevy Suburban with the gray primer. Don't do anything but open the door and sit in it."

"How do you know I won't take off?"

"Paul," Platt said, "don't you think it would be stupid of me to hand you car keys and then not have any way to prevent your taking off?"

Paul snapped the keys out of Platt's hand and went out. Platt fished in a pocket and came up with something that looked like a pager with a large button on it.

"This was unexpected," Jason said.

"No shit," Martin agreed.

Jason looked at Platt and said, "Swofford and Tennant. The earth turning."

Platt looked surprised and nodded. At the sound of a large engine starting in the parking lot, he looked annoyed and pressed the button. The engine cut off.

"See you," he said, and went out.

Jason, Robert, and Martin stood in the pseudo-kitchen. After some time, the mini-refrigerator's compressor kicked in, and the noise made it seem even quieter.

Robert's little chess set rattled as he pulled it from his pocket and clanked when it hit the bottom of Jason's trash can.

Martin leaned against the wall, shaking his head slowly.

"Check fucking mate," he concurred.

50

I'm very glad to see you made bail," Hibbit said experimentally. His arms were tied behind him.

Jeffrey punched him in the stomach. As Lowell gunned the rental van east and looked for a desolate turnout, Jeffrey eyed Hibbit and assembled his ugly new gun.

Coming soon from Walker in the Fall of 1999,

to be published as a Dell paperback,

Keith Snyder's newest Jason Keltner mystery,

TROUBLE COMES BACK.

Please turn the page

for an exciting preview.

The Manor was a huge turn-of-the-century boardinghouse. Or it had been, at the turn of the century. Now it was a leaking, drafty wreck. Jason, Robert, and Martin had lived in it for four years because rent was cheap, but their time was up; it had been sold, and the students and artists who lived there had to leave.

Martin had moved out almost immediately following the announcement, taking a job doing page layout for a small offroading magazine in Long Beach, where his family was. Jason and Robert were supposedly looking for another place to live, but they weren't trying very hard.

Jason popped the back of the camper shell on his little brown pickup, tossed his backpack in, and leaned against the fender.

"Let's go!" he yelled at the Manor's second floor.

Robert's voice called, "Hold on!"

Jason drummed his fingers impatiently on the camper shell and looked at his old Plymouth. It had been sitting for a year on the dead grass between his flimsy back steps and the parking lot, and it had that soulless look that said it had made the transition from vehicle to geological formation. The Manor's residents had complained on and off for eight months. He really needed to do something about that.

Robert's door banged open and he came down the rickety back stairs with a bulging green backpack and slung it into the covered pickup bed. Jason closed and latched the back and they got in the cab and left for Long Beach, a forty-five-minute drive.

"What did he say, exactly," Robert asked when they were on the road. He was concentrating and tapping the dashboard with both hands, but he repeatedly fumbled and started over.

"You're still trying to think of it as one pattern," Jason said. "It's two. The three even beats with your left hand should take up the same period of time as the two even beats with your right hand."

"Shut up."

"They're separate. Sort of."

"Shut up. What did Martin say was wrong?"

"He didn't say exactly."

"You didn't ask?"

"Were we going to help him either way?"

"Of course."

Jason gestured *so* with one hand. He pushed a cassette in and the old Cuban men of the Buena Vista Social Club accompanied them beautifully out of L.A. County on guitars and pianos, with Robert guest artist on dashboard.

THE TAPE WAS in its third encore when Jason parked in front of a charmless apartment building distinguishable on a street of charmless apartment buildings only by address and trim color. He let "Pueblo Nuevo" finish before he killed the ignition, so as not to be disrespectful to Rubén Gonzáles.

He woke Robert and they went upstairs and knocked on Number 20. A boy of about twelve years, wearing shorts and a Bud Man T-shirt, opened the door and said, "Are you Jason?"

"Yes." He offered his hand.

The boy shook it. "I'm Leon."

Robert stuck out his hand and said, "I'm Sonic the Hedgehog."

Leon said, "You are not."

"I'm his brother Phonic. Phonic the Phedgephog."

Jason said, "Can we come in?"

"Okay. Martin's in the bathroom." Leon left the door open and walked away. They followed him in. The apartment was neither comfortable nor uncomfortable; it was rented space with objects in it: couch, carpet, dinette, dishes, shelves, TV.

Martin came out of the hallway, looked happy to see them, and said, "Yo baby, yo baby, yo."

Robert grinned lopsidedly. "Hi, Martin!"

Leon said, "He said he was Sonic's brother."

"Le, buddy," Martin said, touching Leon's shoulder, "I really wish you'd wear a different shirt. How about the one I bought you with those surfing gophers or weasels or whatever they are?"

Leon mumbled something.

"For me?"

Leon flicked a gaze at Robert and Jason but he moped off into the other room.

Robert said, "Grown-ups suck."

"No," Martin said, "I suck for treating him like a child in front of his peers."

Jason said to Robert, "That would be you."

Robert said, "Only emotionally. I am his intellectual superior."

"So," Martin said. "You guys eat?"

Robert shook his head violently.

Martin looked at his watch. "The best place is also the closest one. You mind a gay bar?"

Robert shook his head violently again and almost fell over.

Jason said, "Is it bar food or real food?"

"No, they have a kitchen. It's good."

THE MUSIC WAS loud and thumpy. The plates were black and octagonal and the napkins were yellow. The '90s were scheduled to arrive in Long Beach after the millennium.

They sat outside under unlit patio heaters, away from the dance floor. Their waiter, neat and midwestern with bad skin, said, "Good evening, gentlemen. Can I get you some drinks?"

Jason and Martin ordered soft drinks. After waiting for Robert to study the menu, the waiter finally said, "And you, sir?"

A moment later Robert looked up and said, "I would like the blood of a freshly killed gazelle."

"Very good," the waiter said, and left.

Jason looked amusedly at Robert. "The funny part is now you have to drink whatever he brings you."

"I trust him."

Jason said, "So, Martin, what's your trouble?"

"It's a long story. Let's just chat and get relaxed a little and I'll tell you after the drinks come. Robert, I hear you were on TV."

Robert described his day on the *Joanna* set and how the other actors had been, and Jason talked about the computer game music he'd just finished for Light Wizards. The waiter brought their drinks.

"Two colas," he said. "One gazelle blood." He bowed efficiently. "I'll be back to take your food orders." He pounded his chest with one fist. "*Salud,* strong hunters."

He left. Robert's drink was something red in a snifter with a flexy straw and a leafy celery stalk with a blue paper umbrella stuck into it. He made a show of getting his lips past the celery and took a large gulp.

Jason said, "So?"

"'Ninety-eight," Robert said. "Summer." He made smacking noises. "The Sahara, I believe. Springy, but robust. Graceful." He swirled it under his nose. "O-positive." He nodded. "Excellent legs."

"Speaking of Light Wizards," Martin said, "have you heard from Platt or Paul recently?"

Jason said, "The last time I saw Platt was when he introduced me around at Light Wizards, maybe a year and a half ago."

"And Paul?"

"Not a word."

Martin looked at Robert, who shook his head.

Their waiter returned. "Are you ready to order?"

"Grilled cheese," Jason said.

Martin said, "Chef salad."

Robert said, "Filet of wildebeest."

The waiter wrote on his pad. "How would you like your wildebeest?"

"Medium charred."

"Dark meat or light meat?"

Robert said, "Uh . . ."

The waiter said, "The light meat is less gamy."

"Good. Dark meat."

"Very good choice, sir." The waiter looked Robert over. "I'm partial to light meat, myself." He scooped up their menus and left.

"I do believe," Jason said, "that you have just been cruised."

Robert acknowledged with a lift of his eyebrows and sipped past his celery.

"So," Jason said. "What's your trouble, Martin?"

Martin leaned forward on the table. "My trouble is my brother."

"Leon?"

"Actually Ed is my trouble, Mom's boyfriend. Leon thinks he's great. He's starting to act like him."

Robert said something unintelligible around the foliage of his celery.

Jason said, "Drink or talk. Don't do both."

Robert emerged from his celery and repeated, "But you don't think Ed is great."

"Ed abuses," Martin said. "Ed uses. Ed deals, Ed steals, Ed lies, Ed swindles. No, I gotta say I do not think Ed is great."

Jason said, "What can we do?"

"Two things," Martin said. "First, I'm hoping that if Leon sees some men around who are cool and don't do all that stuff, he'll have a healthier outlet for those role model feelings."

Robert said, "The current term for cool is 'da bomb.' "

Jason said, "It was anyway. What about you?"

Martin said, "Me? No, I can't be da bomb. I'm da mom."

"Why isn't your mom da mom?"

"She's too busy trying to get her life straight. Mom's not a great judge of character. You know? Her taste in boyfriends pretty well sucks. Ed's a real winner. When you meet him, you'll get the drift in about four seconds. Here's the other thing: Ed put his hands on my mom the day before yesterday, in front of Leon, while I wasn't there. I was hoping you'd kind of back me up when I bring it to a head and maybe hang around for a few days and be like a strong male presence."

Robert said, "Put his hands on as in fondling, or put his hands on as in hitting?"

"As in gripping, and shaking."

Jason said, "Does 'strong male presence' translate as 'deterrent force'?"

"That's a pretty good translation."

Jason and Robert exchanged a glance, each to confirm that the other was okay with it.

Martin said, "I'll feed you."

"Okay."

When their waiter came with their food, Robert complained that his wildebeest wasn't hairy enough. The waiter offered to exchange it for the hyena plate, which he promised was excellent and should be suitably hirsute, but Robert said he would make do and ordered another gazelle blood. The waiter gave Robert his phone number on their way out. Robert stuck it in his back pocket and apologized for being straight. The waiter said that wasn't a problem for him.

THE WINNER BOYFRIEND wasn't there when they got back.

"Mom's shopping," Martin said, plopping onto the couch. "She'll be back in time to make us dinner."

Jason pulled a chair around from the dinette and sat on it backward. "It'll be nice to see her again."

Leaning against the wall, Robert stopped tapping his hands awkwardly on his thighs enough to say, "It'll be nice to meet her, finally."

Jason looked at Robert's hands and said, "You should isolate the two patterns."

"Shut up."

Martin said, "She goes for the wrong guys. There ain't a dang thing I can do about it, and I accept that. But Leon's a different story. I been here three weeks, just watching and seeing. Well, now I'm done watching and seeing. I'm the breadwinner in this house and I say he's out of here. I just don't want to stand up to him by myself because frankly, he's really big."

Robert gave up tapping and sat down. "What about the cops?"

"Mom'd never press charges."

"You're paying the rent, right?"

"Yeah, but it's her name on the lease."

"How did it happen the day before yesterday, when he put his hands on her?"

"I don't know, man. She's not talking, and Leon won't give me any details."

Robert said, "They're afraid you'll do something."

Jason stretched his legs out. "Which you will."

"Damn skippy."

"If nobody's talking, how do you know he put his hands on her?"

"At first it was just a vibe? Then yesterday I saw bruises

on her upper arms, like thumb and finger bruises, like a grip. She tried to hide them, but then when she saw me looking, she said she bumped into the car door."

"Eight times," Robert said, "then twice the other way."

"Against that fingerlike protrusion all car doors have at bicep level," Jason said. "When do you want to confront him?"

"Tonight. We have to stay for supper first, though, or Mom will be upset."

"We doing it here?"

"No, I don't want to do it in front of Leon, and I don't want Mom interfering. Also, I don't know if he'll be here. If he is, we'll hook up with him later in the evening. If he's not, we'll go to him right after supper."

Robert said, "You think she'd interfere?"

"Who knows? For all I know, she let me see the bruises so I'd ride to her rescue. But that doesn't mean she wouldn't stand by him while I did."

"Too complicated," Jason said. "Jase protect tribe. Bad men come, Jase make many head knocks, knock-knock."

Robert grunted, "Who there?"

Martin supplied: "Fuckwit."

Robert said, "Fuckwit who?"

"Fuckwit my family, and you go down, Jack."

"Martin make joke," Jason said. "Joke funny."